THE ELECTORS

A Novel by Roy Neel

RECOUNT PRESS

Recount Press
Washington, DC, USA

First Recount Press Printing, January, 2016

Design & illustrations © 2015 by Tucker Neel
tuckerneel.com

Printed in the United States of America

ISBN 978-0-692-65134-6

PUBLISHER'S NOTE
This is a work of fiction. Names, characters, places, and incidents are the product of the
author's imagination or are used fictitiously, and any resemblance to actual persons, living
or dead, events, or locales is entirely coincidental.

For more information, or to order copies in bulk please visit
electorsbook.com

For Jenny

CONTENTS

THE ELECTORS

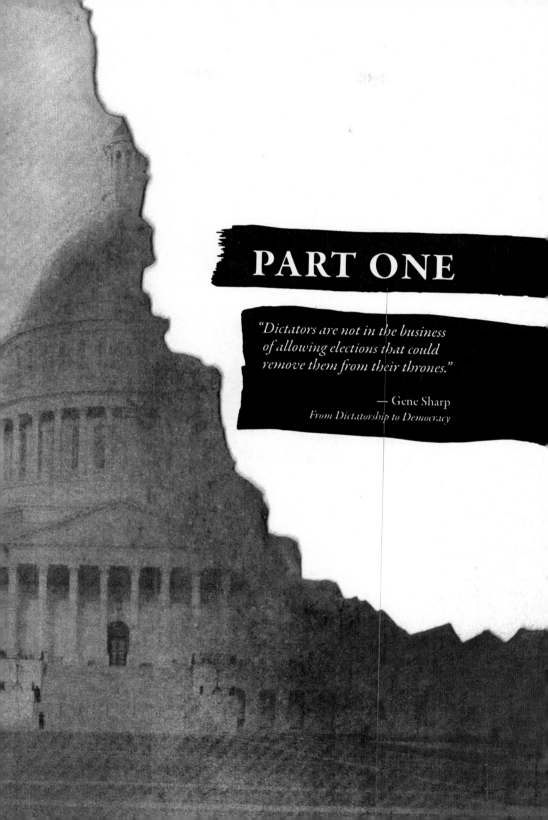

PART ONE

*"Dictators are not in the business
of allowing elections that could
remove them from their thrones."*

— Gene Sharp
From Dictatorship to Democracy

CHAPTER 1

As Air Force One made a sharp turn for its landing approach, the President fell out of bed trying to untangle his breathing machine.

"Goddamn sonofabitch!" he yelled at the device, now blasting air into the compartment. He struggled to his knees as an attendant knocked and asked if the Commander in Chief was okay.

"Yeah, yeah, I'm fine," growled Grady Holland. "Why didn't I get a wakeup call? You guys are killing me!"

Holland slipped on sweats and a tee shirt and slammed the button to order coffee and summon an aide to review the day's activity in Cleveland. Or was it Columbus? *At least this goddamn campaign is almost over. Last debate. Last rope line. I win. I lose. I don't give a shit.*

"Good morning, Mr. President," said Holland's advance man. "We'll have a group of local Republicans on the tarmac for a grab and run handshake. Then you've got a visit to a small manufacturer, before the speech to an American Legion convention. With teleprompter. Here's the draft. A lunch with donors and local officials. Then we're back here wheels up at two pm."

"All right," said Holland, half-dressed, disheveled, and hung over. "I gotta shower and get dressed. Hold the plane on the ground." He dismissed the advance man with a wave and stumbled into the bathroom of the flying White House.

In his private compartment behind the President, Eldon Mann reviewed the overnight tracking polls. The Democratic challenger's lead had shrunk to five points, but the deficit hadn't improved for two weeks. Mann punched up the electoral map, which projected a 320–218 win for Senator Calvin Bridges.

With two weeks until election day, Holland's Chief of Staff resigned himself to the looming defeat. Other than keeping the President sober and on message, there was little Mann could do to turn around a floundering campaign.

During an interview, CNN's John King asked Mann to explain the President's lackluster performance at a recent event.

"Mr. Mann, the President slurred his lines. He seemed distracted. Is he suffering from some kind of illness?"

"John, the President is fine. Just a little cold," said Mann, forcing a smile in the defense of his boss. "He's excited about these last few weeks of the campaign. A lot of voters are just now getting interested in this race, and they like what they're seeing in President Holland's leadership."

As he removed his earpiece Mann clenched his teeth and ignored the thanks of the camera technician as he thought *How much longer do I have to cover for this asshole?*

At eight am, Calvin Bridges sat at the desk in his home along the Severn River overlooking the U. S. Naval Academy. He had finished a two mile jog and a half hour on a cross trainer before pouring over notes for his debate preparation later that morning.

He lifted a large mug of decaf as he leafed through the draft questions his staff anticipated from the moderator, NBC's Savannah Guthrie.

"Senator Bridges," he read, "you voted to authorize President Bush's military actions against Iraq, then you voted to force the President to withdraw troops from that conflict. Then you voted to support President Obama's expansion of the war in Afghanistan."

"Don't you consider that a major flip-flop on the most critical national security decision of the past decade?"

"Well, Savannah," Bridges twisted his face to exaggerate mock outrage. "Them's my views. And if you don't like 'em, I'll change em! And, by the way, may I say you're lookin' mighty sexy in that short dress today. Grrrrow!"

"Hah! That was perfect!" Bridges' campaign manager, Melody Banks, clapped as she came into the room to go over plans for debate prep with the candidate.

"Melody! How long have you been there?" Bridges turned to see the tall blond in skinny jeans, hiking boots, and a *Bridges to the Future* hoodie. She took a chair next to his desk as he turned to face the woman who the political press credited with all but saving his campaign when it hit a wall after the Democratic convention.

"We've moved the cameras and the team into the Annapolis Women's Club auditorium for the mock debate work today. We'll start at 10 am if that's ok." Even in L.L. Bean, Banks gave most men goose bumps. Calvin Bridges was no exception.

"I want to work on the Iraq stuff some more," he said, trying to bring his mind back to the final Presidential debate twenty-four hours away. "Holland hit me hard last time, and I've gotta have a better comeback."

Bridges and Banks reviewed the overnight press and exchanged gossip about the President's recent shaky performance. "He's falling apart," said Bridges. "Let's hope he keeps it going for the debate."

Banks stood and stretched, her attention drawn to the Secret Service agents walking the grounds of the Senator's sprawling estate. "Senator, you'll do fine. I'll see you at ten." She smiled and waved at Bridges' wife as she walked to her car. *This is going to be a good day,* she thought. *A really good day.*

After a backbreaking two weeks on the road with the candidate, Melody Banks had enjoyed the first full night of sleep in her Annapolis hotel room near the harbor. She awoke at six am with her arm across the bare chest of one of Bridges' media consultants. The two downed tequila shooters and a bottle of excellent Brunello at Carlo's Crab House, then stumbled back to her room looking forward to what-the-hell sex. Instead, both collapsed and slept for eight hours.

Stanley Vaughn sat in a booth at the Ice Kingdom Tap Room outside Bismarck, North Dakota, reading the paper and drinking bad coffee poured by a young waitress with a shag haircut and tight blouse that amplified her small breasts.

"Anything else, Stanley?" she teased, fingering the plastic nametag —*Eva, at your service.*

"Not now," smiled Stanley, who pushed an Andrew Jackson across the counter toward the waitress. The bill covered a note on a napkin: "6 pm, at the lake?"

Eva smiled and said, "Well, thanks, Mr. Vaughn. I hope we'll see you again real soon!"

Vaughn left the diner and, favoring a bad knee, walked slowly to his car. He powered up his phone and called his wife Irene, who was this morning chairing a meeting of her fellow Democratic activists. The election was near and Irene and her clan had high hopes for an upset for their Presidential candidate.

"Stanley!" she shouted into his earpiece. "You won't believe it! I've been chosen as an elector! You know, the Electoral College! My name will be on the ballot! Gotta go. I'll have to call you back, hon."

Don't do me any favors, thought Stanley. *The Electoral College? I thought they'd killed that off a long time ago.*

A searing sun rose over the desert surrounding a posh Arizona resort north of Scottsdale. Lizards scurried under freshly washed golf carts and ratllers slithered under rocks as the day's temperature advanced toward the uncomfortable.

Wayne Hartsell, the resort builder and frequent patron, led a foursome onto the first tee, pausing to pour Bloody Mary's into travel cups for his guests.

"Men, we've got a great day here!," he announced before hitting his drive into a cactus off the fairway. "Let's play some golf. Then let's figure out how to make some money!"

After countless meetings of the Arizona Democratic Party to plan election week activities, Hartsell was anxious to jumpstart his next development deal. He had given three hundred thousand dollars to the state and national party organizations, including Calvin Bridges' campaign and SuperPAC. The calls for more donations seemed to Hartsell to be growing, but he figured he had no choice if he wanted to grab a plum ambassadorship. Australia sounded perfect.

What a waste of time, he thought, during a protracted political planning session in Phoenix earlier in the week. *And now I'm a goddamn elector. Big fucking deal. I don't even like these people.*

An early ice storm covered Portsmouth, New Hampshire, making the streets unsafe for locals trying to get to work, to meetings, and morning Mass.

Virginia Sullivan struggled to put on the traction cleats she had ordered on Amazon the previous winter. Grossly overweight, with failing knees and hips, and with limited health coverage, she couldn't risk another fall.

The weather would have given her a pass for one more political meeting, but this particular gathering would choose the party's slate of electors, who would cast the state's votes should Senator Bridges win New Hampshire.

She gingerly navigated the five blocks to the party headquarters on State Street and joined her fellow Democrats. After coffee and pastries and what seemed to Virginia to be mind-numbing chitchat, the executive committee chairman read the proposed electors' names. Virginia's was the last of the four that would appear on the presidential ballot.

Slogging along the treacherous sidewalks back to her row house, Virginia could muster little pride or enthusiasm about her selection. She toiled in the Democratic trenches for decades, but as she hauled herself up the creaking wooden steps to her front porch, all she could think about were the years of sacrifice.

I gave them everything I had, thought Virginia. *And all I get back is this.* Short of breath, aching with pain, she opened the door to a house with peeling paint and rotting windows, and collapsed into a sagging armchair.

Dan West pulled on a dark blue Brooks Brothers suit, straightened his red tie, and pinned a small American flag to his lapel. He sat for a moment on the bed in the master suite of the Vice President's official residence, and tried to temper his resentment at being called away from the campaign. *And for what?* He thought. *To meet a slimy lobbyist and his clients. That's what it's come down to? That's what I've come down to.*

En route to the White House, the Vice President took a call from Eldon Mann, who cautioned him to be especially hospitable to the power company executives. "They stepped up big time for the campaign." said Mann. "When you meet with these people tomorrow, they need to be stroked. Tell them we're looking at some changes at the EPA. That should hold them for now."

West gazed out his limousine window for the short drive to
The White House. With a heavy rain slowing traffic into the city,
he ordered his Secret Service agent to forego the sirens. He was in
no hurry. As the motorcade rounded Sheridan Circle and headed
toward 1600 Pennsylvania Avenue, he revisited the many slights
he had endured since he and Holland entered the White House
nearly four years earlier.

A steady drizzle coated Washington streets around the Capitol
Building, turning the asphalt into a dark mirror of the few car
headlights that cruised the nation's most important neighborhood.
A handful of travelers emerged from Union Station seeking taxis
or cars with waiting friends. Nearby at the Dubliner, weary law
students finished off drinks and exchanged pick-up glances. With
Congress out of town and no major events downtown, Washington was at its quietest.

Ian Wilson, a tall, scruffy young man shouldering a backpack,
waited as the escalator steps brought him outside Union Station.
He couldn't help but think its weight much greater than the
woman had claimed, at least 30 pounds, maybe more. But his
trip was nearly over, his job almost done, and he looked forward
to a beer. The damp midnight air braced his stride as he crossed
Constitution Avenue, past the mountainous Senate office buildings and onto the lawn fronting the Capitol's north portico. He
went unnoticed by Capitol security.

After a short walk, he found the spot, sat on the wet grass and
drew a long tug from his water bottle. He admired the grounds of
the Mall that spread more than a mile before him, framing rectan-
gular pools leading to the Washington Monument and the Lincoln
Memorial. *I've gotta come back here again in the spring*, he thought.

The young man relaxed, slipped the backpack to the ground,
and pushed it beneath a platform under construction for the

coming Inauguration. The woman had cautioned that he had only fifteen minutes after activating the cell number, to walk the quarter mile necessary to avoid any effect of the gadget's detonation. She assured Ian there would be no loss of life. The blast would only release an explosion of blood red paint over much of the Capitol. The mess would take months to remove and represent a warning to U.S. officials to finally take seriously the growing poverty that divided the country.

At precisely midnight, he took a deep breath of the cool autumn evening, drew the cell phone from his jacket and pressed "call" for the only number programmed into the device. He felt and heard nothing as the bomb in his backpack vaporized the immediate area.

CHAPTER 2

As nuclear blasts go, the explosion ignited by Ian Wilson's cell phone was a dud. The conflagration was limited to an area approximately the size of a Little League baseball field. But the visual impact of a gaping hole in the U. S. Capitol was dramatic. A cloud of radioactive dust swirled above the grounds and trailed off into the cold night.

The blast opened the northwest corner of the Capitol, spreading pulverized stone and glass into the Senate chamber. The iconic dome rested precariously over the destruction, cracked like an boiled egg. Across Constitution Avenue a dozen office buildings housing various labor unions, law and lobbying firms had windows shattered. The Russell and Dirksen Senate office building facades were pelted with debris, but the buildings were left mostly unharmed.

However, the blast produced catastrophic radiation levels, in the range of the Fukashima disaster a decade earlier. The first team to the site measured five roentgens per second, or 40 times the lethal dose. The immediate area around the Capitol would be toxic for at least two years.

The President's national security team and a delegation of FBI officials took over sealed quarters below the West Wing of the White House and began gathering information and issuing instructions to teams in the Washington area and in critical sites around the country. A second group convened at the State Department for secure calls with key embassies in Europe, the Middle East and Asia. The team opened digital communication with hundreds of other offices around the world.

At CIA headquarters in northern Virginia every operative who could quickly get to the building was summoned to work. Recalling the horrific tragedy of Sept. 11, 2001, top Pentagon officials were diverted to a specially equipped work area at Langley to begin what would become many long days and sleepless nights.

Alistair Muse, the President's National Security Advisor, quickly realized this was the moment that would define his career. Exiled to academia by the neocons in the Bush-Cheney White House, he missed the Iraq invasion, the search for bin Laden, tensions with the Pakistani intelligence community, the decade of juggling Soviet relations, and the mounting ISIS threat. It seemed to Muse that every important national security event of the past twenty years had passed him by.

Humorless, 60, obese, with a ravaged cardiovascular system, Muse was rescued from a deadly university backwater by his sole political patron, Eldon Mann. He quickly slipped into his role as the President's most powerful advisor on everything from nuclear diplomacy to terrorism. He jealously guarded the information that would go to a President whose command of foreign policy was, at best, unenlightened.

Muse lived alone in a small rented apartment near Foggy Bottom that allowed him to be at work within minutes. He entered the basement of the West Wing, navigating the narrow hallways to the Situation Room and into the "lockdown room" nearby, where he greeted his team. "What do we know? Who is headed in now? Pretty soon it's going to be nearly impossible to get here. We have to brief the President in fifteen minutes, so let's get started."

The President was awakened in his Orlando mansion at 12:30 am by Muse, who broke the news of the Capitol bombing with such control and calm that Holland was unsure at first if there was indeed an emergency. "Mr. President, we have an incident here in Washington. There was an explosion of some sort near the Capitol and there is evidence of radiation release."

"What? Say that again. You mean a nuclear bomb has gone off in Washington? Where? Are you telling me that we've been attacked?" After three bourbons and an Ambien to wipe out the rigors of the campaign trail, Holland was in no shape to make sense of the news. "How many dead? Do I come back to Washington?"

"Mr. President, you must stay in Orlando. Washington is not secure for you at this time. The Service is adding a dozen men to your detail. I'm with the team in the lockdown room and we'll make an assessment for you within the hour. And we'll have an open line to you so you'll know everything we know as we know it."

"Jesus Christ," slurred the President, as he stumbled to put on his boxers while holding the phone. "I'm gonna take a quick shower and I'll be back."

By two a.m. the national security team had contacted every member of the Congressional leadership with a preliminary report, urging all who were in their home state to stay put and those in their Washington area homes to do so as well. No one, no matter how important in the federal government hierarchy, would be allowed inside the quarantined area unless authorized by the FBI.

"Alistair, you need to know that we're inside the blast fallout coverage." Muse's deputy, a severe former Navy commander, interrupted his boss's conversation with the Secretary of Defense. "Commander, I don't care if we're at ground zero, this is where we have to be," Muse countered. "We'll just have to stay here until it's all clear outside."

"Get me Eldon Mann. And contact Senator Bridges' staff and arrange a call for me to the Senator. And his Secret Service detail's got to be fortified. Where are they now? Annapolis?"

After Muse's call, the President fought off the urge to return to bed. His head was pounding and he debated the merits of coffee vs. a hair of the dog to rouse himself to deal with the crisis in Washington. The decision was made for him when a steward brought a pot and mug into the bedroom of his Orlando estate.

It was bound to happen, he thought, pulling on Florida Gator sweatpants and a wrinkled polo from the floor. *At least they didn't come after me.*

At three a.m., an aide knocked on the President's bedroom door. "Mr. President, Mr. Mann and the briefers are in the study, whenever you're ready. Mr. Muse is on the line."

"Just gimme a couple minutes," replied Holland. "I've gotta get dressed." The President careened his way to a nearby chair and retrieved the pants he had taken off hours before. He pulled on his Commander in Chief bomber jacket and wobbled into a room full of Secret Service agents, a CIA briefing team, and a group of White House advisors.

"What do we know?" he asked.

"Mr. President," began the senior CIA briefer, "at midnight an explosion occurred just outside the Capitol Building. It appears to have been a conventional bomb that also released a level of radiation now being analyzed. A square mile around the Capitol is being cordoned off. We don't yet have a casualty report. Here's an initial video feed from the site."

The agent handed Holland a high resolution iPad, and turned down the sound of sirens in the background. Hundreds of law enforcement and hazmat crews could be seen clustering on Constitution Avenue. The scene reminded Holland of an episode in a Tom Clancy novel.

"Jesus!" said the President, viewing a grainy image that was lit by helicopter lights. "Looks like the whole damn thing caved in."

Holland raised outstretched hands and confronted the group. "Any idea who did this? Gotta be the goddamn jihadists."

CHAPTER 3

Instructional books covering a wide range of subjects, from distilling spirits and installing solar panels to air drying meats and making ricin, filled an unwieldy corner of the rambling brick house outside Casper, Wyoming. A dozen members of the loosely organized Aryan Supremacy called the nondescript building headquarters.

A confederate flag hung over a collection of yellowing bumper stickers— "No Coloreds Allowed", "Hitler Got it Right—He Just Didn't Finish the Job!", "Shoot the Queers—Season Opens Next Week". The meeting room stank of stale beer, cigarette butts, and molding pizza boxes. Guns, ammo, and assorted explosives were stored in a locker across town.

"Now what?" growled Jack Raglan, the leader of the ragtag clan of misfits, as his cellphone blasted its ringtone, the opening bars of "Jumping Jack Flash". He fumbled through the detritus next to his bed to retrieve the phone, and lit a half-smoked Camel before answering. "Who the fuck is this?"

"Jack!" the excited voice was breaking up on the other end. "You watchin' TV? Was that a bomb we was carryin' in the bag? Dammit Jack, talk to me!"

"I don't know what you're talking about. Hang up this goddamn phone and don't call me again." Raglan pulled himself out of bed and lumbered into the next room to turn on a television. He was

greeted with a network news anchor reporting an explosion at
the U.S. Capitol two hours earlier. *What the hell? The damn thing
was supposed to go off at noon, not in the middle of the goddamn
night*, he thought.

A month earlier Raglan had come into possession of an explosive device that the seller characterized as a "nuclear bomb but
not one that would set off a war or anything like that." Raglan
was targeted by the seller after he had read an online article
describing Raglan as "one of the country's most notorious
anti-government, anti-immigrant white supremacists, a wily,
tattooed crank who has successfully avoided prosecution despite
his association with drug trafficking, gambling, and loan shark-
ing." Raglan had read the article with pride, posting a printed
copy on the living room wall and obtaining a desk sign that read:
"Jack Raglan, Wily Crank".

The seller, a somber, bearded man in his fifties, pulled his
barstool next to Raglan one autumn night and tried a line of
chitchat until he was cut off. "Listen, fella, I came here to drink
and watch this fucking football game. You got something to say,
say it. Otherwise get out of my face."

"I have something you will be interested to see," said the newcomer. "Can we go somewhere quiet?" Raglan looked away, now
suspicious that this man was likely FBI or, worse, a rival planning
to do him harm.

"I'm not going anywhere," he said. "You got something to say
to me, let me have it here and now." The man pulled an envelope
from his parka and placed it in front of Raglan.

"I'm at the Four Clovers Motel. After you read this, give me a
call. The number's on the envelope. You can call me Walter." With
that he slipped away from the bar and left the building as Raglan
watched. He looked about the room to see if others were trailing
the man and, seeing none, returned to the game. After a minute
passed he opened the envelope and read what appeared to be a
technical document about a weapon of some sort. As he paged

through the material Raglan grew more certain that the man was an FBI agent and that the encounter was little more than a sting designed to nab the wily crank.

Raglan returned to his house and finished off the remaining whiskey left by the *Guns & Girls* reporter who had interviewed Raglan earlier that week. He fell asleep in a food-stained, moth-eaten recliner only to be awakened by his cellphone. "Did you read the material?" said the voice that Raglan recognized as the man from earlier in the evening.

"How'd you get this number?" Raglan spewed. "No one has this fucking number that I don't give it to."

"Never mind that. I assume you read the material. So tell me if you are interested. If not I'll leave and you'll never hear from me again."

"Go fuck yourself," Raglan snarled, powering off his phone. He stumbled to bed and tried to will himself to sleep, finally downing a sleeping pill, then another. But nothing worked. Soon he gave up the effort and arose to pace the house, which he occupied alone since his girlfriend had left the year before. He found the envelope, reread its contents twice, then sat still with another drink. Within fifteen minutes he had a plan to determine whether the man delivering this document was legit or a Fed.

Early the next morning Raglan summoned one of his Aryan Supremacy flock to the house, and sent him off to contact Walter.

The idea was simple: if "Walter" and his offer were for real, Raglan would cut a deal to keep the man more or less hostage until Raglan's plan for the bomb could be executed. If it worked, he would give Walter his money and send him on his way. Otherwise, all bets would be off. All this would take place with Raglan's finger-prints nowhere in sight. If Walter objected there would be no deal.

Raglan activated a monitoring device to overhear any com-munication or read any text coming from the smartphone Walter had used to call him. He then arranged to have three Aryan breth-ren set up stakeouts around the motel to follow any movements

Walter might make the next day. Raglan's followers were pathetic criminals but they were well trained and tech savvy, and they followed orders. Each owed their financial condition, and even their life, to Raglan and knew any betrayal would be met with unpleasant results.

By the next day Raglan had determined that Walter was not likely an FBI agent, but there was still the matter of his offer and whether or not the device was for real. He now had to meet directly with the seller. Raglan's man returned to the motel and left a note with instructions for Walter with the front desk. An hour later Walter drove away in his rental car to Wilkins State Park along the North Platte River a half hour outside Casper. He was followed by two of Raglan's men, who reported that Walter had arrived at the location—campsite no. 12—and that he was alone.

Soon an aging Winnebago pulled into the adjacent campsite and its driver set up a grill outside, threw on hot dogs, opened a cooler of beer, and unfolded a ragged aluminum chair. With the fire underway, the RV driver yelled to Walter, "Hey, you want a dog and a beer? I got plenty."

"No thanks," said Walter, now irritated with the intrusion as he was waiting for this critical meeting. "Just taking a break here before I get back on the road."

"No, really," said the neighbor. "I think you oughta come over here and join me. You can check out my ride. This here's a great RV. Had it for twenty years now. Come on over. It's cold outside."

"No thanks," responded Walter, looking down the path for the visitor he expected.

"I'm not askin," said the RV host, who downed a Coors and focused his attention on the burning charcoal. "Come on over and go inside my RV. There's someone who wants to talk to you. Now."

After Raglan's hotdog wielding associate was satisfied that Walter was not wearing any recording device, the negotiation took place with Raglan behind a curtain separating the lounge area from a small bedroom. The couch smelled of tobacco and beer, so Walter stood for the duration. Raglan was careful to introduce himself as "someone who knows what you gave Raglan, who wanted nothin' to do with this deal. But I do. So let's talk."

Walter assumed that it was Raglan behind the curtain. They discussed the nature of the weapon and its potential for damage, and a price. For three hundred thousand dollars in cash, Walter would deliver two bombs, each containing ten pounds of highly radioactive cesium encased in a detection-proof ceramic coating, with a detonation device that could be activated by a cellphone. The cesium, explained Walter, had been stolen from a Gammator research machine in a warehouse in Zagreb, where the equipment had been abandoned in transit. Rogue Ukrainian scientists had developed a method to fold the toxic isotopes into small, very nasty devices that could render a substantial area dangerously radioactive for years. Walter had taken possession when one of the scientists desperate for cash unloaded the "dirty bombs" for one hundred thousand hryvnia, or about twenty thousand dollars.

Walter had tried unsuccessfully to locate a buyer in the Mideast, hoping to significantly multiply the return on his investment through one of the fanatical jihadists operating in Libya. Instead of buyers, Walter was met with threats. Fearing for his life, he smuggled the bombs into a Mexican port with lax security. He drove through a checkpoint on the Juarez-El Paso border, and north to Wyoming, where he scoured the ranks of skinheads and right wing crazies who might have more money than caution. An internet search steered Walter to Casper, and Jack Raglan.

Pausing to mull over Walter's offer in the Winnebago, Raglan responded. "If I was interested, and I don't know if I am, how can I know if the thing will work? How the hell d'you guarantee something like that?"

"You can pay me half upon delivery and half when it works," said Walter, expecting Raglan's caution. "I can assure you..."

"I got a better idea," interrupted Raglan, who pulled back the curtain, a 9mm Glock in his grip. "I'll pay you a hundred thousand, but only *if* it works." Raglan knew he had now crossed a line that would get him arrested if this was a sting, but he pressed on. "You give me the package, show me how it works, and then I hold you nearby until I'm finished. If I'm satisfied you'll get your money and you'll be on your way."

Walter backed up to the RV door, hands lifted. He was out of options to rid himself of the devices. He had come too close to detection and capture by U.S. intelligence forces to string out his marketing any longer. Raglan was clearly a dangerous customer, but he was also a bird in hand that he would have to pursue, even if it meant meeting his aggravating and even dangerous demands.

"Okay, okay," said Walter. "The terms are acceptable. And there's one more thing you need to know," said Walter, who with this deal wanted to improve Raglan's chances for success. "The government operates something called NEST—the Nuclear Emergency Support Team. They've got several thousand radiation detectors all over the country, several hundred around Washington alone. They don't always work properly, but they might catch any movement of the device."

"This package is adequately shielded from any radiation detectors. But I have information that once a month they take down their signals for recalibration. It's different for each city or port but I know that the ring around Washington will be down for recalibration on the twentieth of each month. You might be able to use that."

Raglan dismissed Walter, satisfied with the deal, and summoned the RV driver to return him to Casper, where he began his plan for one final violent act. Ever since Timothy McVeigh blew up the Murrah Building in Oklahoma City, Raglan had longed to pull off a similar attack, but not get caught. Martyrdom was not his goal.

Unlike the most notorious terrorists, Jack Raglan was not particularly ideological. He scoffed at the suicide attacks on 9/11 and the countless pawns strapped with explosives to blow up "infidels". "Stupid ragheads!" he yelled to his cohorts on more than one occasion. "Sure, go out and kill people if it makes you happy. But there ain't no virgins up there to fuck if you blow yourself up. That's just goddamn crazy."

A few days later Raglan gathered his clan. "I figure it'll take six or seven days to get the bag to Baltimore," he said, addressing no one in particular. "You gotta be careful and not get stopped or break down anywhere, stay under the speed limit. We've gone over all this, but we gotta get it right or all this goddamn work and money and all the other shit won't matter. Jojo, you and Delores will do the trip. Take the baby. A couple heading cross country with a two year old won't draw attention. Use the Impala, it's legal, the registration is good and it'll get you there. I figure you'll need about two thousand for gas and motels and food. And for fuck sake don't fight all the way to Baltimore. And no fucking drugs, OK?"

"So let's go over it one more time," growled Raglan, unfolding a road map with the route highlighted for the couple. "You leave tomorrow. Stay on interstates the entire way, up 25 then east on 90 all the way to Chicago. But stay out of Chicago, go south on 39, then east on 80 into Pennsylvania. Take the exit to Harrisburg then down to Baltimore. You'll take 83 right into town and get off on the Oliver Street exit. There's a Days Inn right there. All this is on your goddamn Google Maps. Check in no later than October 15 and call me when you're there. And keep the bag in your room, not in the car. In case anyone asks, what are you doing on the road?"

"We're going to Baltimore to look for work. I've got Craigslist ads for jobs and apartments," said Jojo, anxious to show Raglan he was up to the task. "I fix cars and motorcycles. Delores is hopin' to get on somewhere cleanin' offices."

"OK," responded Raglan. "On the morning of the twentieth a woman will come by the motel. You don't need to know her name. Stay in your room until she gets there. She'll take the bag. Then what do you do?"

"We stay and watch the Ravens game and get drunk and rob a bank," joked Jojo. Raglan didn't laugh. "Just kiddin'. We check out of the motel and drive south to Florida. No speedin', no accidents. When we get there we call you on the phone marked with the date. By the way, where'll you be?"

Jojo and Delores knew not to question Raglan about the contents of the bag or where it was going. They had posed those questions earlier in the week and were firmly rebuked. "You don't need to know," he said. "In fact, you don't wanna know."

Raglan had declared October and November no-drug months for the ragtag group, certain that if his plan was to succeed and his gang's role not detected they would have to stay sober for a while. Determined to keep the most sensitive details of his plan to himself, he explained that he had information that the Supremacy would likely be raided soon, and that drugs and other misbehavior needed to be set aside until the coast was clear.

It'll be a fucking miracle if those two even get to Baltimore, much less deliver the bomb, he thought.

CNN was reporting damage from the explosion to be massive. Radiation covered the city, now in chaos, which pleased Raglan to no end. *Hell, this is better than 9-11*, he mused.

Raglan had spent days fine-tuning the statement he intended to release to the press, and when completed, he congratulated himself on the product.

Today the Aryan Supremacy detonated a nuclear bomb at the U.S. Capitol. This action sends a clear signal that our government has gone too far in destroying the freedoms that every American cherishes. And what are these freedoms?

1. Freedom to associate with whoever we please.
2. Freedom to own and operate any kind of weapon we choose to purchase.
3. Freedom to keep to our race and kind.
4. Freedom to keep the money we pay in taxes to the government, which spends it on those who don't carry their weight, the freeloaders and minorities who drain our country's coffers.
5. Freedom to build our homes anywhere we want.
6. Freedom to operate our businesses in any manner we want.

And finally,

7. Freedom to worship with whoever we want, and to keep homosexuals out of our churches.

As Jack powered up his laptop to forward the message to the press, CNN reported that two different Islamic extremist groups had claimed responsibility for the bombing. A third added its own claim and threatened to behead two German journalists. A prominent evangelist appeared on Fox to cite countless immoral trends in American society as God's excuse for dispatching the bomber to Washington. An MS-13 Salvadoran gang member put out a video stating his group had masterminded the attack. By eight in the morning more than twenty individuals and terrorist groups would lay claim to the Washington bombing.

"Once again, America has been attacked," reported the CNN anchor, "and once again, Americans are in panic."

"Bullshit!" Raglan yelled at the TV monitor. "You don't even know who the fuck America is. I am America, asshole!"

Trumped by the flood of impostors taking credit for his brilliant work, Raglan decided to forego the release of his statement. Maybe later. In the meantime, he needed to get the hell out of town. After making one final tour of the house to eliminate any evidence of his role in the bombing plot, Raglan tossed two duffel bags stuffed with cash into the rear of his old Jeep SUV, next to Walter's second bomb, and drove north to the Canadian border.

Unpacking her bag in a St. Croix beachside hotel, Jack Raglan's daughter reflected on the past week in Baltimore. *It was too bad. The boy was sweet. He even cried when we fucked. But he was stupid. He bought the bit about a social justice protest, hook line and sinker. So it's over now and I can move on.* She pulled off the skintight tank top, revealing a shoulder and butt covered with tattoos celebrating momentous occasions in her twenty-eight years. *I'm getting these removed. So yesterday,* she thought. Draining a bottle of Evian, she walked a short path to the pool and washed away the stress of her unusual day with a dozen brisk laps. Tomorrow she would consider the rest of her life. Her father, who had taught her well, could take care of himself.

CHAPTER 4

Melody Banks received the White House call as she was falling asleep after her draining session preparing for the coming debate. "This better be important," she answered, eyeshade still in place.

"Miss Banks, this is Alistair Muse, the President's National Security Advisor." The efficient White House operator found Melody within moments of the instruction from a Muse assistant. "I couldn't reach Senator Bridges' liason to our operation, so I've called you. I need to speak to the Senator immediately. We've had an incident near the Capitol, a serious national security breach. I need to brief the Senator and any advisors he deems appropriate. Do you want to arrange this call or should we do it for you?" Muse's tone was imperious and condescending but Banks thought better of pushing back.

"No, I'll call him and get the right people on the line," she said, rubbing her red eyes as she dragged herself from the bed and into the bathroom. "Fifteen minutes, okay?" After taking down numbers for a secure conference connection, she called the cell phone Senator Bridges maintained for urgent contact.

"My God, Melody, do we know what happened?" came a weary voice on the other end. "No, Senator, I assume we'll get all that from Muse in a few minutes." She signed off and called Senator Bridges' longtime foreign policy advisor, an expert on the Middle

East and terrorist activities, and now a Fellow at Brookings. She then located other senior staff and arranged a telephone link for the team to receive Muse's briefing. Bridges' running mate, Texas Congressman Javier Alvarez, was nowhere near a secure phone line.

At the appointed time Muse came on the line. He noted to the group that his team in the basement of the White House was joined by phone with Eldon Mann in Orlando. "Senator, the President has asked me to bring you up to date with what we know about the incident near the Capitol ninety minutes ago."

President Holland had groused about the briefing for Bridges' team. "Godddamit, Alistair, can't we figure this out before we call those people? Am I not still the President?" Muse countered that, like it or not, Senator Bridges could be the next Commander in Chief, and protocol, if not law, dictated that an immediate contact was in order. In any event, Bridges would receive a routine national security briefing later that morning, as had been the case since Bridges became the party's nominee in August.

Muse asked if each had the appropriate security clearances. When satisfied, he continued.

"At approximately midnight, an explosion occurred near or at the Capitol building. The northwest corner of the Capitol is destroyed; the Senate office buildings and several others nearby were damaged as well. However, there appears to be little damage to those on the House side along Independence Avenue, nor was the residential area to the east and northeast seemingly affected by the blast. "

"We believe the explosive device was nuclear, as there is significant radiation detected in the area north of the Capitol. The data from our monitors are coming in now. We do not yet have a count of casualties."'" Muse's tone was formal, his words drawn out to establish authority and control. "Senator, we have no reason to believe that radiation will extend as far north as Annapolis, but we're monitoring its movement. Nor do we have any reason to

believe you are personally at risk. But to be cautious we've asked
the Secret Service to deploy a significantly larger security detail
to your home and headquarters, with helicopter flyovers soon
to be in place."

Senator Bridges and his advisors peppered Muse with questions about the incident, actions underway around the Capitol,
and what the President was doing to deal with the matter. Muse
answered these with little elaboration, assuring the Bridges team
that regular updates would be forthcoming. Mann inserted that
the President had been fully briefed and would be making a public
statement from his office in Orlando at 8 am.

With Congress in recess for the election, the affected area was
relatively simple to quarantine. As soon as the authorities evac-
uated every affected building, the situation around the Capitol
seemed under control.

Away from the blast site, however, order quickly deteriorated.
Television, cable, and radio broadcasts in the Washington market
were up and running, but cell and landline telephone transmis-
sions were jammed. By six am, ambulance, police, and fire engine
sirens blared throughout the city, adding to the panic. The 9/11
attacks two decades earlier were still fresh for many residents, who
assumed that a new terrorist incident was underway.

Streets and freeways leading from the city clogged as thousands
of Washingtonians attempted to evacuate in every direction. With
reliable news at a minimum and uniformed authorities preoccupied with the events around the Capitol, law enforcement officials
feared that many of the city's six hundred thousand citizens could
become an uncontrolled mob.

"The casualty count is now under a half-dozen deaths and
as many injuries," Wolf Blitzer reported, anchoring a non-stop
broadcast from the network's headquarters only a half mile from

the blast site. "Mostly security guards, a taxi driver, and a few late-night customers in nearby bars who wandered outside to see what had happened."

CNN scrolled the casualty count and fed commentary from national security experts. "Had the blast occurred mid-day, loss of life could have been in the hundreds or thousands as tourists roamed the Capitol and the surrounding grounds. We will stay on the air until we are forced to evacuate this building," said Blitzer.

Despite reports of nominal casualties, Washington, D.C. entered a virtual lockdown, with all government employees forbidden to report to work and all businesses closed. Transportation in and out of the city was suspended. Only those involved in the investigation or rescue efforts would be admitted to the quarantined area between the Potomac and a mile north, south and east of the Capitol. The federal enclave soon resembled a war zone populated by technicians in airtight jumpsuits and respirators, recording every square inch of the territory with radiation detectors and high-definition cameras.

As Washingtonians clamored to leave the city, the country glued itself to television reports. Fearing more attacks, law enforcement operations in countless cities struggled to combat an unseen enemy. In Alabama, four Muslim men praying at a small mosque were herded into the street and beaten by a crowd whipped up by a local preacher calling for retribution against "Allah's Terrorists".

Thirty miles from the Capitol, Bridges' senior staff huddled in the study of the Senator's home as a hazy sun rose above the river. A dozen Coast Guard patrol boats motored near the Senator's dock and farther down Little Round Bay near the entrance to the Chesapeake Bay. Two Blackhawk helicopters circled above.

The Bridges compound, enlarged over the years by savvy purchases during economic recessions, stood as one of the region's most desirable locations. Bridges' wife filled their home with comfortable antiques, local art, and landscaped the grounds with gardens full of brilliant colors and inviting paths. A faithfully reproduced Zen garden occupied a corner spot overlooking a small pond stocked with fat, colorful koi, the initial specimens presented to Bridges by the Japanese ambassador. It was a stunning home and would make a fine Presidential residence in the coming years.

"This is one hell of a mess," Bridges began. "Washington has been attacked with a nuclear weapon by God knows who. The city is shut down and we've got no way to get involved in any decision being considered by Holland's people. For all we know they're planning a counter attack as we speak."

"Aren't we supposed to have our people working alongside the President's staff in a situation like this?" Bridges asked.

"Don't everyone speak up at once."

"Cal, you're right, it's a nightmare," said Bridge's national security aide. "I've put in a call to Muse to clear our people into the Situation Room as soon as possible. We've reached out to the FBI and CIA to find out what we can, and I expect to hear back soon."

"We've drafted this statement from you to release to the press as soon as possible," injected Banks. "It doesn't say much but it should buy us some time while we figure out what's happening."

"What do we do about the campaign?" asked Bridges. "We're coming down to the wire. I should call the President myself."

"As far as the campaign goes, we don't have much choice," said Banks. "Holland will almost certainly stop campaigning and make a big deal of it."

"And he's got nothing to lose," chimed in another aide." We're kicking his ass, so he gets to play Commander in Chief."

"Jesus Christ," Bridges sighed, his voice now lowered as he pondered a political and national security situation that was without precedent and almost impossible to fully grasp. "I'll call the President and tell him I'm suspending our campaign and that he has my full support in dealing with the crisis. We'll meet here in an hour."

"Fucking nightmare," Bridges exclaimed to no one in particular. He turned from the group and looked into the rising sun across the river.

CHAPTER 5

The year had been a political nightmare for the President. The U. S. economy was in a ditch, the stock market continuing its slow slide toward pre-Obama levels. Interest rates were up. Housing starts down. Unemployment had risen to ten percent. Mideast tensions roiled the region and African conflicts continued. The sword rattlers in Congress and the media pounded Holland to deploy more military forces in the Gulf region to squeeze Iran and root out ISIS. Bad news dominated streamers across the bottom of cable programming, night after night.

Seven Southern states reversed half-century old voting rights laws and five others legislated severe restrictions on abortion rights. The Supreme Court upheld all the reversals of progressive laws; its conservative balance strengthened by three conservative President Holland appointments.

Mass shootings in shopping malls and schools produced new calls for controls on assault weapons and fueling a hugely successful fund raising campaign by the National Rifle Association. NRA lobbyists torpedoed legislative measures to restrict assault weapons. Billboard slogans—*The only deterrent to an unlawful attack is a fully armed citizenry!*—lined the highways of states with wavering lawmakers. Dozens of southern and western cities enacted new laws allowing the open carriage of firearms. A Texas local school board added gun training to extracurricular offerings for middle and high school students, and nominally trained guards roamed school hallways.

The hurricane season hammered the Gulf, and the western states' decade long drought spawned massive wildfires. Bitter disputes over water rights gave rise to severe rationing and widespread moratoria on development. Catastrophic typhoons in the Pacific left millions without shelter. Several island nations began permanent evacuation operations.

Climate scientists once again determined that atmospheric temperatures were now out of control. CO_2 levels arising from the U.S. and developing countries had pushed the world far beyond the tipping point. New reports revealed that the Greenland ice shelf was dangerously close to sliding into the Atlantic. A projected ten feet sea level rise threatened millions living in low-lying areas around the globe.

The issue, however, remained far down the list of voter concerns, well below illegal immigration, "religious freedoms", gun rights, regulation of the internet, and, of course, the economy. Consequently, all legislative measures to slow the planet's mass destruction were defeated as job killers, or threat to the "American way of life".

Democrats, relegated to the dungeon of minority status in Congress, nevertheless found themselves with an attractive presidential candidate. Emboldened by President Holland's muddling performance, and a bulging war chest from frustrated liberals, Senator Calvin Bridges emerged from the primaries with a head of steam. A successful convention gave Bridges a modest lead in the polls, bolstered by the first Latino vice presidential nominee. Infighting among conservative splinter factions left Democrats giddy with optimism about the coming election.

As the candidates prepared for their final debate, political reporters trumpeted the event as a make-or-break opportunity for Holland to draw closer to his Democratic opponent.

"This is a big one for both candidates," said MSNBC's Chris Matthews. "The first two were mostly a draw, so Holland has to come out swinging if he's going to get any late momentum. Otherwise, he's toast."

"This race is moving away from Bridges," opined a conservative talking head on Fox. "He's an empty vessel and voters are starting to see that. The President has a much deeper understanding of foreign policy and national security, and that's going to come out tomorrow night."

Both camps set up mock debate operations, the President in Orlando and Bridges in Annapolis. Surrogate opponents came briefed with their toughest challenges. Applause lines were crafted. Opening and closing statements were scripted. Calvin Bridges' personal assistant scheduled a massage and a discreet tanning session. JFK's youthful bronze complexion for his last televised debate with a pasty faced Nixon in 1960 was not forgotten.

As the radioactive dust began to settle around Washington, none of the preparations would be put to use. A final, conclusive presidential debate would never happen.

Driving cautiously over an icy stretch of interstate, Jack Raglan stopped for pancakes in Billings, Montana, then made the long, boring drive north, crossing the Canadian border in early afternoon. Fortified by a thermos of strong coffee, he cranked up the volume on his Sirius XM player and sang along with angry country lyrics from Toby Keith, *my kind of kick ass singer,* smiled Raglan. *Takes no shit from anyone.*

Raglan would make Saskatoon by dinner and settle in for a few days to assess the aftermath of his scheme. He would call Jojo on one of the dozen new untraceable cellphones he had purchased weeks before, to calm his package messenger as he and Delores were driving away from Baltimore. That phone would then be destroyed, as would others as their utility was exhausted. He figured to keep his daughter out of the loop from here on.

Raglan had planned every move down to each day, each meal, motel, and phone call, each dollar spent. No guns, no credit cards, no stops where cameras might follow his movements. Fortunately, he thought, the Canadians had not yet caught up to America's obsession with law enforcement cameras on every corner. He would drink in bars only moderately and avoid all confrontations with locals. Keep the conversations to hockey, football, and the weather. Beard and ponytail trimmed, he would dress like every other middle aged Canadian getting ready for another brutal winter. The second bomb, stuffed into a ratty suitcase, would stay hidden in his trunk. In a few days he would find a place to quietly disappear.

CHAPTER 6

The President's speechwriters and senior advisors huddled in Holland's Florida estate, crafting the words he would soon deliver to a country reeling from the bombing of the Capitol. Holland swiveled in an oversized executive chair and plopped his boots on the wide oak desk.

"This is good stuff!" he bellowed to the room, as he finished a new draft of his remarks. "Damn good! I don't need to do a run through. I've got it!" Holland slammed down the text, spilling a pot of coffee onto the smooth, finely crafted surface.

While governor he had the desk made with decking sold to him as planking from the WW2 battleship USS Florida. He'd heard from an aunt that his grandfather served on the ship during the Korean War. An elegant framed photo of the warship hung nearby. Holland delighted in telling the story to visitors to the Governor's office.

In fact, the boards were from a barn outside Tallahassee. Holland gathered political memorabilia and created plausible stories that claimed an association with bits of history. While campaigning for the presidency, he made a point of conducting televised visits to the presidential libraries of the men who served before.

Both Roosevelts, Kennedy, and Reagan. Political party didn't matter. It was the history he sought to appropriate, the men whose reputations and stature he hoped to channel.

"I greatly admire FDR," he said, on camera, peering over a glass case filled with the wartime president's correspondence with Churchill. "He was a leader, a courageous leader." As he moved upward through politics, Holland mastered a wide smile showing off a row of bright white choppers. He had seen film clips of FDR and unselfconsciously practiced the look until it became part of his public persona.

And Holland was not without remarkable political skills. He deftly handled his more conservative primary opponents in every race by never allowing them to get to his right on hot button issues. Realpolitik might force him to govern like a centrist, but few could match his ability to own those issues that inflamed the base. And he drove liberals crazy by winning elections.

Over the past year Holland had been unmercifully satirized in editorial cartoons picturing him as the reincarnation of William Howard Taft, by far the nation's heaviest president. And in a world dominated by vanity, Grady Holland was among the most vain. A barrel-chested, perpetually tanned man nearing his sixtieth birthday, Holland had let himself go since entering the White House. To conceal the rolls of fat collecting around his middle, Holland secretly wore a customized version of Spanx. A discreet cosmetic surgeon removed a growing fold of flesh under his chin.

"Where is the Grady Holland who clawed his way to the top?" read the lead in an influential conservative blog as the reelection campaign began. "Where is the fire that propelled a young Florida lawyer into the Florida governor's mansion? The man who held so much promise to turn around a bloated government, the man who would reverse the unconstitutional excesses of the Obama years? The President is now himself a bloated shadow of that leader."

Stung by such attacks from otherwise friendly sources, Holland surrounded himself with staff and old pals who would help him ignore his fall from political grace.

"Hell, Grady, if they can't take a joke, fuck 'em" shouted one law school friend who had joined the President for a September afternoon of televised football games in the White House. The two sat alone in the front row of the hundred-seat theater waiting for a half dozen compatriots flying in to prop up the president's spirits. A suited steward brought cocktails and popcorn to the two men, and hurried to the rear of the cavernous room.

"Billy, they just don't get it," complained Holland. "This is a goddamn miserable job, and all I get is whining from the press, from Congress, from all those fucking talking heads. Some days I just wanna say fuck it, they can have it. I'm outa here."

"Aw, man," said his companion, waving both arms. "Just look around you. You've got it all – this place, that amazing plane – you're the most important fucking dude in the universe!"

As the rest of his guests ambled into the theater, all dressed in football jerseys of their beloved Florida Gators, Holland's mood lightened. Hugs all around, the President of the United States led the group in a raucous version of "The Orange and Blue" fight song.

＊　＊　＊

As he prepared to address the nation, Holland rearranged the photos behind his desk so the camera would pick up not only his family but also portraits of the country's greatest commanders-in-chief.

"My fellow Americans," began the President's televised address, with a line he envisioned as the moment that would define his presidency, "once again we have experienced a day that will live in infamy. Early this morning our nation came under attack. A device was detonated at the United States Capitol, causing massive damage and releasing radioactive particles."

"Let me say first that there is no cause for panic." Thanks to expert makeup, Holland looked refreshed. "Federal and local authorities have the area under control, and decontamination crews are already neutralizing the radiation."

"I've ordered the head of Homeland Security to provide regular reports to you as our investigation proceeds. We are treating this incident as an act of terrorism." The President paused for effect. "I can assure you that we will not rest until those responsible for this heinous crime are brought to justice."

"Now, as you know, we are nearing the end of a presidential campaign. Given the grave situation facing our country, I have decided to immediately suspend all campaign activity. I spoke to Senator Bridges this morning and he has agreed to do the same. This is no time for debates, no time for raw politics. It is a time for all Americans, regardless of party, to come together as one people dedicated to preserving our nation's freedoms."

"I will be back with you as new developments arise. In the meantime, know that we are working around the clock to deal with this crisis. God bless you, and God bless America."

Eldon Mann watched the President's address from an adjacent study and realized, despite Holland's lackluster campaign performance, and his sheer incompetence as a leader, this election was not yet lost.

CHAPTER 7

On the floor in a makeshift office in Calvin Bridge's guesthouse, Melody Banks went through a routine of stretching exercises to fight off the stiffness that came from eighteen-hour work days. Athletic, long limbed, she twisted her body into a shape a ballet dancer would admire. She held the pose and focused on the coming two weeks until election day, grasping for a strategy for a campaign stuck in neutral.

"Head turning attractive, disciplined, with a cerebral intelligence," wrote one dazzled reporter when her promotion to campaign manager was announced. "She may be just what Bridges needs to build some momentum."

"She may be smart," countered a TV analyst. "But Banks is a relative newcomer to presidential politics, and it remains to be seen if she can handle the rough side of the game. And this race is going to get rough."

Reluctantly, Banks became Bridges' *uber* aide when the Senator's original campaign manager had crumbled earlier in the summer. What others saw in her potential was, to Banks, a mask.

"I can't do this!" she cried to her therapist after getting the call from the candidate. "I'll fail. And the campaign will fail because of me."

"So you fail. What's the worst thing that can happen?" responded the therapist, whose patients ran more to depression than the worries of a woman about to take over a half billion dollar political enterprise.

"The worst?" said Banks. "I'll tell you the worst—Grady fucking Holland wins reelection and continues to send this country down a rat hole. Everything I care about"—she held up a hand and ticked off finger by finger the focus of her fears—"the environment, women's rights, poverty, social justice, gun violence, you name it—it all goes to shit!"

"I don't have the experience, I'm not tough enough, and I sure as hell don't have the confidence to do this job," Banks was now sobbing. "What am I going to do?"

Eyes still reddened from tears, she left the therapist's office, exited onto a blazing hot Washington street and stumbled straight into Jackson Cripple, an old friend and occasional political associate.

"Jackson!" she practically threw herself at the rangy, bearded man in jeans, a fitted tee shirt and dark sunglasses.

"Melody Banks! Nice to see you, too! Whoa! What's wrong?" Banks clung to Cripple, crying again. "Let's get off this street."

Over a cup at an upstairs corner table at Teaism, a popular Dupont Circle hangout favored by local writers and students, she poured out her anxieties to Cripple. He listened patiently, paused and ran both hands along the rough wood table between them.

"Dammit, Melody!" Cripple pounded the table. The room was now empty of the morning crowd. "You've got doubts? You worry about handling that campaign? Let me tell you something, sweetheart. Everyone has doubts! These people who seem to be supremely confident? They're all frauds. It's just a cover up. We all have anxieties!"

"I'll tell you what you're going to do," he leaned halfway over the table, holding both of Banks hands. "You're going to get your ass to Annapolis and tell Calvin Bridges you're ready for this challenge, and you're going to help him win this goddamn election. You understand?"

She stood and reached across the table to hug her old friend. Her therapist charged two hundred dollars for a crying session. Cripple had cost her a cup of iced chai tea.

That encounter was the last relaxed moment in Melody's life as she took the helm of Bridges' campaign. There was no textbook to prepare her operation for the post-bombing confusion facing *Bridges to the Future.*

Banks worked through the night at her cluttered desk. As the bizarre developments unfolded over the past few days she had no sleep, nominal grooming, and a diet of cold sandwiches and bad coffee.

With four video monitors alongside her desk locked into news channels, she flopped into a chair, feet propped on a side credenza, and groaned at her appearance in the nearby mirror.

Fifteen years earlier she moved to Washington after an unbroken run of success at Brown, where she graduated *magna cum laude* and starred on the university's nationally ranked field hockey team. Enrolling in American University's law school with plans to become a diplomat, she bartended nights at Blue 44, a local eatery in northwest D.C. There she met Paul, a young congressman, a recent widower, and began a two year affair that would end her interest in foreign policy and launch a passion for politics.

"Why don't you come work on the Hill this summer?" he asked Melody as she studied in his bed for an exam in contract law, a subject of no interest for her. "I know this terrific congresswoman from New York who'd love to have you on her staff. It'd be great experience, and she has a real future, probably be Speaker some day." Banks looked up from her text and smiled. "No? At least let's talk about it tonight." Hearing a child's cry he threw off the covers and walked naked to his young son's bedroom to comfort the child. He returned and slid under the sheet, caressing Melody's thigh.

"That's sweet, Paul. Hold that thought." She smiled at his lean, athletic body and considered a break from her studies. "But I've got this exam, and you have babies to feed."

Her time with Paul ended on friendly terms when she left for a three-month trek across Italy after her graduation. He needed a wife to help with his three children and soon married a Bethesda occupational therapist. The job with the New York congresswoman led to a much sought-after position in the White House Counsel's office after her graduation and Obama's election. The day after meeting the President at a White House dinner, Melody's mother died at the hand of a deranged gunman who had bought his semiautomatic pistol at a gun show. Melody emerged from her grief with a determination to elect candidates with guts to face down the gun lobby.

Three years later she joined a prosperous political consulting firm representing progressive candidates and left the legal profession for good.

A year before the Bridges campaign began, Banks was featured as one of "Washington's Most Beautiful Insiders" along with a handful of lobbyists, Hill staffers, and four buff congressmen who spent more time in the House gym than in committee hearings. At five-ten with a face some likened to a glamorous, brainy, much admired Australian actress, Melody was a showstopper at every event she entered.

A "well put together, good looking woman," as her father once described her. Others had been more explicit in their compliments.

"Totally fuckable!" crowed a young lobbyist watching the campaign coverage over the din of a Thursday night bar crowd. With no ball games on the dozen flat screens that evening, politics offered consolation entertainment.

"I would, like, switch parties and go door to door for Bridges if I could just suck those tits!" said another twenty something Republican staffer crowding into the Hawk & Dove, a Capitol Hill institution.

Now approaching thirty-eight, Melody vowed to friends that the Bridges campaign would be her last. But as the operation began to find its footing, as Bridges' lead steadily increased into the early fall, she started to feel the rush.

"Just remember," noted her old boyfriend Paul, when he learned of Banks' sudden promotion, "the fleas come with the dog. There won't be many easy days from here on. And when it's going really well, don't let it go to your head. There's always a bear lurking behind a tree."

After Banks completed a review of urgent staff memos for the candidate's attention, she picked up a semi-scholarly magazine article entitled "Power Workouts: The Next Orgasm?"

Her mind drifted to *her* last orgasm some months ago. After a particularly unsatisfying night of sex in Paris with the U.S. Embassy commerce attaché, a man twelve years her senior, she slipped into the bathroom to cleanse herself of his mess. Frustrated but still highly aroused, perched on a bidet, she directed the stream of warm water to her clitoris and soon felt a delicious spasm rush through her body. *Wow!* She thought at the time. *Someday I MUST get one of these.*

That was eight months ago, and it was the best sexual experience she'd had since then. The Bridges campaign – in fact, all her campaigns and policy fights – had fulfilled her passion for liberal causes, but also overwhelmed her desire for a normal life. The lack of good sex was only part of it. She longed for a committed relationship, evenings binge watching television, weekends of bike trips, theater, movies, wine tours, even Europe. *Why can't I...* she began to muse when a Secret Service agent opened her door.

"Miss Banks, the Senator asks that you join him in his study." He extended an arm, indicating some urgency. Banks thought the agent looked like a college student, but he was soldier rigid and a bulge in his coat covered a large pistol. She thought better of flirting with him, and grabbed her laptop, following the agent into the house.

CHAPTER 8

With downtown Washington shut down, tourism, shopping, and dining disappeared. The city settled into a communal paranoia as government officials struggled to assure residents that radiation from the bombing was contained, but that everyone should be on the lookout for unusual activity. The meaning was left to the citizenry's imagination. More than half the population, those with the means to do so, fled Washington to await further developments.

"So how will this crisis affect the election?" asked John King of his panel of political talking heads, now relocated to a safer northern Virginia studio. "Our latest poll has Calvin Bridges holding on to a lead that has narrowed just above the margin of error. Both candidates have suspended their campaigns after the Capitol bombing, but the election is only twelve days away."

While the talkers opined along predictable left-right lines, Eldon Mann gathered the President's political advisors over sandwiches and ice tea in his Orlando hotel suite. Mann had sworn off alcohol years before, realizing that strong drink would impair his ability to control situations. At this critical point, control was paramount.

"We've shut down all the President's travel, canceled all the events, told the field staff to stay put," noted a senior campaign aide. "What now? We're still five points down. What CAN we do?" The other men looked up from their cellphones and waited for Mann to respond.

"We wait," said Mann, to the howls of the political team. He raised both arms to calm the outcry. "Just hear me out. The bombing has scrambled the race. A few days ago we had a lackluster incumbent going nowhere in the polls, and an opponent who was on a roll."

"Now we have a Commander in Chief taking charge of a national crisis, hunting down terrorists, protecting the country. And we've got a challenger who can't shoot back. We have an open field, at least for the next few days."

The meeting broke up with a million dollar team of political consultants shaking their heads and grousing as the group filed out of the room. Mann smiled, stroked his cheek with a cold glass of tea, and closed his eyes for a full minute.

Eldon Mann had navigated Washington politics as an inside operator who quickly figured out what made his bosses tick. He worked hard to exploit their strengths and suppress their weaknesses. With Holland that challenge was huge. But he had plenty of tools. In the Holland White House it was clear he had unquestioned authority.

"He never yells," noted a Mann protégé. "But if you fuck up there won't be a second chance. He'll fire your ass before you know what happened."

Consequently, he was respected and feared. After Holland's first election, a *Washington Post* profile described Mann as, "part Karl Rove, part H. R. Haldeman, a tightly wound, consummate political pro. With a broad, square, unsmiling face, he could pass for an even more humorless, mid-career Dick Cheney. You wouldn't want to pass a lazy day at the ballpark with him, but if the President needs to get something big done, Eldon Mann would be the right guy."

Mann seemed to have no close friends and few outside activities other than a regular early morning workout in the White House gym. Few were surprised when his marriage dissolved midway through the first Administration. Weary of playing second fiddle to his political life, Mann's wife moved to San Francisco and into a Pacific Heights flat with a celebrated artist she had been seeing while Mann served the President.

"Why do you care what happens to that man?" As she left, his wife stood in the door of their comfortable Chevy Chase home, holding two bags and shaking her head. "He's a total asshole, you've said it yourself. He treats you and everyone around him like shit."

Mann watched her Uber drive away and thought, *good riddance. She knew exactly what she was getting into with me.*

CHAPTER 9

Extensive internal polling by both campaigns revealed alarming news. When asked "Does the recent attack on the U. S. Capitol affect your support for either presidential candidate?" Holland's numbers rose and five percent of Bridges' support had dropped from "committed" to "leaning". Those still "undecided" grew by five percent.

"This is a disaster," said Bridges to the advisors assembled in his dining room, which was now functioning full time as a campaign war room. "We need to get on TV, and now. We need a message that is tough on terrorism, gives statesmanlike support to Holland, blah, blah, blah. We need to get on top of this!"

"Right," responded the candidate's media chief. "We're working on scripts now. We'll have something for you later today."

"Well, it better be good. The last drafts were pathetic," said Bridges, running both hands through his hair as if scrubbing his scalp, pacing the room. "Melody?"

"I've been on the phone with every state director in the target states," she said. "These polls aren't as bad as they seem." She turned her laptop so the candidate and others could see what she was reviewing.

"Here's what it looks like. The national numbers are correct, we've dropped, but much of that has happened in states we won't win anyway—the South, the mountain west, and so on. We're holding steady in the six swing states that count. Look at this map, these numbers." Banks ran through the presentation provided by her staff and let the conversation evolve into a number crunching, state-by-state analysis. She needed time to think and come up with something more to overcome Holland's revived prospects. *I can do this,* she thought. *I can do this.*

The White House, the Bridges Campaign, and official Washington arose to a barrage of commentary as the networks' analysts discussed the bombing and the suspended presidential campaigns. The head of Homeland Security bounced between the Sunday talk shows. For politics, Stephanopoulos added the chairs of the DNC and RNC with his regular panel. *Meet the Press* piped in Eldon Mann and Melody Banks. Fox brought on familiar old faces James Carville and former Republican heavyweight Haley Barbour. CBS went with two senior House members and a rising conservative star.

Mann reiterated the President's determination to devote all his energy to the terrorism crisis. "The President is setting aside politics for a more important priority. I'll leave it to the American people to decide the election."

When asked to comment on Mann's statement, Banks froze. "Senator Bridges supports the President's focus on the bombing incident. But we'll, uh...we'll be back on the campaign at the appropriate time." *Jesus!* She thought. *What kind of dumb comment was that?*

As the show moved to the next round of analysts, Banks removed her headset and sighed. There were few more frustrating experiences than sitting alone in a chair in a dark studio, unable to see your questioner or the other guests. She glanced at a nearby monitor and saw Eldon Mann's tight, restrained snarl as he thanked the host. *He is one scary asshole*, she thought, pulling a parka over her TV-ready outfit. *But he is really, really good at this stuff.*

The partisan sparring between the talking heads was predictable and unenlightening for viewers. It was left to one presidential scholar to make a closing understatement.

"This is President Holland's moment to lead. History rewards those who do so with courage and discipline during a national crisis. Lincoln and Franklin Roosevelt are our best examples. Hoover, and perhaps George W. Bush, are examples of another kind."

"It's unclear if Grady Holland is up to the challenge."

TOP SECRET MEMORANDUM   October 25, 11 am

To: The President
Via: The Chief of Staff
From: Director of Intelligence Services, Central
Intelligence Agency

In advance of the regular security briefing, we are
forwarding the following information resulting
from our lab tests, extensive screening of
surveillance equipment around the Capitol, and
intelligence sources in the Mideast.

The device exploded at the base of the Capitol was
a crudely constructed "dirty bomb", containing
ten to twenty pounds of highly radioactive cesium,
likely obtained from discarded medical equipment.
As we have discussed in the past, several hundred
pounds of cesium and other radioactive materials
have disappeared from laboratories and commercial
facilities over the past thirty years. The
explosive was Semtex-H, manufactured in the Czech
Republic.

A Caucasian who appears to have been in his
twenties placed the device under a wooden bleacher
under construction for the Inauguration at the
northwest corner of the Capitol. He was killed
instantly by the blast. We are now analyzing
clothing, bone, and tissue fragments near the site.

At this point we have no evidence that the
incident was carried out by any known terrorist
group in the Mideast, despite claims to the
contrary coming from the region.

Homeland Security is forwarding separate memoranda
relating to the damage and radiation exposure in
and around the Capitol.

CHAPTER 10

"Eight days! Eight days, people!" An eager young Bridges staffer stood on a table in the campaign's Annapolis headquarters and tried to rally the hundred or so schedulers, field coordinators, press and online staff, administrative aides, and volunteer gofers. "We're still up! We're gonna win!"

To Banks, the applause seemed more perfunctory than excited, as she climbed on the same table for her morning update. "I hope everyone got some rest this weekend. You're going to need it."

"It's true, we've formally 'suspended' the campaign." She made quotation marks in the air. "But we're not stopping. We're online in a big way—you guys are doing a great job over there." She gestured to a corner of the room housing two-dozen veterans of past online campaigns, led by a renowned cyber genius from the Howard Dean campaign. "Geeks for Cal" were responsible for a virtual nonstop conversation with the candidate's fourteen million "friends".

"Our field staff is reporting great numbers. We have twenty-six thousand volunteers taking people to the polls next Tuesday." Banks felt the energy rising in the room when she closed, with a pointed finger in the air. "And this weekend the campaign will be back on the air with the strongest ads yet. It takes more than a bomb to stop this campaign!"

Walking back to her office, Banks met her lead pollster in the hallway. She grabbed Melody's arm and steered her into a nearby room.

"We have a problem," began the pollster, a Lily Tomlin looka-like who was the Party's most respected data analyst. She pulled Banks to a large monitor displaying six spreadsheets. "We just finished analyzing the two-day tracking numbers. We've held more or less steady in the six swing states, but Holland's numbers are up sharply among independents. And it's all about the terrorism stuff. His speech yesterday drove his numbers up big time."

"We've now got a dead heat, and it's trending the wrong way," she was still holding on to Banks' arm. "Melanie, we've got to get back on the air, get Bridges out there doing something!"

"Eldon, dammit! Get me out of here!" The President screamed at Mann, who had returned to Washington after federal officials declared the White House secure and out of radiation danger from the Capitol blast. Holland circled his pool in flip-flops and a robe that barely covered his bulging girth. A morning swim, followed by French toast and a Bloody Mary, did little to ease the President's restlessness.

"I've made three televised addresses. I've talked to every goddamn world leader. I've called almost every fucking member of Congress and given interviews to every asshole reporter you've asked me to." Holland spat out an olive pit and continued his rant.

"You wouldn't let me go to the Florida-Auburn game on Saturday. I can't play golf. I sit around waiting for the next CIA briefing, which gives me not one damn thing that makes sense."

"They're now telling me it was probably some dumb white kid who planted the bomb. Can you believe that? I want some other opinions. Get that guy from the Heritage Foundation down here. And that agent who wrote the book about ISIS plants in the U.S. I want some other...some other ideas. And by the way, the kid could've simply been an ISIS plant!"

"If I'm going to be a leader, I've gotta lead, goddammit!"

"And another thing," said Holland, taking a long gulp from a second drink. "Get the fucking Vice President off my ass. He's driving me crazy, calling every day wanting to be briefed, to be involved. Just what I need, his bleeding heart liberal ass fucking up my work."

"Jesus, Eldon, you talked me into putting him on the ticket. What were you thinking? I'd've been better off with Sarah fucking Palin."

Mann considered reminding Holland that, four years earlier, the nominee needed a mature, steady hand to balance the ticket. And West's credentials were impeccable: a 100% Chamber of Commerce rating, pro-life, fiscal conservative. His left-leaning environmental record was of little concern, for, after all, he would only be the Vice President.

Holland's tirade reminded Mann to get Vice President West to reschedule the meeting with coal company executives and their lobbyist, a former congressman who had been extremely helpful. The bombing had canceled all White House activity for a week, but this meeting was important for the President, and to Mann personally.

CHAPTER 11

Dan West carved overhand strokes through the warm current streaming from jets inside the lap pool adjoining the Naval Observatory, the grand antebellum home that housed every Vice President since Walter Mondale. A dedicated swimmer since childhood, the slim, fit, seventy-year old managed at least a half mile daily in the heated waters. Normally he would have listened to the Eurythmics or Sting on his waterproof iPod while finishing his laps, but this morning he used the time to think through his current predicament.

I'm so tired of this, he thought.

He paused and draped one arm over the tile slab, where a tall glass of juice awaited him. He downed the orange and mango concoction and smiled at the recollection of his late wife's favorite morning drink. The cold air was bracing as he slipped back into the pool.

Holland's an arrogant prick, he thought, rolling into a breast-stroke for his final laps. *And then there's Eldon Mann. Pure goddamn evil.*

Like many vice presidents before him, West had often been ignored and isolated from the President's business. When

approached by Holland to be his running mate four years earlier, then Senator West extracted a personal commitment to be
included in every important meeting and to play a significant
role in making administration policy. After the election he consulted previous vice presidents who had similar agreements. Each
cautioned West that once elected, the President's commitment
could be quickly forgotten.

"It's great when they need you for something," counseled
Dan Quayle, who had been relegated to the Space Council as
his primary public role under President Bush. "Don't expect any
real support from the President's staff for what you want to do,"
warned Dick Cheney, still smarting from W's refusal to pardon
his felonious Chief of Staff. Biden had offered the only marginally
optimistic observation.

"Dan, you're gonna be a great Vice President. I gotta tell ya, it's
a great job. Just watch out for all those assholes on Holland's staff
who'll fuck you in a New York minute if you let 'em. Otherwise,
it'll be a lot of fun."

West threw himself into those tasks deemed too insignificant or
unseemly for the President. After their Inauguration, he attended
every fundraiser, chaired every meaningless commission, and took
on every meeting blown off by the President. He even conducted
personal tours of historic offices in the Old Executive Office
Building and the West Wing for major donors who expected
special treatment from the White House.

"Mr. Vice President, here's how it will work." Soon after moving
into the West Wing, a Holland aide met with the Vice President to outline the discreet policy toward "special friends" of
the Administration.

"We've got a staff assistant over at the RNC who does nothing
but screen the financial contribution and political importance
of each visitor. There's a rating system to determine how they
should be treated: 90–100 gets a sit down in the Oval Office,
80–90 warrants a few minutes with you or Eldon Mann, and

maybe lunch. 70–80 gets a visit with a Cabinet member. Below that level and they're shuffled off to a staff assistant."

"This seems bizarre," responded an alarmed Vice President. "What if it gets out?"

"Don't worry." The aide smiled and shook West's hand as he left the Vice President's office, a few steps down a narrow hall from the Oval Office. "We'll handle that. It's all in a data base that only Eldon Mann can access."

West's age and experience as a respected Midwestern Senator, and his acceptable conservative credentials had earned him a spot on Holland's ticket, but the party's extreme right wing groused about West's political temperament and especially his environmental record and support for modest gun control measures.

Early in his term, he proudly framed a profile declaring him to be "a true conservative, an environmentalist of the Teddy Roosevelt school. He is expected to steer the President and his cabinet in that direction."

As the reelection campaign began, he had encountered an Appalachian family uprooted from their home as a result of toxic waste from the mountains of coal ash dumped from nearby utility operations. The family brought all five children to a political rally with the hope of cornering the Vice President with their dilemma. Hugging a rope line as West made his way from the stage, they beseeched him to hear their story.

West did more than listen. Much to the aggravation of his campaign handlers, he ordered his staff to arrange an impromptu visit to the family's home before leaving for the next event.

After coffee in the dilapidated double-wide house trailer on the outskirts of town, the parents accompanied West to the nearby power company grounds. Large black pools held the coal ash that had been leaching into streams and groundwater aquifers.

"They know it's making people sick around here, sir," said the pale, sunken-eyed father, who looked more like seventy than his forty-five years. "But the state people won't do anything about

it. The EPA was out here last year, but nothin' happened. The
company's just got too much power."

West took it all in and promised the family he would look
into the problem and get back to them. Sending them home in
a staff van, the Vice President slumped in his SUV, rubbing his
aching temples.

"Can I get you anything, sir?" His traveling aide opened a bottle
of water and fished two Advils from his bag. West took the pills
and drained the water bottle.

"It's okay," he said, after a long silence. "Let's get back
on schedule."

Returning to the White House, West ordered a review of the
family's complaint by the Council on Environmental Quality, a
White House operation staffed with energy industry sympathizers.
These officials assured the Vice President that the West Virginia
family was exaggerating the coal ash problem.

Dissatisfied, West dispatched an aide to be briefed by career
scientists at the Environmental Protection Administration. They
confirmed that the agency's internal findings revealed massive
clean water violations at the West Virginia site. When pressed,
they noted that EPA political appointees and White House officials had stalled any regulations, much less Justice Department
prosecution of the company. The Council, using industry data,
warned of "catastrophic job losses" in the region if the industry
was forced to reduce its operations.

The Vice President sent a personal letter to the family, noting
his ongoing investigation, and vowed to take up the matter with
the President. However these private meetings were more often
than not canceled due to "scheduling conflicts."

With the fall campaign underway, the President held a rare
cabinet meeting as a photo opportunity to bolster his sagging
poll numbers. He used the event to express his condolences to the
ten families who lost relatives in a mass shooting at a children's
soccer game near Atlanta.

After cameras were ushered out of the room, West challenged the President and his colleagues to revisit the administration's lockstep support for the NRA and the gun manufacturers.

"How many times do these killings have to happen before we stand up to these people?" he asked the group. "I know we've supported the gun crowd. Hell, I'm a lifetime NRA member. But it's gone too far. How many more children have to die before we do the right thing?"

An awkward silence enveloped the Cabinet Room before President Holland spoke.

"Dan, we're all concerned about this. But we've got a lot on our plate, and we can't get distracted. Besides, even if we did propose new gun laws, our friends on the Hill would go berserk. There's no sense wasting our political capital on something that just won't fly."

West renewed his appeal to Holland over lunch later in the week, an hour on the President's schedule grudgingly granted by his staff. "Grady, this gun violence has just gotten out of hand, and we haven't done a damn thing to stop it."

West was unable to eat the meal prepared for the two, alone in the President's study next to the Oval office, and nervously pushed the greens around his plate. Seeking the right words to move the President, he looked across the table at Holland, who was happily shoveling grilled salmon, seemingly oblivious to West's pleading.

"Dan, my friend, I appreciate your passion on this. I'll give it some thought, but I just don't see how we can take the lead. Maybe you should meet with the Republican leadership and see what they think."

Holland pushed back from the table, wiped his mouth, and dismissed his Vice President. "Now I gotta run. This has been great. We gotta do this more often!" He slapped West on the shoulder and walked through a side door back to his office.

West lingered in the President's study to calm his growing anger. As he rose to return to his office he overheard Holland's conversation with Eldon Mann as both men entered the Oval Office, a door separating the two rooms cracked slightly open.

"Jesus, Eldon," said Holland, "he's gone bonkers! Wants us to go after the NRA. Can you believe that shit?" Mann nodded but suppressed a response.

"Look," said Holland, punching a finger into Mann's chest. "I don't want to see him. I don't want to read his fucking memos. I don't want him anywhere near me for the rest of this campaign. If I could get him off the ticket, I would. You understand?"

The Vice President was shaken. He knew Holland had little use for his help or advice, but he was rocked by the rawness of his insult. He knew then that, one way or the other, his days in the White House were numbered.

Weeks later, returning to the White House compound for the first time since Homeland Security had cleared the building for priority occupants, West reluctantly agreed to Mann's demand to meet with industry lobbyists. Executives from the nation's second largest coal-burning utility were ushered into the Vice President's ceremonial office.

West greeted the group with an introduction to the magnificent room that had served sixteen Secretaries of the Navy, pointing out the historic gasolier fixtures, with gas globes on top and electric lights below. "These ceilings and walls are decorated with allegorical symbols of the Navy Department. There are some great photos of FDR working with the war cabinet," noted the Vice President, who ordinarily enjoyed giving guests a tour of one of Washington's grandest rooms.

Steve Barnes, their walrusy Washington lobbyist, introduced the five dark suited men as "close friends of the President". Barnes had long questioned the Vice President's commitment to the administration's pro-energy positions. As the executives took seats around the long cherry table, the lobbyist pulled West aside.

"Dan, thanks for seeing us. These guys are very, very important to me, and they're important to the President. They're looking forward to some encouraging news." He flashed a forced smile and gave West a sharp pat on the back as he returned to his clients at the table.

The lobbyist opened the meeting with an overview of his client's "good faith" efforts to clean up toxic waste in West Virginia and other locations in which their utilities operated. The utility's CEO claimed environmentalists were distorting the scientific evidence and that local activists were ignoring the company's commitment to resolve a minor problem.

The Vice President interrupted his visitors' presentation. "I know this is the industry position, and I know you're just doing your job. We've always tried to be supportive of you folks, and we've given you special opportunities to make your case with this administration. But this toxic dump in West Virginia is going unchecked and it's happened elsewhere. You can't stonewall EPA or the Justice Department forever." West opened the file he had brought to the meeting and distributed copies of the EPA report to the group.

"Mr. Vice President, you know these claims are just part of the conspiracy to kill coal," responded the lobbyist, waving off the EPA documents. "We just need EPA to get the message to back off. And by the way, Dan, no one has been quicker to support the President than these businessmen. I don't have to tell you how deep that support goes."

"Well, we'll just have to disagree about this issue." The Vice President rose to indicate that the meeting was over. "I'll be advising the President to take a closer look at the EPA findings. We'll get back to you. Thanks for coming in."

West shook the hands of his stunned guests as they were ushered from the office. He canceled his next appointment, left by a side door and exited two floors down, and onto 17th Street. With his Secret Service detail in tow, he walked toward the Washington Monument, then west toward the Lincoln Memorial, for more than an hour. With severe security precautions still in place, and a tall fence cordoning off a half-mile in every direction from the Capitol, there were no tourists in the area. He walked unnoticed, deep in thought, for nearly an hour.

A light rain turned to sleet as the Vice President reached the awning leading to the entrance to the West Wing. He slowly climbed the steep stairway to the first floor, and entered his office. West informed his secretary that he was heading home to rest. He pulled on a heavy topcoat and waved off an assistant who expected to accompany him with briefing material for the next day. As West's limo headed for the Naval Observatory he pulled out a notepad and listed the points he intended to make to the President as soon as the staff allowed him into the Oval Office.

The limo's secure telephone trilled. Eldon Mann's call was not unexpected. "Mr. Vice President, I just spoke to Steve Barnes. He isn't happy."

"I don't give a damn what you heard from those people," responded West. "I'm sick and tired of this shit. I want to see the President and I want to see him right away."

"That's not possible," said Mann. "He's getting ready for the weekend fly-around. We're jump starting the campaign."

"What the hell?" said West. "I haven't heard anything about this. My staff doesn't know about any campaign schedule."

"Mr. Vice President, we've decided it's best that you sit this out. It's going to be a rough three or four days."

Seething at the last straw in his long-running humiliation by Holland and his staff, the Vice President slammed down the phone. He leapt from the car as it pulled up to his home, and vaulted the stairs to his porch, two at a time.

As he entered his home and began the climb to his study, West was hit with a powerful chest pain and lightheadedness. He slumped to the floor, too dizzy to stand. A Secret Service agent knelt by the Vice President and spoke into his lapel microphone.

"We have Badger down at NavObs.," the agent called, using West's security moniker, harking back to his Wisconsin roots. "I repeat, Badger is down! Require medical aide immediately."

"I'm fine!" West responded. "I just can't breathe." Struggling to rise, the Vice President slumped back to the floor and passed out.

Within minutes a Navy physician entered the residence and ran a cursory check of West's vital signs. An ambulance appeared shortly, its team rushing to load the Vice President onto a gurney for the trip to Bethesda Naval Hospital. As the motorcade sped through the security checkpoint, West regained consciousness and confronted his medical handlers.

"Where are we going?" he said, confused and struggling against the body restraints. "Why am I in an ambulance? I'm fine. Just a little under the weather. Let's go back home."

Certain the Vice President had experienced a stroke, the physician cautioned West to relax. "You're going to be fine, sir. But we need to do some tests. We'll have you back home as soon as possible."

"I...I have to speak to the President. It's urgent." West faded into a deep sleep as the doctor injected a strong sedative into his patient.

"Dan! How you feeling!" The President's blustery phone greeting rattled West as he was emerging from a drug-induced snooze.

"I'm fine, Mr. President. All this was unnecessary. But I'm glad you called. We have to talk."

"Sure, sure, Dan. But that can wait. You just get some rest and follow those doctors' advice. Those guys are really good. I love those guys. I'll come out to see you when I get back to town." Holland rang off and called Eldon Mann.

"Keep him at Bethesda as long as possible," growled Holland. "He can't hurt us out there."

During a break in the battery of tests, West borrowed a laptop from a staffer who was summoned to Bethesda. Fighting a powerful headache, he checked his anger for a moment, stared at his computer, and fired off an email to the President's personal account.

FOR POTUS ONLY

Mr. President. I have reached the end of my rope. My advice is ignored. I'm little more than an afterthought in this Administration. And now I am told by Mann to "sit out" the rest of the campaign.

I'm informing you that I intend to resign as Vice President`. Though I am on the ballot as your running mate, if you win next Tuesday I do not expect to serve a second term.

I intend to make an announcement to this effect as soon as possible.

I wish it had all turned out differently.

Sincerely,
Dan.

West paused for a moment, the cursor hovering over the "Send" command. He looked out the second floor window onto Rockville Pike as a car rear-ended another on the icy road.

Fuck it. He clicked the mouse.

A continent away an unkempt twenty-something—known as "Jumbo" to his online fans—slouched in his mother's basement and fired up one of four oversized computer monitors.

"Hel-lo!" he spoke with glee to the empty room. "What do we have here?"

Email from Number Two/Encrypted 1645 EST

Flashing on the young hacker's screen was Vice President Dan West's resignation message to the President.

CHAPTER 12

"Welcome to Election Countdown! Our campaign update about candidates who are not campaigning!" Fox TV's Megyn Kelly opened the network's evening political show with a mischievous tease. "Let's get right to it!"

Since Holland and Bridges canceled their final debate and all public appearances, reporters grasped for coverage angles. Left to analyze campaign ads and spots aired by the many SuperPACs and interest groups, news outlets turned to nightly polls to report voters' leanings.

"This race is now a tossup!" crowed Sean Hannity. "If this trend continues, President Holland will win reelection in a race he was doomed to lose three weeks ago."

Every major media outlet led with similar predictions, though one – *Politico* – ran a sidebar hinting at a major development in the campaign's final days. "Sources report that Vice President Daniel West may not serve in President Holland's second administration," read a column in the wildly popular Washington insiders' journal. The hacker Jumbo had contacts in all the important media outlets. "White House spokesmen deny this rumor, and the Vice President was unavailable for comment."

"How the hell did this get out?" The President railed at Eldon Mann. "Who knows about this? Goddammit, Eldon!"

Mann was equally furious but knew better than to feed Holland's tirade. "We don't think it has legs, Mr. President. We've made sure his staff denies it all. We just have to keep the Vice President under wraps for a few more days." Mann rustled some papers, coughed, and tried to change the subject.

"The campaign is sending some new television ads for you to review. I think you'll be pleased," Mann pushed a folder across Holland's expansive desk and tapped the first page. "Look at the text for the retired generals' testimonials. Good stuff."

"Yeah, okay," Holland grumbled. "What about the new briefings on the bombing? I told you days ago I wanted a second opinion. The CIA report makes no sense to me."

Mann assured the President that the memos countering the CIA analysis were forthcoming and walked him through the schedule for the coming days. He made a mental note to pay a visit to the Vice President as soon as Mann returned to Washington. After his stroke and the ill-timed email to Holland, West became a clear liability, and Mann was determined to limit any public damage arising in the final days of the campaign.

After receiving the anonymous message, attaching West's email, *Politico's* editor ordered his top reporter to seek confirmation from the Vice President or other sources. Pima Grantham struck out with every call to White House and campaign officials and decided to take a more aggressive approach.

Tall and reed thin, Grantham had a broad smile and engaging wit that won admirers among reporters and the political class she relentlessly pursued. A tireless investigator, she was recruited by nearly every national media outlet. Instead she preferred the intimate work environment of *Politico* and the freedom she had to maneuver wherever she chose.

"My name is Grantham. I'm a reporter for *Politico*. I'm here to see the Vice President." The Marine positioned at the entrance to the Naval Observatory took her identification and called into the residence. She waited calmly as they processed her request. *What the hell,* she thought. *All they can do is say no.*

"I'm sorry," said the Marine, handing her ID through the window. "There's no record of you on the Vice President's schedule." As he moved back into the guardhouse, he took another call.

"Miss, hold up," he said, raising his uniformed arm to motion her to stop her retreat back onto Massachusetts Avenue. "You've been cleared to enter." He pushed a button and the heavy metal fence opened.

"Miss Grantham." West waved off an objecting White House staffer and showed the reporter to a couch in a pleasant sitting room off the entrance foyer. "I only have a few minutes. My staff has plans for me. You're here about the resignation rumor, I'm sure."

"Yes, Mr. Vice President," she said. "I hope you are feeling well. We were all disturbed by the news of your stroke." West smiled but made no response. "We received an email from an unidentified source. Here's the attachment." She handed him a single sheet. "Is this your email message to the President?"

"Good God!" he exclaimed, rising to walk to a nearby window, shoulders sagging in distress. After a long pause, he responded.

"I can't comment on this document. But I can tell you, entirely off the record, that I probably will not serve if the President wins a second term. Might as well get that out." Shaken, he ushered her toward the door.

"I invited you in because I remember a fine, balanced piece you wrote earlier this year about the politics of gun control. You're a good reporter. But I can't comment further about this document, and I hope you will honor my request to make our conversation on background only."

"I'm going to make a public statement tomorrow morning, but you have it first." West rose and extended a hand to the reporter, signaling that the conversation was over. He turned to climb the stairs, then looked back at Grantham. "Oh, by the way, I'm going to send you some documents about a coal mining spill in West Virginia. You might be able to do something with them."

Grantham almost stumbled down the steps to her car outside West's residence and fumbled in her bag until she remembered that her new Prius used only the electronic fob. As she exited the gate, she spoke into the wireless headset, "Call office."

CHAPTER 13

"Eldon, what are you doing here?" The Vice President frowned at the image of Mann entering his home without notice.

"The President asked me to drop by to see how you were doing. He'll come out as soon as he returns from Florida. We were worried about you after the stroke, and after your email to him. Is there anything you need?" Mann stood in the foyer, a heavy leather satchel at his side.

"I'm fine, thank you," said West. "You can tell the President that all is well. If he can find the time, have him give me a call. In the meantime, I've got some work to do, so you can see yourself out."

As West ascended the stairs to his study Mann called out. "I'll just take this call in the library if it's okay with you."

"Suit yourself," said the Vice President, not looking back as the Chief of Staff hurriedly placed a call. A nearby TV monitor scrolled news of the firing of the Washington Redskins coach after yet another dismal season.

Locking his study door, the Vice President managed to reach John King at CNN by Skyping the reporter on West's personal laptop, which had been fitted with its own wireless adapter some months ago when West realized he had no totally private means of communication. It had remained unused until the morning of his call to CNN.

With his high-definition image validating the caller for King's assurance, West quickly laid out his request. "John, I want to speak to your audience right away. There's been a lot of speculation since the *Politico* report. I have something to say and I need to say it now."

King assured West he could put him on the air within minutes once the technical connections were executed. He placed the Vice President on mute and motioned a producer to his office, where he quickly briefed the young woman and sent her off to make the necessary arrangements. "Mr. Vice President, our people are going to hook us into the studio feed in a moment. Can you give me some idea of what you'll be talking about?"

"John, I've had a revelation over the past few weeks and I decided that I had to speak to the country immediately. I haven't cleared this with the President or his White House staff. That's all I can say until we go on live."

The CNN newsroom was suddenly buzzing as the word spread through the staff. The unverified reports about the Vice President's possible resignation, followed by a lock down of news from the White House, had riveted the political press. King sensed that West might be unstable and that his on-air comments could backfire for the network.

Yet to have the Vice President live on his show would be a huge event, a news coup that would drive the other networks crazy. Within five minutes the studio had patched West's video feed into their studio set, with King ready to introduce his guest once the host was cued to interrupt her feature on the east coast flooding.

"Good morning," King began. "We're breaking into our regular programming to bring you an extraordinary appearance by Vice President Dan West. Only fifteen minutes ago the Vice President called me and asked to go on this program to explain his absence from the campaign and to discuss other matters. He is speaking to us from his residence at the Naval Observatory, about three miles from the CNN studios. Mr. Vice President, thank you for joining us."

Eldon Mann watched the library monitor with horror as CNN streamed text about the upcoming appearance by West below the storm news. He ran up a flight of stairs and pounded on the locked door. Mann demanded that a Secret Service agent break down the door, but the agent refused, saying this was possible only if they believed the Vice President was ill or somehow in danger. In fact, West had called his lead agent moments before to assure the team that he was fine and that no one was to enter his room.

"Goddamn it! The Vice President *is* in danger! Do I have to call the Director?" By now Mann had become frantic. West had somehow found a way to beam into a CNN broadcast, and the Chief of Staff was impotent. He called the White House operator and yelled to be put through to the Director of the Secret Service, his last recourse.

Unable to restrain West's determination to go on television, Mann convinced the Secret Service Director to take over the Naval Observatory residence and lock down all communications. Telephone lines were blocked, West's smartphone account canceled, and internet service suspended. The staff at the residence, Mann, and the protective agents settled into an eerie deathwatch of sorts with West alone in his study composing a statement.

As he placed a call to the President, Mann was stopped cold by the image of West speaking live to a national news audience.

"John, I appreciate this opportunity. You and CNN have always been fair and balanced in your coverage of our work." West appeared relaxed, dressed now in a dark suit, red tie, white shirt, and the ever-present American flag lapel pin. "First, I know there has been some talk about my health. As you know, I suffered a mild stroke a few days ago. I'm fine, and my recovery is going smoothly."

"Now, I want to briefly address why I asked John for this time. I have come to believe that our political system no longer serves the people we are elected to represent. It will sound like a cliché to those who have been tirelessly criticizing the corrupting influence of special interests in our governance, but I have been slow to take this fact to heart."

"A few days ago I met with an influential lobbyist and his clients. He demanded that our administration bend environmental rules to allow his company to evade certain pollution laws. These men were clear in stating that the millions they had contributed to our campaigns entitled them to special treatment."

"If this had been an isolated incident it could be dismissed as an aberration, a request that could simply be ignored. However, I'm ashamed to admit that we have received—and granted—hundreds of such requests over the past four years of our Administration. We've placed dozens of political loyalists in key jobs throughout the government to make certain these requests would be honored in ways that may be legal but are surely not in the public interest."

The President, watching the same video feed from his Orlando office, screamed into a telephone, "Get me Eldon Mann, now!"

"Jesus, Eldon! Why haven't you stopped this? I thought you said it was under control. Can't you pull the plug somehow?" Mann turned away to see three Secret Service agents moving up the stairs with a heavy tool to break into the Vice President's sanctuary.

West continued his statement. "I am speaking out today because I believe these remarks will receive considerable attention as we wind down this campaign. I hope that President Holland will choose an outstanding team to lead the country for the next four years, and that part of that leadership will involve a thorough examination—bipartisan and uncompromising—to correct the path we have taken in this government. I...."

CNN viewers were then treated to images of two Secret Service agents bursting into the Vice President's study and slamming down the monitor on his laptop. The feed went dead.

The Vice President's televised remarks sent shock waves through the political community and ground Holland's surging momentum to a halt.

"We're going on the road!" shouted a Bridges campaign aide to staffers in Annapolis. Schedules were revived to reflect polling movement in the remaining battleground states. Advance teams in both campaigns deployed to organize last-minute events that would rally supporters. Thousands of volunteers were piped into conference calls to jump start ground operations. Consultants gobbled up every available minute of television ad space and online advertising spots were prepared.

Like two huge armies restarting their engines, *Bridges to the Future* and *Holland for America* began a seventy-two hour forced march to election day.

CHAPTER 14

After a three-day marathon of tarmac speeches, and blistering television and internet ads by affiliated political groups, the Holland and Bridges campaigns settled into their headquarters in Maryland and Orlando to await the results. The Holland team was bolstered by early returns in Florida and Ohio, but watched the monitors with growing nervousness as Pennsylvania, Arizona, New Hampshire, and even North Dakota showed virtual ties. By ten pm. the networks were projecting the closest presidential election since 2000.

Eldon Mann worked three phones and a laptop in a makeshift office next to Holland in the President's hotel suite in Celebration Village near Disney World. "Eldon, this can't be happening!" screamed the President. "What does it look like in Michigan and Indiana? I thought we had Virginia locked down." Holland fumed as CNN streamed the latest numbers below the talking heads trying to explain the voting patterns across the country.

"We think Bridges' lead in several of these states will collapse as numbers in the suburbs start coming in. Let's hold tight." Mann forced an optimistic tone with the President, even as he knew the incumbent was in deep trouble.

Mann withheld the latest tracking polls from the President. In every contested state the Holland momentum that seemed unstoppable two weeks earlier had disappeared, largely attributed to the Vice President's televised revelations. The day's exit polls were worse. By Mann's most optimistic count Holland could win with a margin of fewer than ten electoral votes. But the possibility that he would actually lose to Bridges was growing as each state's polls closed.

An hour after the western states were in, none of the networks were prepared to call the race for either candidate. But when Arizona and New Mexico reported all precinct counts at two am, Bridges was projected with 271 electoral votes to 267 for Holland. Having led Holland by a comfortable margin only two weeks earlier, Calvin Bridges was called by all five networks to become the 46th President of the United States, in the closest electoral victory in U. S. history.

"What the fuck do I do?" The President yelled at Mann as he paced his hotel suite at eight am, clearly the worse for wear in shorts and a blue and orange U. Florida tee shirt that screamed "National Champions—Forever!" Eldon Mann and a small team of campaign lawyers filled a small conference room listening to the President's anguished rant.

"I've been on the phone nonstop over the past five hours trying to make sense of this election. I want an explanation of how this could happen, how a limp-dicked pussy like Calvin Bridges could win this election. I don't want another excuse about how Dan West fucked us with his...his whatever the fuck it was. I just want answers."

"What I wanna know is this: can we do anything about it? I'm not gonna call that sonofabitch and concede until every goddamn stone has been turned over. Can we challenge the numbers in any of these states? Are we gonna simply sit around with our thumbs up our butts and turn over the government to these assholes?"

"Mr. President, we have some ideas but we need a few hours." Mann responded. "We're putting out a statement now that says we're still reviewing the returns from the states and that there will be no further news for now." Mann was tempted to remind Holland that only a few weeks before, the President, after several cocktails, stated that he could care less whether he won or lost.

"All right," said Holland. "But you better bring some legal dynamite to turn this thing around. Otherwise I'll have to go out there tonight and concede this shitball election."

Deep into the night, after the election had been called for Bridges, Mann fought off exhaustion to come up with a plan for the coming day. A concession was simple. Holland would call Bridges to formally concede. Holland gives a gracious speech. Everyone goes home and prepares for an orderly transition of power.

But something kept gnawing at Mann. He struggled to remember a book or a lecture or journal article that recounted an unusual quirk in the presidential election process. Googling "election disputes" he scrolled past "2000 Recount" and "Gore v. Bush" and found what he was looking for. By mid-morning Mann had drafted a game plan. He was confident that his assessment was valid, but he needed an expert to help him convince the President.

Nearly thirty years earlier Mann had listened to a luncheon speaker describe a Constitutional anomaly. In twenty-one states, presidential electors were under no legal obligation to cast their vote for the candidate who carried their state. The speaker, now an election scholar at a conservative think tank, was Lyndon Polk. His presentation on the potential for "faithless electors" was forgotten by the attendees before coffee was served.

In the rear of the room a young congressional aide focused intently on Polk's remarks. As an undergraduate, Eldon Mann devoured all he could learn about the Presidency and wrote his senior thesis on the workings of the Electoral College. His professor had encouraged the young Mann to pursue graduate studies, but Mann wanted to dive into the political pool as a practitioner, not a scholar. As for Lyndon Polk, over the next three decades no one ever asked for his advice about the Electoral College, until now.

Mann reached Polk at six am at his home in Washington. After a brief introduction, Mann was direct. "The President needs your help. We've got a problem and we think you can help us figure it out." Within minutes a car met Polk for the drive to Dulles Airport where two campaign attorneys and a Gulfstream VI awaited, courtesy of Bloch Partners, an oil and gas holding company with special relationships throughout the Holland administration.

During the three-hour flight, Mann called into the plane to prepare for the session with the President. The presentation had to be compelling, as Holland was becoming unhinged as the hours since election night wore into morning.

"Let's go over this one more time," he said to the three men assembled in the plush cabin after the attendant had poured more coffee and laid a large platter of fruit and pastries on the table fronting the swiveled chairs. "I see the numbers from these states. They're the most recent reports from our people on the ground, right? And I understand the distribution of electoral votes. All this still comes out with us three votes shy of a 270 majority. What I need to be clear about is this concept of faithless electors."

"Let's say several electors did vote against their state's popular vote." Mann "You've assured us this is possible in a number of states, so let's say that happened, and it reverses the vote. What happens next?"

"Well, all sorts of things could take place," said Polk, who was clearly overwhelmed by the circumstance of his journey to Florida to meet the leader of the free world.

As he launched into a nineteenth-century electors' rebellion in Virginia, Mann interrupted again. "Let's skip that part. It's interesting but it's not relevant now. And you should probably edit out some of the more complicated slides here, especially the historical stuff." The President's attention span was painfully short.

As the Gulfstream touched its landing gear onto the runway at the Air Force base outside Orlando, Mann cut off Polk's preview. *It's crazy, but it just might work*, he thought.

After the President received Lyndon Polk's overview, the scholar was dismissed with a tour of Universal Studios before flying back to Washington. He had hoped to return on the Gulfstream but was unceremoniously booked on a commercial flight, economy class. Yet his whirlwind briefing trip was a thrill nonetheless, and he vowed to write about it someday. President Holland was polite, even charming, and seemed to fully grasp the complexity of Polk's presentation.

"Can we trust that guy to keep his mouth shut?" Holland asked Mann after Polk left the President's suite. "I hope you're on top of this, Eldon. If he goes and talks about this stuff we're screwed."

"This is all just too fucking unbelievable," said the President, still stunned by Mann's proposal. "I still don't think it can be done, but for now I'll take your word for it. And that it's all totally legal, right?"

November 4

"Let's get this transition underway," said Bridges as his circle of key advisors assembled in the President-elect's dining room. Mike, let's start with the files on the lists of people you've identified for the first round of appointments. We'll need to name a national security team right away. Then the economic team."

Mike Malloy was Bridges' closest friend from their days at Princeton. Months earlier, the candidate had asked Malloy to begin discreetly gathering background information for a potential

Bridges cabinet. Malloy was well prepared for a review of his material. He had consulted every Democratic—and some Republican—transition directors from past campaigns.

"By the way," continued Bridges. "You'd better talk to Gore's guy to see how they handled their work during the 2000 recount. I doubt it'll come to that but we need to be prepared."

"You're gonna be swamped by all the wanna bes—all the donors, all the strivers who want to promote themselves or their clients into the administration." said Gore's transition director, tracked down in Perth, Australia, where the former political aide was vacationing.

"You'll have new best friends who used to never return your calls. People who didn't do jack for your campaign will be buzzing around Bridges and his family, trying to get into his head, gossiping, trying to blow up good people. They'll be a royal pain in the ass. Get some deputies to hand hold 'em. Keep your time free to meet with Bridges. Pick a chief of staff right away. Make Bridges take a vacation. They all fuck up by not doing that."

"And one more thing, Mike. You may be in for a long, horrible stretch before all this is over. Take all the good news with a giant grain of salt."

Malloy stacked the binders on Bridges dining room table, awaiting a session to review potential cabinet appointments and senior staffing prospects. Ambassador postings and the plethora of ceremonial committees could wait. He glanced at his cellphone and noticed 123 missed calls and 90 texts. He reminded himself to set up another cell account to screen petitioners. *Gore's guy was right. It's going to be a bitch.*

Melody Banks and Bridges walked the short distance from the steps of the Maryland Statehouse to the campaign offices three blocks away. Bridges had specified, at considerable campaign expense, that the neo-classical building, a fine nineteenth century structure, would be renovated for the campaign, LEED-certified and equipped to provide a high-tech welcoming space for staff and visitors, a site that pleased the environmental community in particular.

Bridges delivered brief remarks at the Statehouse acknowledging the election outcome, thanking his team of staff and volunteers and the American people, and confirming that he had not yet spoken with President Holland. A Secret Service detail cleared their path through hundreds of press and cheering supporters.

"Have you reached out to Mann?" Bridges asked Banks, who once again had gone without sleep for twenty-four hours.

"Yes, I talked with him a few minutes ago as you were speaking. He blew me off, said they are still looking at the numbers."

"What do you think they're doing? Planning to call for a recount somewhere?" Bridges stuffed his hands in his overcoat and shivered in the bitter cold that had set in overnight. Storm clouds covered the mid-Atlantic region, with rain and sleet predicted for the coming days.

"We've got almost a hundred election lawyers on the ground in eight states to start preparing for legal fights. We'll have a briefing for you later today." Banks suppressed a bone-tired yawn and continued. "But I've got to tell you, I don't see where they make the challenge. None of these states seem to justify a recount scenario."

"Right." Bridges stopped the scrum of security and staff and placed his hands on her shoulders. "Whatever happens now I want you to know that I couldn't have done this without you. You've been terrific, and I will never, ever forget it."

"Thank you, Senator. It's been an honor. But we've got a long way to go before it's over." Banks heart was pounding. She couldn't determine whether she was simply excited after winning the election—or scared shitless that it wasn't over.

PART TWO

"It is not truth that matters,
but victory."

— Adolph Hitler

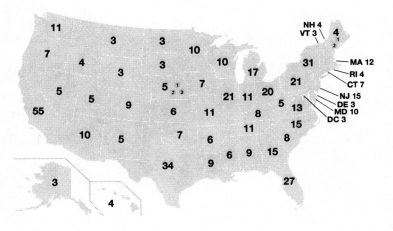

11

7   3   3
                              10
     4   3   10
          3   3   17
                                                    31   ── MA 12
5   5 1   7   20   21   ── RI 4
     5   9   2 3   21 11   5   ── CT 7
55   6   11   8   13   ── NJ 15
                                                          ── DE 3
                                                          ── MD 10
10   5   7   6   11   15   8   ── DC 3

3   34   6   9   9   15   27
          4   9

NH 4
VT 3   4
          2 1

CHAPTER 15

To run the elector project Mann turned to Carlton Espy, a tough Dallas lawyer who had helped Mann bludgeon Holland's Democratic opponent in his first presidential campaign. Mann's file on Espy included an insightful memo from an aide, who was asked to vet Espy for an administration post three years earlier.

CLASSIFIED

For Chief of Staff Mann Only

Carlton Espy has a successful practice representing energy and manufacturing clients. Other than the usual legal battles, he has not been targeted by any state or federal entity for illegal or unprofessional behavior.

One press account noted: "Espy is a brutally effective political infighter and a passionate libertarian. He is also a clear-eyed realist, a Duke law review scholar who understands the limits of a fight. During the Reagan years it was James Baker's portrait that hung on Espy's office wall, not the President's."

During the campaign Espy was especially helpful. Using his network of investigators to produce sensitive information about the opposition, Espy provided surrogates and conservative media a wealth of material to embarrass the Democratic candidate.

His work was discreet enough to be largely ignored by the political press, but our vetting located one Democratic operative who knew of Espy's involvement.

"He tagged our guys with pedophilia, arrests, financial mismanagement, general whoring by campaign staff, and a host of other charges, all unsubstantiated. But the press ate it up, and the damage to our candidate was done."

Espy is married, with four grown children, but seems to take little interest in family matters. A background check produced at least four extramarital affairs over the past few years. It is unclear that he has any interest in joining the administration in any capacity.

Mann returned to Washington after three grueling days with a President who was alternately ebullient, angry, depressed, and frequently sloshed. As the Citation taxied to the private terminal at Dulles, Mann found Espy on his ranch in the Texas Hill country.

"For Christ sake, Eldon, I thought we were winning," Espy hit the off button on a skeet machine with the butt of his shotgun. "What happened?"

"Not now, Carlton," Mann was in no mood for election analysis. "I have a job for you. You'll need to clear your desk for this one. How soon can you come to Washington?"

After a brief description of what he had in mind, Mann forwarded Lyndon Polk's Electoral College memo to Espy and scheduled a call for later that day. The delay was unnecessary, as Espy rang Mann within minutes of his review of the memo.

"Damn, Eldon! This is amazing stuff. I'm in!" Espy had recently completed a successful, lucrative defense of an energy conglomerate that had been sued by the Justice Department for antitrust violations. He was ready for a new challenge.

At Mann's direction Espy recruited a dozen investigators to sift through data on every Democratic elector who could not be legally bound to vote for their candidate when the Electoral College would meet on Dec. 14. An empty floor of offices in nearby Leesburg was rented by one of Espy's discreet clients.

The data deep dive required special talent. Two years earlier Mann had been urged to bring an eccentric young computer expert from Cal Poly Tech into the White House. Jonas Stanning's dissertation on rising cyber warfare capabilities of Muslim extremists had attracted the attention of a conservative professor at Pepperdine who had connections to major Republican donors in California.

The referral soon made its way to the desk of the White House Chief of Staff. During their interview, Stanning chewed his fingernails down to the nubs. Mann worried that Stanning might be a poor fit for the infighting inside Alistair Muse's National Security Council, so he shuttled Stanning to a protégé at the Defense Department. Stanning's skills soon sent him to the National Security Agency, where he developed a complex program to produce an astounding array of sensitive information on any citizen of any country at a moment's notice.

The Stanning system had proved invaluable to intelligence analysts and senior administration officials, who had lost many of these capabilities after the Snowden scandal a decade earlier. Invisible to Congressional oversight, Stanning's operation produced personal and professional background nuggets that would have made J. Edgar Hoover salivate.

Mann pondered making the call to the man he had helped enter government three years earlier. It would be a delicate conversation—the elector project was not only sensitive but fraught with legal uncertainties – and Mann was determined to keep the knowledge of its existence, much less its actual workings, a closely held secret. Yet the scope and urgency of the project demanded risks be taken.

Mann waited on a bench overlooking the Potomac at a turnout along George Washington Parkway. Stanning arrived and stumbled as he extended a hand to shake. "Oh, sorry about that. I don't get a chance to meet with the White House Chief of Staff too often." Stanning laughed nervously as Mann smiled and motioned him to a seat. Mann took note of his ragged wool scarf and mustard stained tie and made a mental note to send him a gift from Lord & Taylor.

"Jonas, it's great to see you!" Mann gave the younger man an avuncular pat on his shoulder and inquired about his work, relatives, and Stanning's two much-pampered Bishon Frise puppies —all information he had obtained from the conversation with Stanning's NSA boss. "I'm sorry to hear about your mom. That's a tragedy."

After a few minutes of casual conversation, Mann got to the point, describing the activity now underway in Leesburg and Stanning's possible role. "We need you to run this operation, Jonas. Its success depends on your skills."

"I'm honored," responded Stanning, now rocking on the bench, looking back and forth at the sky and the ground, anywhere but in Mann's direction. "But why me? You must have dozens of intelligence specialists like me. People who've been doing this sort of thing for a long time, probably better than I can."

"No," replied Mann, "there isn't anyone else like you. Without you this project won't get off the ground, much less be successful. And, frankly, there's no one else I can trust—no one else the President can trust."

Stanning shook his head back and forth, indicating a negative response, but then blurted, "Well, of course! If you want me I'll do it!" The two men stood, Mann grabbed Stanning's arm and looked at him with a broad smile under cold gray eyes. "You're going to make history, Jonas." *He's an odd duck*, thought Mann, *but he'll do whatever we ask.*

Within twenty-four hours Stanning presented a budget of fifteen million dollars to cover equipment, specialized dark software that he could not easily lift from his NSA operations, and private jets to fly a dozen skilled hackers to join the boiler room operation in northern Virginia. With one call, Mann got the money from a wealthy California hedge fund manager, a donor who had been rewarded weeks earlier with the implicit promise of a plum ambassadorship for his new wife during the next Holland administration. The donor was eager to double down on his contribution to a new, secret, political education fund, created by Espy, for unspecified "research".

Mann instructed Stanning to start with objective data to locate targets—how long had the elector been an active partisan? Had they held elective office? Did their families have a political legacy? Along with the basic information- age, sex, race, education, financial assets, etc. —the legal team was expected to find and recruit three Democrats who would face the wrath, potentially violent, from their fellow partisans by switching their vote from Bridges to Holland. Start with older men; avoid women, Latinos, and African Americans—they were most likely to be rock solid liberal electors.

Stanning and his team of cybergeeks worked through the first days organizing their systems, collating easily obtained information on the targeted names. A team of lawyers assembled by Espy culled a list of 130 Democratic electors from states won by Bridges – ostensibly party loyalists, but who would not be bound by their state laws to vote for Calvin Bridges.

"You won't believe what these guys can do," said Espy, calling Mann after his first debriefing with Stanning. "We used to think that digging up arrest records or FBI background information was great stuff, but they can find just about anything. Believe me, Eldon, nothing, I mean nothing, is now secure."

But the initial results were not promising. Only eight names offered any lead for the first phase of outreach, and even those were considered long shots.

Unfazed by the team's first probes, Mann and Espy knew what they really wanted was not empirical but deeply personal, psychological, even unrealized by the targeted electors themselves. The project needed to unearth a small slice of emotional motivation that could produce electors willing to betray their party.

"I need affairs, financial problems, mental issues, grudges, political slights," Mann challenged Stanning. "Anything that opens a door, anything that gives us an edge. They can't all be happy, all-American guys."

CHAPTER 16

November 9

Brad Cantwell pushed the Nissan rental to ninety along a deserted highway headed to Bismarck, North Dakota, for his meeting with Elector #3, identified by the Leesburg team as a tier one prospect. It was the job he wanted, when Eldon Mann was divvying up the tasks for the team eighteen hours earlier. But he wasn't counting on ten below in a car better designed for Texas. Galveston was his home since Cantwell's effective work during the 2000 Florida election recount. Sent to the state by Republican House Majority Leader Tom "The Hammer" Delay to disrupt the recount in Dade County, Cantwell had proven a most able—and discreet—operative.

As he left the highway and entered the city limits of Bismarck his GPS directed him to a modest house with lights still blazing at midnight. Intrigued by the request from his hunting partner earlier in the day, Stanley Vaughn would be waiting up for his visitor. He opened the door before Cantwell could knock.

"Come on in. It's too damn cold out there for anyone, much less a Texas lawyer." Vaughn took Cantwell's hand and steered him to a deep armchair in a living room that reminded Campbell of his grandfather's home. "Bum Stinson says you've got an interesting story for me and that I should listen carefully. That's good enough for me. Bum's a good friend and I trust his judgment. I suspect this has something to do with this damn election and what's happening in Washington, am I right? Or am I right?"

Cantwell knew he must put Vaughn at ease quickly before he got down to business. "Do you have a cup of coffee, Mr. Vaughn? I've been driving for several hours and nearly drove off the road a ways back."

"Jesus, look at me! What kind of manners do I have?" Vaughn lumbered to a nearby kitchen and returned with a mug. "Tell me if this is burnt and I'll make another pot."

"This is fine, thanks. Boy it's cold out there. Is this normal for November?" Cantwell managed the chitchat for a few minutes until Vaughn interrupted.

"Mr. Cantwell, I can stay up all night shootin' the shit about weather, fishing, and so on. But you came here to talk about something else. What you say we get into it, okay?"

"Yes. Well, you know that our nation's capitol has been attacked. The damage to the Capitol is extensive and the entire area has been hit with severe radioactive fallout. We don't yet know who is responsible and we don't yet know if more attacks are in the works."

Cantwell had calibrated his alarming message to draw Vaughn into the drama, stopping short of a sense of panic. He had to demonstrate that the government—President Holland—was in charge and effectively managing his role as Commander in Chief.

"Sounds like 9-11 all over again," said Vaughn. "Damn outrage."

"Absolutely." Cantwell stirred his coffee and paused for effect. "The thing is, Mr. Vaughn, we have a Constitutional crisis. And our national security team believes we're facing more attacks just as we have a presidential transition that could make matters much, much worse."

"So what does that have to do with me, Mr. Cantwell?" Vaughn's expression began to harden as he waited for this visit to make some sense. "I assume the government is functioning and that Senator Bridges is on top of all this as well."

"Please, Mr. Vaughn, call me Brad." Cantwell now had to choose his words carefully or he would be out the door and headed back to Fargo and Washington before his coffee got cold.

"We've been approached by a number of senior elected officials—Democrats and Republicans—as well as top national security advisors who believe that turning over the entire federal government to a new administration in a few weeks will be catastrophic."

Cantwell paused again, taking a sip of his coffee. "Especially to Senator Bridges and his team. With no foreign policy experience, no leadership on terrorism issues, no proven stature in an extremely dangerous world, we believe the country could face a new round of horrifying attacks, and likely a deep recession that would be far worse than the 2008 meltdown."

Stanley Vaughn scratched his chin and nervously gouged his ear. "So what are you saying? That Bridges shouldn't take office? He won the election, it's a done deal. Why are you telling me all this?"

Adding to the knowledge that Vaughn was little more than a nominal Bridges supporter, Cantwell carried national security documents designed to convince his target that Bridges was unfit for the highest office.

"I'll get to that in a moment. But first, read this memo. It came to us from a worried source from Sen. Bridges' campaign policy team." Cantwell handed Vaughn an impressive binder with a bold seal of the National Security Council. Inside was a single sheet of paper with an email from one of Sen. Bridges' foreign policy advisors to the candidate.

CLASSIFIED

FOR SENATOR BRIDGES ONLY

Pursuant to our conversation this morning, I have inquired into the possibility of a meeting between you and President Holland to discuss the terrorist attack and how you could be helpful in managing the crisis during the transition period. It appears that the President's team may be willing to arrange a session if it is limited to only the two of you, with a photo op but no press questions afterward.

We must prepare carefully for this meeting, but most of all, you must adhere to your decision (reached yesterday during our phone conversation) to NOT assist the Holland administration with this crisis. As you noted, these are his problems and, if you keep an arms length from him and his team you cannot be blamed for negative outcomes. And there will surely be negative outcomes.

We must take office with a clean political slate. The Holland administration will undoubtedly take the brunt of public criticism for the state of affairs following the attack, and you should not be painted with the same brush. There is virtually no political capital to be gained by inserting yourself or your national security team into the mess that Holland is facing.

So we strongly advise that you stick with your earlier assessment of his offer—that is, meet with the President but make no accountable offer to assist him in executing a response to the events earlier this week.

Vaughn closed the binder and stared at a wall in the near distance, gathering his thoughts before addressing Cantwell.

"I'm not sure I understand this memo, Mr. Cantwell. Brad. Terrorism policy isn't my area of expertise. I'm a Bismarck car salesman."

"Please, now read this," said Cantwell. He took the first binder and handed Vaughn a second one, similarly official, with another one-page memo inside, this one stamped "Top Secret".

```
NSA Intercept, 0420, 9 Nov.  COMNET.
Text from ARMASCO to TEHRAN contact.  Source affirmed.
Read as follows:


"Strong reason to believe Pres.-elect Bridges will
take no tactical action against our interests after
inauguration. Planning should go forward."
```

The Midwestern car salesman now looked weary. He shook his head, paused and turned to Cantwell. "I still don't understand."

Cantwell took the two documents from Vaughn's grasp, and spoke in the most compelling voice he could muster. "What these two memos state is that Senator Bridges will refuse to engage with President Holland to deal with the attack and that there are forces planning additional attacks with impunity in the face of an incoming Bridges administration."

"OK," said Vaughn, now visibly disturbed by the conversation, "but as I said, what does any of this have to do with me?"

"Stanley, you are a Democratic elector from a state that cannot force its electors to vote for a particular candidate when the North Dakota electors meets next month here in Bismarck," Cantwell then leveled his challenge. "We want you to consider casting your vote for President Holland."

＊ ＊ ＊

Cantwell drove through the icy North Dakota night determined to make the 8:20 am flight from Minneapolis to Washington. Fortified by three cups of coffee and a bag of Dunkin

Donuts, he reviewed every moment of his late evening with Stanley Vaughn, trying to be objective in assessing Vaughn's response to Cantwell's presentation. How he characterized the meeting and his target's reaction would substantially impact the team's strategy.

The brief on Vaughn was extensive, and spot on. Sixty-five, a modestly wealthy retired car dealer, a Lutheran but not especially religious, registered Democrat who voted for Reagan twice before marrying at fifty to Irene Bunson, a Burleigh County Democratic committeewoman whose first husband had been a friend of Stanley's since high school. The research also revealed Vaughn hated Irene's politics and her candidates almost as much as he hated spending time with Irene. She had dogged Stanley into helping with party organization for nearly a decade. He could barely tolerate the countless chili suppers, rallies, and endless speeches, and increasingly found excuses to be occupied elsewhere.

"Stanley," she implored, as she headed to Fargo for a gathering of her fellow Democrats. "Come with me. It'll be fun!"

Vaughn groaned at the thought of a weekend with Irene's earnest liberal activists. "Maybe next time, sweetheart. I need to get up to the lake to do some work."

Stanley had not been with her when a massive heart attack took Irene. Unbeknownst to Irene or anyone else, he was in his hunting lodge on Lake Sakakawea, and he wasn't alone. Before starting the drive to the lake he parked behind the double-wide trailer next to the Ice Kingdom Tap Room to gather a thirty-five year old waitress he had been seeing for the past year. Irene's frequent political travels around the state, combined with his well-known longing for days in the duck blind, gave Stanley considerable license to pursue a tryst with the agreeable woman who lowered her head into his lap as they drove away, partly to avoid being seen, partly to welcome Stanley in another way.

Vaughn felt no guilt about his fling with Eva. She was attractive, even beautiful from some angles, clever and irreverent, and an energetic free spirit, especially when it came to sex. Eva was everything Irene was not, giving Stanley an extra spring in his step as he ushered Eva into the cozy cabin that overlooked birches lining the lovely lake Stanley had increasingly frequented over the past few years.

As he nuzzled into Eva's warm, soft body, he failed to hear the buzzing on his silenced cellphone, a call from Bismarck to let him know his wife had died shortly after accepting the vote of her fellow Democrats to represent North Dakota in the coming Electoral College.

Returning to Bismarck and depositing Eva at her trailer, Stanley fished the cellphone from his coat to check messages. He was greeted with more than a dozen frantic texts from Irene's colleagues—"Please call me. Irene has fallen ill." "Stanley, where are you? Please pick up. Irene has been taken to the hospital." "Urgent. Check your VM." And from his brother Barney in nearby Menoken—"Stanley, call me immediately. It's about Irene. We need you."

Stanley was now shaken, worried not that Irene was in trouble but that his absence from any communication might somehow expose his philandering. He spoke into his SUV's Bluetooth speaker – "Call Barney" and soon his brother came on the line.

"Where the fuck have you been, Stanley?" his brother was breathless and angry. "We've been trying to reach you for eight hours. Irene's dead. Heart attack at the hotel where they were meeting. You understand? Stanley, you there?"

Whole minutes seemed to pass as Stanley froze at a stoplight after his brother's announcement. Cars behind him began to honk, shaking Vaughn back to the moment. He pulled off the road a few blocks short of his home. "Yeah, Barn, I'm here. I don't know what to say. I've been up at the lake and I didn't realize my phone had died. I'll be home in a minute and I'll call you right back."

Before returning the call to his brother, Stanley poured himself a large tumbler of whiskey and sat to collect his thoughts. Irene dead. Seemed fine when she left the house the day before. His wife of fifteen years, dead. Irene, whose political work he had come to loathe, dead. The woman whose passion for politics was bottomless, but whose passion for him had long ago ended. Now dead.

There were no children to call to comfort. Neither he nor Irene had ever been a parent though Stanley suspected that Irene regretted not having had a child during her first marriage. Not so Stanley. Never could understand the joy that his friends took in their children. He only saw the pain and misery and expense they caused their parents.

"Barn, I'm devastated," he called. "I just saw Irene yesterday morning and she was fine. I don't understand how this could happen. Where is she now?"

With the basic information in hand Stanley called the funeral home and arranged to have Irene's body brought back to Bismarck the next day. He then placed a call to their Lutheran pastor and asked his help with arrangements. He took calls from Irene's sister and welcomed three sets of neighbors and friends who dropped by to offer condolences. A state party official called to tell Stanley the party had chosen him to replace Irene as an elector. It was only fitting. Stanley then turned off the lights, locked the front door, and called Eva.

How all this information came to Brad Cantwell was a deep secret known only to Eldon Mann's team in Leesburg. Stanley Vaughn's photo, one of nine under investigation by the team, occupied a wall that was beginning to look like a police detective's command post. Espy pulled Stanley's headshot and moved it to a clean whiteboard and wrote underneath: "Elector # 1".

CHAPTER 17

The President was noticeably calmer when he took the early morning call from Mann, who was fighting off severe fatigue after a long night of research with the Stanning team. "So Eldon, what've you got for me this morning? Do we have a shot at turning this thing around? Or do I get the speechwriters down here to draft a concession?"

"Mr. President, a few days ago I would have said we should pack it in. We had no realistic vote challenge in any state," Mann recounted. "But the bombing of the Capitol scrambled the situation, and it gives us an opening."

"Keep going," said Holland. "I just got my CIA briefing and it looks like the worst of it is over. But that goddamn Muse took it on himself to call Bridges again and brief him on what we're doing in the Mideast. Before we could figure out the politics of the thing."

"Yes, of course," said Mann. "But we've made significant progress with the elector project since we met last week. It's still a long shot, but we're working on it. We'll know more in a day or so."

"At this point we should just put out a statement that we're still looking at the state vote counts, but that whatever the outcome, the Administration is responding effectively to deal with the terrorist attack, to find those responsible, and so on."

"Right," said Holland. "And I guess I should say that we're keeping Senator Bridges abreast of all these developments. But for God's sake, make damn sure Muse keeps his mouth shut about the FBI report on the Capitol bombing. You can handle that."

Mann had managed his relationship with the President for six years by never over-promising, but this political crisis would test that tactic, for if the President went off script, the entire project could fail, and the outcome for Mann would not be pleasant.

"I'll be back to you at noon with an update. Until then, sit tight and trust that we're doing everything possible to turn this around." Mann signed off and returned to the Stanning boiler room to prod the team for more progress.

"What is Holland doing, for Christ sake?" President-elect Bridges paced the living room of his Chesapeake Bay home in sweatpants and pullover after an intense workout. He leaned against a chair and stretched his hamstrings as he confronted Banks and the five men. "He's using the Capitol bombing as an excuse to delay his concession. Todd, is there any, and I mean *any* possibility they can successfully challenge the vote count in any state?"

Todd Campbell, the campaign lawyer, was nearing fifty and anxious to leave his huge Baltimore firm and enter a new career in a Bridges administration. He was a short, bespectacled man with a thinning hairline and a bulging waste fed by too many morning doughnuts and fast food lunches at his desk, and rare exercise. As the post-election drama took an unprecedented turn, Campbell struggled to convey confidence and control. To Bridges' question, he shook his head and spoke as forcefully as possible, addressing not only Senator Bridges but also the team of six senior aides gathered around a large table strewn with papers and coffee cups.

"Senator, we've spent three days canvassing not only the state election officials but down to the county coordinators of every state you won. About the only place remotely in play for them is Virginia, and even there they'd have to pick up 4,500 votes in a recount. All the absentee ballots have been counted and the contested ones resolved. I've challenged each of our attorneys to come up with a strategy they might use and not one can produce a realistic path for the President."

"I just don't see how they can make this happen," he concluded.

"So what the hell are they up to?" Bridges was visibly agitated. "The Democrats are going nuts in Congress and on the talk shows, the media have piled on, all but calling Holland deranged for not conceding. Even his own leadership has been lukewarm in defending him."

"And this bombing has only made matters worse for us." Bridges bent over to press his palms to the floor to complete his post-work-out stretching. Toweling off the sweat, he leaned over the table. "It creates a distraction Holland can exploit while he figures out what to do. What's worse, he can use it as an excuse to bomb the hell out of the Mideast and get credit for it. By the way, are they giving us anything more on the Capitol bombing? Do we have a source for the bomb?"

Bridges national security team, calling in from the Pentagon, had little to offer. The cooperation had been cordial, but the President-elect's team had largely been kept in the dark about Holland's retaliation strategy.

"Melody, have you heard anything more from Mann?" Bridges frustration was growing. "Can we get any Republicans to light a fire under Holland?"

Banks sat upright and smoothed her jeans as she relayed her latest non-contacts with the White House. "No, Senator, since your briefing with Muse we've had nothing other than that one text from Mann saying they'd have no news until further notice. I've checked with a few mid-level sources I have in their campaign and I get nothing. They're keeping it very close to the chest."

"So what do I do? What do we do?" asked Bridges. "Should I hold a press conference and call on the President to end this delay and allow an orderly transition to begin? I'm sick and tired of sitting out here twiddling our thumbs. Fact is, the country has been attacked, the markets are going crazy, and the leadership of the federal government is in limbo. Can't we make that case?"

Each of the gathered advisors attempted a contribution to the discussion, none presenting any creative idea to resolve the dilemma Senator Bridges found himself facing, days after winning the election. The group consensus was to wait for Holland's next step. Surrogates would keep pounding the President to concede and talking points would continue to flow hourly to the media, campaign supporters, donors, and friendly talking heads around the country. But Bridges would make no public appearances and simply...wait.

Melody Banks called a deputy and put those routine actions into motion, then retired to an empty room in the Bridges home to make a different sort of call.

"Jackson, it's Melody. I need to talk to you. I _really_ need to talk to you, it's urgent. Please call me." She left the voice message for Jackson Cripple, her old friend she hadn't seen since their encounter on the street months earlier. After losing his law license in the wake of a questionable investigative project, Cripple had branched out to develop a discreet practice for special clients with highly sensitive problems. Melody had used Cripple to research political corruption allegations in a campaign that went the right way. Her candidate won after the opponent's bribe taking became public, thanks to Cripple's high-tech sleuthing.

"Hey, Melody, who's trying to get into your pants these days? You're gonna have 'em all over you once you get in the White House!" Cripple's greeting was more irreverently flirtatious than offensive. Banks let it pass and got immediately into the purpose of the contact.

"Jackson, we have a huge problem over here. As you know the President hasn't yet conceded. We're going crazy waiting to start our transition operation, but we have no idea what's going on with the President. They're freezing us out, probably while they try to figure out if they can reverse the vote in a couple states, sort of a Gore v. Bush deal in reverse."

"Yeah, I got that," replied Cripple. "So how can I help?"

"I need you to help me find out what they are doing over there in the White House and their campaign. It's that simple."

"Sure," he said with a hint of a chuckle. "Piece of cake. I'll just tap a few phone lines into the White House, plug into the President's email and text and that of every senior staff around him, and I'll have you an answer by supper time."

"I'm serious," Melody replied. "This is really critical stuff and, in fact, the country's future might depend upon it."

Cripple turned serious. "All right, I understand. Get me the names of everyone you think might have information. And if you can, their cell numbers and email addresses. Not the official White House numbers. Their personal numbers. They'll stay off their government-issued devices for anything sensitive. Maybe you have a friend in that campaign who has access to that stuff?"

"I'll get back to you," she said. "In the meantime, you can start by thinking about what you'd have to do. Of course, it all needs to be legally defensible. Seriously. I don't want to go to jail and neither do you."

"And one other thing. Find out anything you can about the Capitol bombing, Who, how, whatever you can dig up. Holland's people are stiffing us."

Melody signed off the call and lay on a nearby bed, closing her eyes, trying to make sense of the past week's unfathomable events. *We're winning the election. Then, Jesus, a nuclear bomb goes off at the Capitol and Holland gets a huge bump. Then the Vice President trashes the Administration and all hell breaks loose in the final few days of the campaign. Holland's numbers go south and we win, but he won't concede. And here we are. Unfuckingbelievable.*

She threw some water on her face and reluctantly checked the mirror, grimacing at her pasty, tired reflection, hair that had not been properly cared for over the past month She sighed. *At least all this will be over soon and I can crash.* At midnight she set the timer on her phone for a ten-minute nap. Sleeping through the alarm, she was awawkened at six am by Jackson Cripple, with alarming news.

"I don't have specifics, but before I go any further you need to know something that may make you want to drop this whole thing," Cripple was all business now. "It seems the White House Chief of Staff has assembled a bunch of scary computer pros out in northern Virginia. Totally a non-official enterprise. At least a dozen guys—I know one of them, worked with him on a nasty project a few years ago. Managed to get him by text, then voice a few hours ago. Before he could catch himself he told me he would be tied up for awhile, had a major job that would last a few weeks, recruited by some dude from NSA. I shit you not. Those were his words—*some dude from NSA.*"

"How did you get all this?" she asked. "No, strike that question. How do you know Eldon Mann is involved?"

"My hacker friend made a mistake. He took my call on a cell I could locate later. I won't tell you how I know he had also taken a call from a very serious guy at NSA, who only yesterday had met with Eldon Mann."

"OK, hold on, I'll get back to you as soon as possible. I need to talk to someone." Banks was reeling with Cripple's revelation. She ran through the implications of seeking counsel before going further. Involving others would increase the chances of a leak. It could require her to reveal her source in Cripple, which she did not want to do. Discussing this intelligence with the campaign lawyers could blow up any thoughtful planning while waiting for Holland to concede.

And what if it was just not relevant? she thought. The NSA-Eldon Mann contact could be nothing. It could simply be another effort to find out who masterminded the Capitol bombing. There wasn't enough information to open the discussion with the Bridges team, much less with the President-elect. She would give Cripple the green light and wait to learn more.

CHAPTER 18

Three days into the project Eldon Mann began to see hopeful signs. Stanning's team had turned up another dozen prospects, several of which showed special promise. Brad Cantwell's positive report on the outreach to Stanley Vaughn—a kind of beta test for a more extensive set of contacts—led Mann to believe the strategy now had at least a twenty percent chance of success, a nineteen percent improvement over its start.

Mann figured the timing of any commitments from Democratic electors was as critical as their actual willingness to take the remarkable step of reversing their state's partisan outcome. If promises were obtained too early, second-guessing could prevail. The project had entered uncharted political territory in the extreme, and caution and urgency had to be balanced with precision. Even Eldon Mann, one of the most successful, consummate political operatives of his generation, could not predict with any confidence what the hell would happen next.

"Anything new?" Mann asked Stanning at the top of his regular call. Both were now carrying hyper-encrypted devices for their communications after Stanning found two of his hackers talking on their personal smartphones. After reading the riot act to his team he broke out three of the prototype NSA sets he had recently tested for the agency. One for himself, one for Espy, one for Mann.

"I just sent a new file to Mr. Espy," Stanning said. "Some interesting data."

Mann desperately needed to be with the legal team to review the next step for outreach, but he also needed to be more visible around the White House, to assure the staff that he was on top of things, to speak for the President where necessary, and to give background on the election issue to friendly reporters. With President Holland holed up in Orlando, Mann had to give the impression that official White House business was being well managed.

Over lunch with Alistair Muse, Mann got an earful about Muse's efforts to quell an uprising among the staff and national security press after his last background briefing. *I'm dealing with the future of the Presidency and this asshole can't shut up about how hard he's working,* thought the Chief of Staff, barely concealing his contempt for the President's national security advisor. Insecure, politically tone deaf, Muse had been a constant burden.

"Alistair, you're doing a great job," assured Mann. "I know it and the President knows it. We can't get through this without your leadership. Just try to keep everyone calm and let 'em know we're on top of the attack. Don't worry about the political stuff, the election, you know. We're handling this. You've got your plate more than full."

"But Eldon, you've seen the CIA reports. It was some kid, a college student. They can't find any link to ISIS or Al-Qaeda or any other Mideast terrorist group," Muse clinched his fists repeatedly and scratched his forearm, a tic that soon annoyed Mann to the point of distraction.

"I know, Alistair," countered Mann. "But the President wants to be absolutely certain about this before he pulls back the military strikes. He's taking it seriously, and he needs your help."

With Muse temporarily calmed, Mann turned to the crush of phone messages his frustrated assistant had demanded he must return. He ignored all but two, one to the CIA Director who wanted to know why an NSA staffer had been detailed to the White House, and one to a particular donor who asked for an update on the prospects for reversing the election results, passing along his wife's respects and the note that she had been working hard on her Spanish.

Mann arrived at the Leesburg office building by early afternoon, dismissing his regular driver and taking his Camry to avoid attention from the gaggle of media on the north lawn of the White House. Little noise came from the twenty cubicles arranged in the open space on the top floor of the Leesburg building. He was met by Espy and got down to work in a makeshift private office, furnished with folding tables and some plastic chairs.

"We learned a lot from Brad's visit with Stanley Vaughn," began Espy. "We see him as almost there. We've monitored his calls and texts to be sure he hasn't spoken to anyone about Brad's meeting, and he's been quiet, even with his mistress. Brad will call him regularly to check in, and go back out there next week, or earlier if necessary."

"Good," said Mann. "What does the list look like now?"

"I want to send our folks to make contact with these electors," Espy handed Mann a single sheet with three names and brief profiles, without any sensitive material included. "Middle age men, each with at least two of the factors that raise questions about their complete loyalty to the party or their candidate."

"OK, let's go through each one," replied Mann. "Winston Granberry, Hazard, Kentucky. I know that place. Spent a night there years ago while I was running Joe Comstock's Senate campaign. Grim coal town. Claim to fame was Elizabeth Taylor choking on a chicken bone while campaigning with John Warner."

"Actually, Eldon, that was over in Wise County, Virginia," corrected Espy, whose recollection of political events rivaled that of Google. "But the place is similar. Granberry's seventy-one, a lifelong Democrat, held a number of state and party offices, but he was rejected by the state party to chair the national convention delegation from Kentucky. They chose a black professor and a young gay student from Centre College as co-chairs instead. The party gave him some nominal title—delegation platform policy chairman or some such—but we know he's still bitter and that he's told a number of friends he's had it with the Democratic Party and the tree huggers in particular."

"And get this," continued Espy. "His father owned one of the last large strip mine operations in eastern Kentucky. Obama's EPA put him out of business. Something about mountaintops he wouldn't rehabilitate. The father died last year. Granberry believes the loss of the coal operation killed him in the end."

"Remarkable," said Mann. "How do you want to make the contact?"

"Just like with Stanley Vaughn, we found a friend of his in Hazard who will make the introduction. One of Granberry's father's business partners who's known him since he was a child. He now runs the Save our Energy Choices group down there. They're both big Wildcat basketball fans."

"OK, good plan," said Mann. "Richard Moulton, Pittsburg union rep. What do we know about him?"

"On paper Moulton looks like a non-starter," said Espy. "Long time union organizer, college educated, led anti-war protests in the early seventies. Publicly clean as a whistle. Wife is a social worker, six kids, all Catholic. But there's one thing not even his wife knows. Moulton is violently pro-life. And I don't mean write-your-Congressman pro-life. I mean burn down the abortion clinic pro-life. Last year he gave $10,000 from his pension fund to Randy DuPont."

"You mean the guy who shot that abortion doctor in Georgia?" asked Mann.

"One and the same," said Espy. "And get this—we think Moulton was with DuPont when the shooting happened. We know for a fact that Moulton was in Ringgold, Georgia that day, and that he made a half dozen calls from there to DuPont's lawyer, and to another pro-life organizer nearby. Then he wired money to DuPont's lawyer. All the time he was supposed to be on Kiawah playing golf."

"OK," Mann continued. "We're getting somewhere. Webb Cusimano. New Orleans city councilman. How's that going to work?"

Espy was looking forward to a discussion about Webb Cusimano. The background developed by the elector project was the deepest and darkest of the lot.

"Cusimano wants out of Louisiana, and soon. He has big problems with a drug gang from Honduras he has, let's say, disappointed over the past few months. There's a lot of money involved, and people have even died as a result of our man Webb's actions—or non-actions."

Espy stated the upshot of Webb Cusimano's dilemma and the project's opportunity. "He needs a million dollars to make the Hondurans go away, and he needs to be relocated somewhere in Europe, preferably Sicily, where he has relatives."

"Why doesn't he go into witness protection?" posed Mann. "They handle this stuff all the time, right?"

Espy shook his head. "Cusimano is a dead man if he goes to the feds. Some of that Honduran smack killed the daughter of a Ponchatoula police chief. We turned up info that the chief has vowed to have the person who caused his daughter's death killed like a rabid dog. Cusimano knows this and he's been frantically trying to call in favors to buy off the Hondurans, and go missing."

"What about family?" asked Mann. "That would seriously complicate his exit."

"Estranged from his two children," replied Espy. "Wife is in a nursing home with early stage Alzheimer's. He's convinced flight is the only answer."

"So we're looking at money and safe passage to Sicily, right?" Mann frowned. So far the team had been focusing on hot-button issues as the currency of persuasion with Vaughn, Granberry, and Moulton. The interception of telecommunications could be buried after this was over. But money and fugitive flight were another matter, with disturbing criminal implications. "Let me think about this one before we proceed. But go ahead and get people out there to see Granberry and Moulton. Both look good. And let's turn up a few more as soon as possible."

"Eldon," said Espy, leaning on Mann's desk, "what if Bridges' people get wind of what we're doing? They could turn our converts around, or get the state party to replace them, right?"

"It could happen," replied Mann, "but only if they know well in advance of the vote. So we're going to put them to sleep until the very last moment, so they won't have time to act."

Mann stuffed a sheaf of memos on Espy's prospects into his ancient leather briefcase and returned the White House for a six pm staff meeting and a call from President Holland to buck up the staff. With Leesburg Pike jammed with traffic, he took White's Ferry across the Potomac and made the slow, but pleasantly diverting drive through the Maryland countryside before picking up River Road and George Washington Parkway for the run into downtown Washington.

Trailing a Mercedes sporting a "Save Democracy—Impeach Holland!" bumper sticker, Mann frowned and thought, *Rich lefties. They deserve what they're about to get.*

CHAPTER 19

November 17

The President struggled to stay calm as the calls for his concession mounted to a flood of editorials, speeches, and talk show
bullhorns, and not only from his traditional political opponents
but from a few Republican members of Congress. The more
measured criticisms were manageable: the *Wall Street Journal*,
Chicago Tribune, and various regional newspapers praised Holland's achievements in office and encouraged him to formally call
for a recount of votes or step aside.

Fox, a dependable supporter for most of Holland's presidency,
continued to blast the "liberal establishment" demand for his concession, calling Holland a strong leader who was likely defeated
by widespread voter fraud, especially in African American and
Hispanic precincts. "And let's not forget," concluded the host, "it
was Al Gore who held up the election of the president for five
weeks in 2000."

"If these Democratic Senators and Congressmen were true
patriots," screamed one Fox talking head, "they'd be calling for
legal intervention to freeze the ballot boxes in hundreds of locations to root out the corrupt voting practices of local Democratic
party bosses."

"At a time when the nation has once again come under terrorist attack," said the *National Standard*. "Senator Bridges and the liberal elite should put the interests of the country ahead of a raw partisan power grab. President Holland is correct to challenge the initial outcome of this election."

These friendly voices were of little comfort to the President as he considered his options. Two weeks after election night, states were now certifying vote counts, and the media would soon be calling the outcome official. "Not since the 2000 recount has there been such uncertainty in our nation's leadership," led the *Washington Post* editorial. "The terrorist attack on Washington magnifies the crisis, which is far greater than the question of who becomes our next president. President Holland must end this drama and move to an orderly transition with President-elect Bridges."

"Jesus fucking Christ, Eldon!" shouted Holland over Mann's phone call. "I can't keep this up any longer. If you can't give me something to justify my refusal to concede this election, I've gotta end it now." Mann couldn't see the President's face on the secure audio feed but he knew that Holland was seething and possibly losing his grip.

"Mr. President, we believe we may have three Democratic electors, and possibly more, who'll switch their vote to you when the Electoral College meets in a few weeks," Mann spoke without any hint of uncertainty for the benefit of his now-unhinged President. Keeping Holland resolute for the next twenty-four days was essential to the project's success. "You have to understand that we've got to be disciplined and discreet with everything we say and do between now and then if we're going to have any chance of pulling this off."

"And by the way," lied Mann. "we're doing all this above board, nothing that could be remotely challenged legally. No money offered, no promises of jobs or legislation or anything. We won't risk a Watergate here." The infamous White House cover-up needed no clarification for Holland. That dark incident was burned into the mind of every American who lived through the impeachment of Richard Nixon. But Mann wasn't about to reveal the manner in which the project had unearthed critical information on the targeted electors. Only the Chief of Staff, Jonas Stanning, and Carlton Espy held those secrets.

"Well, that's reassuring," said the President. "But I've decided I've gotta make a public statement. I'm gettin' hammered."

Mann was prepared for this demand. "We've got a draft for you to look at. The speechwriters are down there, and they'll come over to review it with you as soon as you're ready. We're looking at a good venue there. You can do it as early as this afternoon, but I'd suggest you spend some time to get the tone right and get some exercise and rest. Tomorrow evening makes sense so the talkers won't be all over it all day. "

"And there will be no questions. This won't be a press conference," concluded Mann. "Does all this work for you?"

"I guess so. But I gotta tell you, we can't keep this up much longer. And I need Muse down here so I can stay on top of this goddamn bombing thing. It'll be a fuckin' pain having him around, but I don't have much choice."

After signing off, Mann checked to be certain the encryption code was still active on his device. This was not a time to have his conversations overheard.

"Alistair, the boss needs you in Orlando," Mann spoke on his less secure phone to the President's harried National Security Advisor. "How soon can you get down there? Fine, get the Mil Aides to arrange a Lear for you. " He knew that Muse would be ecstatic about the summons. Briefing POTUS was his catnip.

After returning a handful of calls to nervous Republican senators, Mann rang Espy, hoping to find more prospective defectors had been uncovered. "We don't have much new data to go on, Eldon" said Espy, "but we've turned up something from another source that may be helpful. Are you coming out here anytime soon?"

"I'll be there in two hours," Mann replied. "We need to lock down at least two more targets, and soon. POTUS is coming unraveled."

November 18

"So this is the best we can do?" Senator Bridges addressed his senior aides over crab cakes and salad, with the late autumn colors framing a perfect view of the Severn River outside his dining room.

"I'm the President-elect. We won the election. But for two weeks now we've been twisting in the wind, waiting for the President to concede or at least show his hand in demanding a recount somewhere. Not only hasn't that happened, there doesn't seem to be any prospect for a concession." Sen. Bridges stood and walked to the wide window overlooking his boat hanging above its slip on the Severn. His last pleasant sail on the Chesapeake was a distant memory.

"What the hell are they doing? And what can *we* do to end this mess?"

"Senator," responded Melody Banks, "on the second point, Todd has had his people researching the laws that govern this situation. There's a timetable that kicks in—state certification of vote counts, then the meeting of the Electoral College in December – but there is no legal requirement that compels President Holland to concede. It's only precedent that makes this happen. He can wait as long as he wants until the vote is reaffirmed in the Electoral College, and that's still three weeks away. Even if every state official has certified that you've won that state's election, it's not official until the College meets."

"I know all this," Bridges snapped. "Remember, I was a poli sci professor before I first ran for office. What I want to know is, what are they doing that might disrupt the process? And what can we do now? What tools do we have other than public outcry? Which, by the way, seems to have shrunk with all the paranoia about terrorism."

"We're looking under every stone," Banks said. "I have some sources who may have something for us soon."

"Well, I hope so," said Bridges, now with his back to the group, seeming to have suddenly tuned out from the conversation, gazing into the distance. "That's all now. We'll get back together as soon as we have something more to go on."

Banks returned to her makeshift office in an extra bedroom the Bridges family had organized for her. She hadn't seen her Washington apartment for weeks, as the work extended far into every night since the election. Her clothes, makeup, and bicycle were off limits until the hazmat teams could clear the area for reentry. A staffer had made a shopping run into Annapolis to buy essentials for her, and she had all the communications gear she needed. But she was bone tired and sluggish, functioning without exercise or proper sleep, and feeling entirely inadequate to the challenge facing Senator Bridges and his team. Somehow she would have to muster the stamina to keep the team on track. And she had to jumpstart Jackson Cripple's investigation, wherever it might lead.

CHAPTER 20

The Lear jet descended through heavy clouds over a bleak, denuded landscape that announced eastern Kentucky coal country. Lydia Elving, the plane's only passenger, removed her eyeshade and stretched.

She checked her face in a pocket mirror and ran a brush through long, dark hair. Satisfied, Elving opened a file with information about her coming appointment, a Southern gentleman who had become a potential electoral defector. She organized the papers in the order to be presented to her target and ran through the checklist she had received from Carlton Espy two days earlier.

"No hard sell," he stated. "Use your charm. He'll be attracted to you, like an uncle to a favorite niece. Give him some time to get comfortable, then use the memos."

The jet taxied to the small corporate terminal where a black Escalade met her for the short drive into town.

"Miss Elving, I'm Winston Granberry, so pleased to meet you." The tall, imposing Kentuckian showed Elving to a Queen Ann couch next to his massive desk. "This couch belonged to my grandmother Rebecca Ann, who brought it from England and had it reupholstered with material she bought in Paris early last century while she was studying in Europe."

"It's beautiful," said Elving, stroking the worn but still elegant covering. "Your grandmother must have been a remarkable woman."

"Yes, like all the women in my family. All remarkable women, all strong, no-nonsense types who kept their men in line, saved the money and spent it wisely," Granberry poured coffee from an ancient electric percolator he kept filled next to his desk. "I hope this is ok. Never got a new coffeemaker. My father had this one going the day he died."

Lydia Elving was the team's "Go Girl", as designated by Carlton Espy, a little joke she not only tolerated but a distinction she enjoyed. A Vanderbilt University-trained lawyer with clients under fire for asbestos mismanagement, coal mine accidents, and most recently, another massive Gulf oil spill, Elving had become one of the Southeast's most celebrated young attorneys. And her post-feminist personal views stood her well in staunch Republican circles.

Elving had worked briefly but profitably with Carlton Espy on a case involving a Texas chain of exterminators under prosecution for dumping toxic waste in the Corniche River. The defense managed to convince the court that the chemicals in question could not be certifiably traced to their client and that the video evidence may have been tampered with by the government. The EPA was not a popular institution in East Texas. So when Espy began recruiting his team of outreach lawyers for the elector project, Elving immediately came to mind.

A committed free market conservative, skilled in both rhetoric and tactics, Elving was also a good-looking woman, with a svelte athlete's body. She gave the team an ideal weapon—a woman who could charm the socks off men of a certain age. And for a kicker, she abhorred the idea of a Democratic president and all the smug liberals he would bring into government. Elving could care less about the national security crisis and who might best defend the interests of the country. She wanted passionately to keep liberals off the bench at every level, and certainly off the Supreme Court.

"So, Miss Elving, what brings you to this remote corner of Kentucky," Granberry was in no hurry to rush his visitor's response, and he was intrigued. He never had a visit from an important lawyer who flew into the tiny Perry County airfield on a Lear jet. An old friend had called the day before to ask Granberry to meet an interesting young woman coming to town on business.

"Mr. Granberry," she began, rearranging her legs and sensible pumps to present a proper, well turned out image to her target. "The election confusion in Washington—and then the bombing—has created a crisis that could set the country back a decade or more. Of course, I know that your candidate seems to have won the election, and that you supported him. And you're an elector from Kentucky."

"Well," interrupted Granberry, "yes, I voted for Bridges, and yes, I'm a Democratic elector. But from what I hear I'm worried about where he might take the country. I have a lot of doubts." His friend had alerted him that Linda Elving was a conservative corporate lawyer, and a Republican.

"So do we, Mr. Granberry, so do we," she clasped her hands as if to pray. "Sen. Bridges is an honorable, decent man, but we now know what kind of team he'll bring into office, and what his legislative and policy agenda will be, and we are very, very concerned."

"Go on," he said, now moving from behind his desk to the chair next to his grandmother's loveseat.

"Take the EPA for example. President Holland has tried to help the mining and extraction industries recover after the damage done by the Clinton and Obama administrations. I don't mean to insult those officials if you were a supporter, but..." He waved a hand to stop her.

"I supported Bill Clinton, and I supported Obama. But they both let me down. Let the country down. We got over Clinton's skirt chasing—no one died there. And thank God we didn't get Al Gore. But Obama," Granberry shook his head, "his people simply destroyed the economy down here. Shut down practically every coal operation. Thousands of good people lost their jobs, their homes. And it hasn't come back yet. Never will."

"That's right, sir." She decided to leapfrog the rest of her buildup and go right for the kill. "And here's the worst. We've found out that Senator Bridges plans to bring back the Clinton-Obama people to run EPA, the Interior Department, and the Justice Department environmental division."

Elving pulled out her trump card. "You remember Carol Browner?" Elving recalled the name of Clinton's EPA head and Obama's White House environmental czar.

"Who doesn't?" Granberry replied. From Jonas Stanning's memo Elving knew her target had told more than one close friend that he blamed Browner for the demise of his father's company. "She killed this part of Kentucky and practically all of West Virginia," he paused to grasp the prospect of Carol Browner in a Bridges administration.

"It doesn't make sense," he said. Granberry's hand began to shake as he rubbed a tabletop. "Senator Bridges was pretty clear that he would be a different kind of Democratic president. He said in Richmond last month that he'd bring pro-business, common sense people in to run the agencies. I was there, I heard him. I believed him."

"So did a lot of people," she sighed. "I want to show you something." She withdrew a small electronic pad from her purse, turned it on, and handed it over to Granberry. "I don't have this on paper since I just received it on the plane coming down to see you, but it will be clear."

The memo was addressed to Senator Bridges' transition director for environmental appointments, from Carol Browner, now an attorney and university lecturer in Vermont. It was brief and to the point."

It read, *"Please tell the President-elect that I would be honored to serve in the capacity we discussed in Maryland last week. We'll have a great team to enact his ambitious agenda. I'll look forward to hearing from you once the transition begins in full."*

"'I'll be damned!" Granberry's face turned bright red as he handed the pad back to Elving.

"Mr. Granberry," she spoke softly now, not wanting to overplay her hand as he had taken in her information exactly as she'd hoped. "Senator Bridges' is not a moderate agenda. And the country will pay a huge price if he takes office."

"So what are you saying? That there's some alternative to Bridges becoming president? Short of impeachment, I don't see how you can stop it from happening."

Elving then laid out each circumstance that could intervene, noting that the election would not be official until the Electoral College met in three weeks, that a few electoral votes moved from the Bridges column to Holland would reverse the original count.

"So you want me to switch, that's it, right?" This was the dangerous moment Elving now had to maneuver to not send Granberry howling to his Democratic friends, to the press, to the Bridges campaign team, even to the FBI. She steeled herself and said nothing, waiting for Granberry's next response.

"But if I said yes—and I'm not saying that—it's not possible, is it? Aren't there rules, laws that prevent an elector from switching?" His tone wasn't adversarial, thought Elving, a good sign at this critical stage in the conversation. "I remember when we met in Frankfort for the vote after the 2012 election some of the people joked they could get a lot of money from Romney if they switched sides. But that was just ridiculous stuff."

"No," she said. "It's not ridiculous. Taking money to switch, yes. But electors here in Kentucky are not bound by law to vote for the candidate who won the popular vote in this state. Democrats here would be upset, for sure, but you can vote any way you choose, and no one can do anything about it." She placed both hands on Granberry's and spoke forcefully. "Winston, you can do this. You can help save this country."

She left Granberry after a quiet lunch in the Coaltown Inn near his office, during which they agreed to set aside the more delicate topic of the election for a casual meal before her departure. He was pleased she ordered, and finished, a plate of ribs he especially prized. *No shrinking violet, this one,* he thought. *Just wish Maureen could meet her.* His wife was in Louisville with the grandchildren. She rarely involved herself in her husband's business or political affairs.

Elving reconstructed her conversation on her IPad as the Lear climbed through the haze and cruised back to Nashville. Granberry made no promises other than to keep the conversation to himself until they talked later in the week. Yet, she was confident she had seeded enough doubt in the courtly Kentuckian.

CHAPTER 21

Melody Banks pulled on a lined windbreaker borrowed from Mrs. Bridges and laced her running shoes for the two-mile jog into Annapolis, explaining to staff that she needed some exercise to clear her head for the day ahead.

The Crab Hole served an all-day breakfast menu, and when Banks arrived, Jackson Cripple was already in a corner booth, digging into an omelet, sausage, and a side of pancakes. "That's disgusting," she frowned, ordering coffee and a muffin. "How can you eat like that? Didn't your mother teach you anything about nutrition?"

"Comfort food helps the libido, Melody," Cripple mouthed through a forkful of eggs. "And at my advancing age I need all the help I can get." After a minute about the frigid weather, the news of the bombing aftermath, and the Washington Redskins' continued descent into football oblivion, they switched to a more pressing topic.

Cripple pushed a file folder across the table. "This is an outline of what would be needed to do this work. The numbers there are plus or minus 20%, given how much skilled manpower I would need. It's tough to project cost because there are so many unknowns here, legal questions, and so on. But that's pretty close."

"The real problem is getting past the heavy security that these people undoubtedly have in their devices. We could get just so far and hit a wall with virtually no information you can use. But we'd have to spend a bundle to get to that wall." Despite his extraordinary success in mining sensitive data in past projects for Banks and others, Cripple was conservative in promising results. His was a profession that was plagued by unexpected roadblocks. His office was decorated with a framed needlepoint: *Shit Happens. Deal With It.*

"Jackson," she said, "we don't have much choice. Not a single source has provided any real information about what Holland and his operatives are doing. "I have a friend who works for a Republican congressman who tried to see Holland down in Florida. They blew him off, said the President was jammed with meetings about the bombing and wasn't scheduling any visits."

"We're picking up recount noises in a few states but in general the Republican campaign operations are quiet as far as we can tell. Routine conference calls from Holland and others to keep them upbeat. But nothing that gives us any idea why the President is not conceding. We're going crazy here in Annapolis."

Cripple nodded and presented a devil's advocate assessment. "Have you considered the possibility that they really aren't doing anything to reverse the election results? No recount plans, nothing. And that this NSA stuff in Leesburg is entirely related to the bombing and the national security team needing to get out of the White House for its work. After all, that area is still quarantined off limits for everyone else."

"Yeah," she said, "of course I have. I'd like nothing more than to believe that Holland and his crew are just arguing with each other about how to mount a recount. That way I'd know this will end, and that their string'll run out and he'll either concede or not. Regardless, Bridges could start his transition and take office in January. That scenario would make me completely happy."

"But Jackson," Banks said, both hands spread across the Formica tabletop, leaning into Cripple, "I don't believe it. I just don't believe that these mean, conniving bastards in the White House are letting this go. I think they're looking for some way to blow up the election and keep that asshole Holland in office."

Cripple cleaned up the last of the syrup-drenched pancakes, folded his napkin beside his plate and responded, "Maybe so. But we're gonna need a break to find out. And then there's the budget. Can we do that, Melody?"

"I don't know," she said. "We don't have a bunch of billionaires who would write checks like this with no questions asked. Can't do it with campaign funds. I'm told our SuperPACs are tapped out, and that's where this would have to come from. I'll make some calls this afternoon. Problem is I have to do this myself. No one else can know about this for now."

Cripple paid the bill and drove away in his new all-electric Tesla convertible, top down, heater blazing in thirty-degree weather. *A total contradiction*, thought Banks. *But this guy may be our best chance to get the information we need, maybe our only chance.* She walked the first mile, then ran at full speed to the Bridges home where she would resume her vigil with the President-elect.

■　■　■

Clay Harper, *Politico's* editorial director, convened his staff to plan the day's coverage. "We'll need something from Holland's people about a concession. And a follow-up from the Bridges campaign."

"We've got reports that Holland's campaign has begun a recount process in at least three states, including Virginia, but have any formal papers been filed?"

"I think they're looking at New Mexico and Ohio, too," added Pima Grantham, whose scoop on Vice President West's possible resignation had shocked Washington days earlier. Hired away from the *Washington Post* when Amazon's owner bought the paper six years earlier, Grantham came to *Politico* with a computer full of leads and sources.

Once the meeting concluded, Harper ushered Grantham into his glass-walled office. "Pima, what do you think is happening with Holland? Does he have a chance with these recounts? This is crazier than Gore 2000."

"I've talked to dozens of people here in Washington and around the country," she responded. She mussed her hair with both hands—an unconscious habit that left her looking like a tousled kid. "I bought drinks for the party chair in Albuquerque till one am last week and got nothing. He said he thought the campaign would seek a recount there, but he didn't see it making a difference since the margin was over the number that could justify the expense. They challenged every absentee ballot possible, and not only did they not pick up votes, they lost a couple hundred. He was clearly confused."

Grantham slouched in the deep cushioned chair offered to visitors likely to stay awhile. Tall and painfully thin, uncaring about her looks or clothes or posture, Grantham's spunk was her allure. Her ability to get the story, when others had long given up, was a source of constant admiration among political journalists.

"Pima, I want you to lead a team to manage the recount story. We need to get out front of it now." The editor was eager to beat the *Post* and the *Times* as the election debacle unfolded. "None of the papers or television or even the bloggers have broken anything new since election night. The analysts and talking heads are clueless and we haven't done much better."

"Take anyone you want, other than the terrorism team, and find out what you can. Let's plan to be online and on TV within twenty-four hours. And put out updates every four hours after that. Can you manage that?"

"Sure," she said. "But don't get your hopes up. I don't see a tsunami here. I just think they're putting together a massive legal effort. God knows they have the money to recount every vote in the country. "

"I talked to Melody Banks last night," Grantham continued. "She's now running everything in that operation. I like her—she's smart and tough and honest. But I don't think she knows any more than we do."

"Pull out all the stops," pushed Harper. "This is the biggest political story of the decade, and you're gonna get it right. This is Pulitzer stuff."

CHAPTER 21

The Stanning team worked through the weekend without new leads to feed Espy and the outreach lawyers, and Eldon Mann was becoming impatient, and worried. *How much longer can we keep up this charade,* he thought. *When will the press and the Democrats realize that the only play we have is the Electoral College? How long can we keep the two converts we have from getting cold feet? Will Stanning's team be secure, especially when they figure out what we're doing?*

Mann tossed down a lukewarm cup of mint tea- he had long ago quit coffee and most nerve-jangling caffeine drinks – and focused on Espy's new list of prospects. Vaughn and Winston were not enough to ensure a reversal of the vote, even if they commit to switching. The team needed three solid Democratic elector votes on Jan. 14 and at this point they were one short of the 270 needed to declare a Holland reelection. Two votes would put the count at 269–269, which would throw the election into the House of Representatives where the outcome could be difficult to control. To cover the likelihood that one or more of the converts would bolt, Mann figured he needed four or five electors who would promise to drink the Kool-Aid.

"You know, Eldon," said Espy. "Even if we pull this off and come out of it with the numbers, all hell will break loose in Congress and even in the courts. Each of these state Democratic parties will file lawsuits to reverse these electors. It could go to the Supreme Court, but it would be much more complicated, even though we have the Court."

"I'm aware of that," said Mann. "But we're now deep into this and we're going to see it through. I've got campaign counsel putting together a group of election lawyers ready to deal with all this when, and if, the time comes. They don't know what they'll be fighting, but they'll have a plan as soon as we've locked down the three votes." Mann knew the hurdles were huge, and mindful of the blowback that would occur if their plan was successful. There were moments when he hoped the project would hit a dead end and that would be it. A long vacation from politics wouldn't be so bad.

"What's the best we have at this point?" Mann wanted to get back to the target electors and take his mind off the prospect of failure.

"OK, the list isn't long, and only one of these looks as promising as the first group," said Espy. "Let's talk about Wayne Hartsell, Scottsdale, Arizona. Rich developer, big Democratic donor, gave Bill Clinton twenty-five thousand, raised another hundred for the DNC, wanted a cabinet appointment or at least Costa Rica but only got the Kennedy Center Arts Commission. Stayed out of Obama '08 and 2012 but jumped on Bridges this year. We figure he gave or raised three-fifty for the campaign and another million for their SuperPAC."

"Doesn't look too promising to me," responded Mann. "Guy's gonna get something if Bridges takes office. "

Espy smiled and raised his index finger to note an objection. "Right, but wrong. We know that Hartsell is *persona non grata* with the Bridges transition people. They've got information that Hartsell's company will likely be indicted soon for some kind of building and finance irregularity in Phoenix. A golf course development that's getting built with dirty money. Hartsell's not personally implicated, but his company is in trouble with the SEC. That's not the kind of news an incoming administration wants to deal with when they announce appointments."

"So how do you sell him on the idea that he should come over to our side? Their transition can keep him on the hook until springtime if they want to." said Mann.

"We have an email from one of Bridges' team working on potential appointments, and...a voice recording. They make it clear that Hartsell gets nothing in a Bridges administration."

"All right, let's try to get him," said Mann. "But be careful. We can't promise him anything in Holland's second administration. That's the hard line that protects us when the shit hits the fan. And you have to be careful that he doesn't go ballistic and starts whining to all his friends about getting screwed by Bridges after all he's done, blah, blah."

"We'll send Lydia Elving to see him," said Espy. "D'you know she's a scratch golfer? She kicked my ass in Dallas last summer. She'll have to be careful not to embarrass him if they play."

Mann was curious about what "scratch" golfer really meant, but he shook off the thought, golf representing to Mann a colossal waste of time and energy.

"You go to church, Miss Elving? There's a chapel here." Wayne Hartsell poured coffee for Lydia as the two ate breakfast on the terrace of the Boulders, an upscale spa, golf, and tennis resort Hartsell had developed in the eighties. Elving had landed in the corporate jet late the previous evening and managed a good sleep before meeting Hartsell to begin the political discussion. While under considerable pressure to complete her conversion of the developer, Elving knew she would have to move carefully to keep him interested.

A billionaire real estate mogul would be wary of any meeting he felt was wasting his time. But the weather was spectacular and the desert gave off a seductive aroma from a nearby mesquite fireplace. She would try to enjoy the next twenty-four hours.

"No, Mr. Hartsell, I gave that up years ago. You?"

"Nah, I don't see the point of it," he laughed. "So what can I do for you? My office says you represent some serious financial interests in Nashville. I'm always ready to talk about money."

"Yes, I do have clients who invest in real estate," she replied. "But I'm here to talk about something else that involves you personally and politically." She had rehearsed her pitch carefully, down to her body language as she spoke.

"As you know this presidential election is a mess. Senator Bridges appears to have won but that's by no means assured. President Holland is about to mount recount procedures in at least three states, and his attorneys believe they have sufficient grounds to turn around the result in at least one. Voting machine irregularities, possibly even fraudulent activity by some groups working to defeat the President."

"I'd be surprised by that," said Hartsell, "but go on, I'm listening."

"I know you've been a strong supporter of Senator Bridges in this campaign, and that you may want to be a part of his incoming administration. But I think you should know something about their planning."

"Where are you coming from?" Hartsell checked his cellphone for messages, and looked over Elving's shoulder at two teenagers lounging in bikinis. "Yeah, maybe I'd like to get involved next year, but that's a ways off and, beside, I've got my hands full here in Arizona trying to get a bunch of projects off the ground."

Elving then withdrew a file from a leather case and placed it next to Harsell's plate. Inside was an internal memo from the Bridges transition team, which included a wish list of cabinet and ambassadorial appointments from the campaign fundraising chairman to Senator Bridges' transition director. Hartsell scrolled through the list and found his name on page two, with the notation:

"Interested in Western Europe. Board or commission will be rejected as insult."

"Damn right that would be an insult, after what I raised for these people," Hartsell said. "And most of these assholes didn't do squat for the campaign. I know for a fact that Gonzalez claimed a million that was raised by other people. And Markson? Five million? No way. He did maybe two at the most. I can document every penny of what I gave and raised, and I can tell you it was a lot."

"I'm sure that's true," said Elving, drawing another paper from her thin Dunhill attaché. "But look at this."

The second document was a memo back to the campaign finance chairman, responding to the donors' wish lists. Hartsell read the single page quickly.

"First of all, it's premature to be discussing these donor expectations while the election is still not resolved. I understand the pressure you're under to be responsive, and you should continue to assure these generous folks that we will give careful attention to every request once we take office in January. Everyone on your list will be treated with respect and most will likely be offered a prestigious appointment of some kind."

"However, several of these donors will be problematic, especially Wayne Hartsell. We have information that his real estate development company will soon be indicted for securities fraud in Arizona and that while he personally may not be charged, Mr. Hartsell will face intense legal difficulties for some time to come.

"Hartsell should not be encouraged to seek any appointment during the early stages of the Bridges administration. It will be bad enough that his campaign contributions will be noted alongside his legal problems. Should his legal issues be resolved in his complete favor we may reconsider sometime next year. However, until that time he will not be on any list presented to the President-elect."

"I'll be a son of a bitch!" Hartsell exclaimed. "Goddamn! How did they know about the securities issue? And by the way, that's going away. The state has absolutely no evidence of any wrong-doing. My lawyers have assured me of that."

"I'm sorry," said Elving, placing her hand on his forearm, drawing his eyes back to hers. "I'm sure you're right. But they seem to have a line to the prosecutors." She then played the voice recording for him, a clear voice restating the tone of the memos, with the two participants from Bridges' transition operation laughing at the presumptuousness of Hartsell even thinking he would be rewarded with an ambassadorship at this point.

"I need to make a call," Hartsell heard a loud ding on his cellphone, excused himself abruptly and moved to a nearby patio. Elving watched as Hartsell waved his arms while screaming into his phone. She assumed his attorney was on the other end of the tirade. He hung up, returned to the table, and sat quietly for a moment before addressing her.

"My lawyer just told me he talked to the state attorney general thirty minutes ago. U. S. Marshalls are on the way to my office right now. I have to go. I'll call you in a couple hours. Enjoy yourself here." He ran through the lobby to retrieve his Beemer and drive the twenty minutes to his Scottsdale office, where he was greeted by law enforcement officials brandishing search warrants.

Thrown off by the rapid unfolding of events, Elving returned to her handsome casita to take stock of the situation with Hartsell. The legal bust had overtaken any outrage he had from reading the Bridges transition memo. *How do I get him back to focus on the electoral vote?* she wondered. It could be days, weeks before he calmed down.

After a brief call to Carlton Espy to report the morning's turn of events, she donned her Lululemon workout suit and checked out the Boulders gym. From her treadmill she watched golfers cycle through a golf hole surrounded by water and cactus, on their way to the back nine of one of Arizona's premier courses. *When have I had time to do that?* she thought. *Maybe I'll go hit balls and putt while I wait for Hartsell to call, if in fact he does call.*

The pro shop fitted her with a set of rental clubs, a hat and glove. She worked through two buckets of practice balls, sending precise wedges and mid irons to targets down the range, then banged a dozen drives mostly in the direction she intended. *Not bad*, she smiled. Elving had joined Nashville's most exclusive club earlier in the year, planning to take up the game seriously again, once the work allowed. Most of her clients spent as much time on the golf course as in boardrooms.

As a Vanderbilt undergraduate, she had led her team to an SEC championship and finished in the top ten in the NCAA tournament her senior year. Urged to turn professional, Elving instead enrolled in law school and quickly caught the eye of several prominent national firms. After graduation, she turned down offers in New York, Atlanta, and Dallas to join a Nashville firm known for representing high-profile corporate clients.

The junior associate buried herself in tort law, quickly rising to the top of a firm renowned for defeating trial lawyers attempting to win huge settlements from her corporate clients. Her growing caseload, combined with a torrid, discreet affair with a married partner at the firm, left no time for golf. Now, in the warm Arizona desert, she felt the rush that came from mastery of one of sport's toughest games.

She rolled putts on the velvet smooth practice green before returning to the pro shop and scheduling a massage and pedicure. "Don't put those clubs away yet," she heard Hartsell's booming voice from the entrance to the shop. "We're gonna go play a few holes."

"Now, Lydia, what were you saying about the goddamn election?" Hartsell was smiling and relaxed, showing no discomfort after federal officials ransacked his office. "By the way, they got nothing. Not a goddamn thing!"

Four hours later, after she drummed him by seven strokes, with the sun dropping over the giant saguaro cacti, Elving and Hartsell clicked glasses of a rare burgundy, after a dinner of quail and prickly pear sorbet. Hartsell was not only agreeable to the plan Lydia outlined, he also offered any help the team might need, including money, to make it happen.

Carlton Espy received her report shortly after midnight as he was finally headed to bed in his tri-level condo in D.C.'s trendy Bloomingdale neighborhood, an area of Washington that a few years earlier would have seen few white faces. The widespread re-gentrification of the inner city had brought a wave of clever speculators, including Espy and his discreet girlfriend, a rising staffer for the Senate Energy Committee. Espy bought two drafty, decrepit brownstones three years earlier and undertook a complete renovation. The new units were lauded in architectural reviews and much in demand by affluent young professionals willing to spend lavishly for cutting edge housing. He set aside one unit for his own cozy Washington pied a' terre while away from Dallas.

He had touted the condos to Lydia Elving, who occasionally made noises about coming to Washington to add a prestigious federal title to her resume. *If she wanted,* thought Espy, *I could grease the skids for her with Holland, maybe something serious at Justice, or a deputy cabinet position, or even White House counsel if that idiot Poindexter could be shoved out. And, she would make a great tenant.*

Real estate was not on his mind, however, as he received Elving's call. "Lydia, how'd it go out there? Did you talk to Hartsell after the bust today?"

"Carlton," she purred, "you're going to buy me a huge steak and get me a round of golf at Pine Valley after this is over. I deserve it."

"So?" Espy responded, anxious for some good news. "What's the deal with Hartsell?"

"He's not only on board, Carlton. He wants to play in our sandbox. And I mean *seriously* play. You can count him as a solid vote. I'll need to do some hand-holding between now and then to make sure he sticks to the script, but for now he's one of us."

After a brief round of related news, Espy rang off and started to call Eldon Mann. Instead, he decided to wait until morning, when both men would have clearer heads to consider the implication of a third likely convert.

CHAPTER 23

Thanksgiving week began with another predictable round of criticism of Holland's failure to issue a concession. Joining the partisan howling were multiple editorial calls for the President to formally initiate a vote recount or to end the election limbo. Even Holland's Republican support had gone silent. Senate and House leaders met to discuss the dilemma, though no agreement could be reached to call both legislative bodies back into session.

"What could we do even if we brought everyone back again?" asked the Speaker of the House over poached eggs in the Jefferson Hotel dining room in Richmond, which had become the informal interim congressional headquarters since the bombing. "Until the election is decided by the Electoral College there's no role for us. And I'm told several states are delaying certification in case there will be recounts. This is a totally fucked up situation. Pardon my French, Alice." The House Whip Leader smiled at the unnecessary apology.

Congress had adjourned in October, then called to Richmond soon after the election. The Virginia governor had cleared the premises to accommodate the U. S. House and Senate, though its members were forced to double up in cramped spaces intended for part-time state legislators.

Within a few days the leaders of both parties determined that, other than in the intelligence committees, there was little business that could be done to deal with the terrorist attack. The stalemated election was a problem for President Holland and President-elect Bridges. So all but a handful of the congressional leadership returned to their home states to await further developments. Besides, noted one grizzled committee chairman, the hotels in Richmond were sub-par and the food worse. With the office holders gone, the lobbyists scattered. Except for one Washington lawyer determined to mine the situation for the gold he saw in the disarray that had enveloped the Capitol.

Tommy "The Rake" Thompson made a fortune turning tragedy into business. During a thirty year lobbying career he secured hundreds of clients who had ruined rivers and oceans with toxic chemicals, manufactured cars with deadly flaws, cheated millions of consumers with cartel pricing, and sold assault weapons through gun shows with no background checks. For his most lucrative project he cobbled together a rump association of huge cable television companies to avoid regulation of that industry's monopoly price gouging. The Rake was, in most Washington insiders' opinion, the most successful lobbyist since the Civil War.

"He's like a hulking buzzard on a telephone line," said one colorful profile. "If there's road kill to be eaten, the Rake will be on it first."

Single since his thirties, after a bad marriage got worse, Thompson preferred the company of VIPs who could share his bounty and enhance his influence in the nation's capitol. Finagling a coveted invitation to a Holland state dinner honoring Great Britain's newly crowned King William and Her Royal Highness Catherine, Thompson scored a double by bringing a rising star on the Senate Appropriations Committee as his date. Everything was a transaction for The Rake.

Barely five and a half feet tall, Thompson nevertheless struck a commanding presence in the capitol—his suits made by the most expensive New York tailor, shoes from Milan and ties from Paris. His chauffeured car was the most recent Lincoln sedan, purchased at the suggestion of his good friend, the dean of the Michigan delegation, during a hunting trip at Thompson's Eastern Shore estate. There he maintained not only a substantial supply of pheasant and duck for his guests' shooting success, but also the most extensive collection of assault weapons in private hands.

The Michigan congressman, a powerful committee chairman, loved firing these guns, especially the Soviet Izhmash, a virtual antique among Thompson's stock and the powerful Galil Ace, a recent Israeli product that could destroy a platoon of men in one burst. On a recent weekend visit The Rake provided a small herd of deer to be mowed down by his VIP guest, an event that thrilled the chairman, a favor he would not forget.

On a cold morning in Richmond, as his competitors were scheming to game the arrival of a Bridges administration, Tommy Thompson was concocting a plan to move the U. S. Capitol to a cornfield near Lebanon, Kansas, less than three miles from the epicenter of the United States. He compiled an exhaustive list of potential clients who would pay dearly for his services to make it happen. For Thompson it was simply a matter of making it *appear* that such a move could happen. The idea had been percolating in his mind for years as little more than a fantasy. The bombing two weeks earlier had given it life.

"Jimmy, I hope all this craziness with the election and the bombing hasn't affected your tennis game," Thompson joked to James Lismore, the Kansas congressman who chaired the House Administration Committee, which oversaw operations of the Capitol, among other mundane but politically beneficial decisions.

"Hell, Tommy, I can't imagine when I'll be able to get away with playing tennis anytime soon," responded Lismore. "We must be seen to be doing the people's work these days," he chuckled. "What's going on over there in Richmond?"

"No one seems to know what to do. The leadership is just waiting on Holland to cave. The terrorist thing seems to have settled down but Homeland Security is telling members that the radiation will be around the Capitol for some time." Thompson continued, "We should talk about that idea you mentioned when you were on the Eastern Shore last year, you know, moving some or all federal functions out of Washington to prevent just this sort of attack."

"Damn right!" said Lismore. "I thought of that the moment I heard about the bombing. We'll never be totally safe there. We're a prime target for these nutballs, militant Muslims, whoever the hell they are. It's only a matter of time 'till it happens again. And it could be a lot damn worse, especially with these goddamn drones that just about anyone can buy off the shelf. Why, I read today...."

"And by the way," continued Thompson, "this isn't a totally new idea. Remember the proposal that Nebraska Senator – wasn't it Ben Sasse? Yeah, back in 2014 he ran a TV ad in his campaign, to move the Capitol to Nebraska. We can't let him get the jump on this."

Thompson let the congressman rattle on for another five minutes, citing unverified reports of Islamic militants hoarding chemical weapons, nuclear devices, even missiles. "Jimmy, you're dead on," he interrupted. "Now's the time for Congress to seriously consider a new home. It'll be years before you can get back into the Capitol. And who knows what's going on in the office buildings. I hear that Russell and Dirksen may be shut down for several years too."

"You're onto something, Tommy," said Lismore, warming to the subject. "Why don't you come out here to Topeka and we'll sit down and come up with a plan? Marilyn can cook up that wild boar stew you love, and we'll drink some of that Makers Mark reserve you gave me, ok?"

The Rake hung up, shook off the grim prospect of Marilyn Lismore's inedible stew, and rang his office to book the jet charter service he used for such outings as this. By early evening he was in the air headed toward Kansas.

CHAPTER 24

President Holland glanced down at the speech he was about to deliver in the media room of the Florida White House. He wore a dark suit, blue shirt and red tie, the standard political power garb for television, and stood behind a podium bearing the large presidential seal. Reading from the teleprompter, he began.

"My fellow Americans, I speak to you on this day of families coming together to give thanks for all the bounties we enjoy and for the well-being of those less fortunate. After one of the most extraordinary months in the history of our great country we are all ready for a rest."

"Two weeks before the election, our nation's Capitol building, the very symbol of our democracy, was struck by a lawless terrorist faction determined to undermine our security. The men and women of our emergency teams in Washington have worked tirelessly to contain the fallout from the explosion, a nuclear detonation within our borders, one we have long feared but have managed to avoid since the dawn of the nuclear age."

"I am pleased to report that the radiation has been contained and no longer threatens Washington or the surrounding areas. However, the damage is severe and it will be many months before reconstruction of our Capitol and the surrounding buildings can begin. In the meantime, our Congress has established temporary quarters in Richmond, Virginia, and White House operations have resumed. We're getting back to normal in your nation's capital." Holland paused for effect, and continued.

"We will not rest until all those responsible for this cowardly attack are apprehended and punished. Ours is a resilient nation and our government will respond with every resource we have."

"Our brave military forces have launched successful air and drone strikes against more than a dozen strongholds of militant jihadists in Yemen, Pakistan, Somalia, Sudan, and Libya. Today our commanders have moved the Sixth Fleet into positions in the Mediterranean, Gulf of Aden, the Persian Gulf, and the Arabian Sea, where they will continue to confront the threat we are facing in that volatile part of the world."

"Those who have planned or carried out this vicious attack on Washington are being hunted down and either killed or captured. Terrorist cells in Europe are being flushed out and their leaders apprehended. We have coordinated all these efforts with appropriate leaders in the countries affected."

" I am extremely proud of our men and women in uniform and our intelligence services during this crisis. And I know they have the heartfelt gratitude of all those listening today. I am determined to deploy every tool in our arsenal to respond to terrorism. Our freedom may be challenged, but it will not be broken."

"For this reason, I have chosen to devote my every waking moment to the security of our nation and the steps that must be taken to prevent another horrendous incident such as the one that shook America in the early hours of October 21. I have kept Senator Bridges informed of our every decision and action during this time."

"As to the presidential election, I have chosen to allow the various party officials who have expressed concern about the vote totals in their respective states to take orderly steps to ensure a proper counting of the votes. Some will call for a recount, others will let the early tabulations stand. I cannot predict the outcome."

"If the final count reveals that I have lost reelection, I will move swiftly to transfer the reins of the federal government to Senator Bridges and his incoming administration. I have already authorized federal officials to cooperate fully with his transition team to begin reviewing potential appointees. And I have instructed the General Services Administration to find secure office space for his transition team."

"However, until the state recounts are tabulated I have chosen to forego a concession. I ask your understanding and support as we move through this difficult but necessary task. Whatever the final result, this country will continue to have solid, patriotic leadership responsive to you, the American people."

"I will return to you as new developments arise. In the meantime, God bless our nation during this difficult time." Holland waited for the camera to pan back to show the family photos and the Stars and Stripes in the background. "Thank you, Mr. President," said the producer of the televised address, which was fed to news outlets around the world.

Holland smiled and thought, *take that, Calvin Bridges, you pussy.* After issuing a formal pardon to the Thanksgiving turkey flown to Orlando by the National Turkey Association, the President returned to his office to call Eldon Mann to find out if there was any chance he would return to office on January 20.

Senator Bridges and his senior advisors watched a few minutes of commentary after the President's televised remarks, then turned to the business of assessing Holland's strategy. "Will this work?" he asked, incredulously. "I'm dumbfounded."

One of Bridges' political consultants opened the conversation. "He can keep this going as long as he likes, he can bomb the entire

Mideast. But it won't change anything. The public may like it, but Republican leadership is jumping ship, the media's pounding him, and the clock is running out."

"We have forty-two states about to formally certify the vote count," added Todd Campbell, the campaign counsel. "All but three of the other eight have margins so large they can't realistically be challenged. In those places where they've started recounts we don't see any chance for success. When the Electoral College meets it will be all over but the shouting—and the final vote in the Congress of course. But that's a formality."

"I agree," said Bridges. "What do you think, Melody?"

Melody Banks had been silent through the telecast, scrolling through her email and answering text messages on her official phone. She was more focused on a second phone tucked under her shirt, set to vibrate when Jackson Cripple called.

She looked up from her tablet. "Of course, we should get our transition started. But," she paused. "I think we're missing something. If we're right and Holland has no chance of reversing any state total, then why is he refusing to concede? And why hasn't he called you since right after the election? And his excuse—to devote all his energy to the terrorist attack? I'm sorry, but I think that's total bullshit."

The meeting broke up, Banks and the campaign lawyers departed for the headquarters in Annapolis, and transition staff stayed behind to review prospective appointees assembled for Senator Bridges' review.

"Melody, can you wait a moment?" Bridges nodded to Banks to join him in his study. "Is there something you couldn't share with the group just now?"

"I just think there is more going on here than a recount operation," said Banks, gripping a nearby chair.

Bridges looked down, shuffled some papers, and came up with a note card. The envelope, postmarked a day earlier, carried a simple line above the flap—"The White House".

"Look at this," said Bridges, handing her the note with a brief handwritten message:

"Cal, this is from a friend. I'm sure you're puzzled by the President's hesitation to concede. Just hang in there. But be careful. It's a nasty crowd around him. They'll stop at nothing."

"Do you have any idea who sent this?" responded Banks.

"Yes, I recognize the handwriting," said Bridges, with a deep sigh. "It's from Vice President West."

CHAPTER 25

November 30

Congress—or about half of it—reconvened in the Virginia State Capitol, summoned by its leadership to discuss national security, but mostly to give the public an impression that they were actually working. No legislative business was at hand, and with the presidential election still in limbo, no upcoming agenda could be negotiated with either the president-elect or the incumbent. Yet the Rake and his patron, Chairman James Lismore, were hard at work lining up support for their grand scheme.

"We can't roll these guys," cautioned Lismore over a large ribeye steak and a second bottle of very good Shiraz, which The Rake brought to the working lunch in his suite. "We gotta give 'em a good excuse to go along with the plan, at least to start the process, fact-finding, all the economic studies we'll need to make the case."

"I've already got two think tanks working on numbers that will show a virtual wash in terms of spending," replied Thompson. "And I figure we can claim at least three hundred thousand construction jobs and ten thousand permanent jobs out of this. Here, Jimmy, have another glass of this amazing wine,"

Thompson had toured the Barossa Valley vineyards on a recent junket to Australia and had shipped back four cases of the best vintages, including the rare and very expensive Penfolds Grange. At six hundred dollars a bottle, he poured the wine only for his most valued and influential congressional friends.

The weekend of planning with Lismore in Kansas had proved fruitful. The congressman was eager to pursue the bold, improbable venture. And Thompson knew how to work the levers of power to move it along. All he had to do was nudge the Chairman toward a strategy that would steer the most lucrative retainers toward the lobbyist before others got into the game. Lismore knew The Rake was using him, but it was a symbiotic enterprise. He needed Thompson's creativity and outside resources to convince enough officials to validate the idea of moving much of the federal government to rural Kansas.

Every legislative proposal needed a compelling narrative to have a chance of leapfrogging the thousands of measures that are introduced in the House and Senate each year. For Lismore and Thompson, it was national security, propelled by the recent bombing but bolstered by countless acts of terrorism around the world, and the ongoing heightened anxiety about the potential for another 9-11. Add to those fears the billions of federal dollars that would be required to make such a move and dozens of industry leaders would line up to promote the biggest public works project in U. S. history.

Inflating the federal deficit would present a challenge, but there was always more money to be printed when the threat to national security could be effectively claimed. Bush and Cheney figured this out in promoting the Iraq war, and President Holland followed suit in obtaining billions for a half-dozen new weapons systems and, in the wake of North Korea saber-rattling, a new version of Reagan's Star Wars scheme. It was an easy sell with a Congress perpetually afraid of appearing soft on America's enemies. Spreading the weapons spending around the country to appease reluctant members of Congress made the legislative challenge much easier.

Within a week the Thompson-Lismore plan had become "The National Security Relocation Act of 2020", complete with forty-eight committed cosponsors, mostly from rural states. Thompson's team produced background papers with bold charts, dramatic facts and numbers, testimonials, and flash drives with interactive charts and numbers each member of Congress and staff could manipulate. Each cosponsor was armed with material that could be personalized to make communication back home virtually labor-free.

The legislation stopped short of authorizing an actual relocation of federal facilities, but there was sufficient off budget funding available to jump start the project when the new Congress convened in January. In the meantime, a lame-duck Congress would approve the initial stage of the Relocation Act, assisted by an outgoing President eager to keep the Members at bay while he figured out his own problems. The media would be preoccupied with the post-bombing story and the election fiasco. Lismore began greasing the skids for easy passage when the body convened a few days later and the measure was sent to the President for signature. After all, the Act only amounted to a study at this point.

"What do you think Bridges' people will think of this when he takes office?" asked Lismore. "My guess is he'd try to shut it down, right?"

"Who knows?" replied Thompson. "By then we'll be far enough along with supporters lined up. These things take on a life of their own." *And anyway,* thought Thompson, *it doesn't matter. Whoever is in the White House, I win.*

CHAPTER 26

"We have exactly thirteen days to finish this project," Eldon Mann reminded Espy as the two hiked along a hilly Rock Creek Park trail north of the White House. Washington was encountering an exceptionally cold late autumn. The frozen path crunched under their boots. With little exercise over the past two stressful months, Mann had difficulty keeping up. His speech was labored as he discussed their situation.

"So it looks like we have three solid converts—Vaughn, Granberry, and Hartsell, and Moulton is about fifty percent there, right? If all four hold, we've got a chance."

Espy was cautious in his assurance that all was on track. "We've shut down the larger data mining project and sent half the team away with their money and plane tickets. We set up an entirely new technical operation with a small group in Dallas to minimize any hacking into the program, deliberate or accidental."

Espy climbed the steep trail with ease, leaving his companion wheezing. He stopped to let Mann catch up. "Our four targets are being monitored every minute of the day- phone calls, emails, texts, any credit card charges, virtually every movement they make. Our guys miss nothing. So far the three are solid.

Moulton is more fragile, and we've sent Brad to Pittsburg to babysit him."

"I just don't have a good feeling," said Mann. "There's too much time for something to go wrong. One of them gets a morality surge and blows the whistle. That happens and we're done. Shit, it's cold out here."

"All we can do is hold their hands and make damn sure they don't," said Espy, pulling on his hoodie and jogging in place.

"And how do we lock down Moulton?" Mann was grimacing and bent over, regretting this trek in the bitter cold.

"Obviously it's dicey," said Espy. "He's figured it out that we know about his anti-abortion activity, and he's scared shitless that his involvement in a hate crime'll be made public. I know we can't threaten him with this, and we've done all we can with Bridges' record on the issue. But I think he's no worse than 50–50 at this point."

"Well," said Mann, "if nothing more let's keep him quiet until the votes are counted. Do we have anyone else?"

"A couple long shots we're still checking on, but no, that's probably it. We either turn three of these four or we're done."

"I want to know about Hartsell," said Mann, his shallow breath freezing in the morning air. "He's a little too eager, sounds full of himself."

"No doubt about that," said Espy, taking the steep path with ease. "But we know he's pissed at a lot of people, and not only Bridges. He recently caught his third wife sleeping with one of his contractors. Private detectives, fistfights in an airport, all kinds of nasty stuff."

"Turns out Hartsell got ahold of her cellphone and loaded some software to follow her." Espy flipped through pages from Stanning's latest report. "It's off-the-shelf stuff- you can buy it from one of those airline shopping flyers. Even lets you record texts, emails, conversations, whatever. It's a crude version of what our guys use."

"So he tracks her for a few days – we picked up all this – and records her fucking the guy in his car, in the desert near Sedona, in some motel. She comes home and it gets really ugly. It's going to be a very nasty divorce, 'cause she's got all kinds of evidence of Hartsell fucking around as well."

Mann dismissed Espy's story as irrelevant to the elector project, but wondered why he didn't think of the phone tracker when he suspected his own wife's infidelity. *Women just aren't worth it,* he thought.

The two men climbed the final hill on their hike and returned to the parking lot along Beech Drive. "You know," said Mann, "right over there was where that young woman's body was found, remember her? An intern having an affair with the congressman everyone thought killed her. Turned out it was some Guatemalan day laborer. Illegal of course. But the congressman lost his seat and he was ruined. Tough luck all around."

"Just goes to show you," chuckled Espy. "Don't fuck around with interns."

CHAPTER 27

December 7

Before dawn, Jackson Cripple awoke bleary-eyed from an evening of too much wine and a joint or two. He was anxious to review the new data on his laptop. His techies had worked through the night after settling on a new algorithm to locate and decipher communications to and from the Holland contacts Melody Banks had given his team three weeks earlier. It was painstakingly slow work, a trial and error exercise being conducted under severe pressure. Cripple cross-referenced the information with his own list, as he had erected a firewall to shield his team from the actual names he was pursuing.

By mid-morning, he found what he was looking for—a half-dozen connections that might help Banks begin to make sense of what Eldon Mann's Leesburg crew was up to. He placed a call to her as she was jogging across the Severn River Bridge. Banks' Saturday morning had been an endless session with her staff, going over communications strategies, with the lawyers researching election laws in the states Holland might be contesting with recounts. Carrying the secret of her collaboration with Cripple increased her burden. She longed to attack the crisis as part of a team.

Banks slowed to a walk as the phone vibrated under her running bra with the call she had been expecting for days. "Melody, I may have found something," said Cripple, "I need to see you right away."

"OK," she responded. "Meet me in that back booth at the Crab Hole." Rejecting an urge to shower and change, Banks ran full throttle back to the Bridges house to retrieve her car and head to the restaurant. If Cripple had anything new, she wanted it immediately.

Cripple arrived early and was already tucked into a plate of fried soft shell crabs. Banks slid onto the cracked Naugahyde seat across from his. He began without small talk, his voice uncharacteristically excited. "I think we have something." For the next ten minutes he explained.

"Mann's people have been digging into every imaginable detail on about a hundred people all over the country. Once we had the names it didn't take much to figure out what they had in common. Every one's a Democratic elector from a state that Bridges won," he reported. "And get this—they're all males between fifty and seventy-five. Here's the full list."

Banks scanned the page and looked back at Cripple. "About a week ago," he continued, "the monitoring went silent. Nothing. I tried to call my contact who was working over there—remember the guy who slipped up and told me he'd been recruited by an NSA operative? Yeah, him. But now I can't locate him. No signal anywhere. He's gone completely dark."

"And Mann must have some seriously encrypted toys, since all we get from him is ordinary stuff on his official lines, to and from the White House and campaign staff, nothing remarkable. We tracked his car but the movements aren't giving us anything special either. Parked in Rock Creek Park the other day, but there are no cameras out there to check, so we don't have a clue what he was doing there."

"How do you know where he was?" asked an incredulous Banks. "You now have spy drones, or what?"

"Ah," responded Cripple. "That's easy. Mann's got a smart car, and his navigation system is tied into a central computer at Toyota. We've got the codes." Banks shook her head, continuing to marvel at Cripple's skills.

"But here's where it gets interesting," he said. "Before they shut down the Leesburg operation, we picked up that one of the men they were tracking, one of the electors, is Wayne Hartsell, an Arizona big shot. He's a monster donor to Bridges' campaign, but then you'd know that."

"OK, but what's so interesting about Hartsell?" Banks asked. She remembered him as a man who had rubbed a little too close to her at the Convention, then tried to bring her drinks in the VIP lounge.

"A few days ago he hosted a woman at this resort near Scottsdale. The two had breakfast. But then suddenly he calls his lawyer and learns that his offices were being raided by law enforcement seizing files from his business. He heads there, but then he goes back to the resort to play golf and have dinner with this woman."

"Yeah, that's strange, but maybe he's just got a thing going with her. It's been known to happen."

"Maybe," said Cripple. "But guess who she is? Lydia Elving, a hotshot Nashville lawyer, a real ball buster. And..." he paused for effect, "Lydia Elving is wired into serious national Republican players, with clients that show up on every dirty dozen list you can find. But that's not all."

"Not long after we started our search, Winston Granberry, one of the electors Mann was tracking, was visited in his office in Kentucky by none other than our Miss Elving. Go figure."

"Jackson, this is good stuff. I can't thank you enough. I need to put this together with other information we're getting. Can you keep the monitoring going awhile longer? Just to see if they ramp up again?"

After some mild haggling over Cripple's budget issues, she left the Crab Hole without touching the salad he had ordered for

her. Her mind was racing as she drove back to Senator Bridges'
house, trying to focus her thoughts for the difficult conversation
ahead. By the time she arrived the team had reassembled for a
debriefing of the day's events and review of the upcoming weekend talk shows.

Banks waved at the crew and hurried to her bedroom, where
she stripped off the running clothes and quickly showered. She
pulled on clean slacks, turtleneck, and a sweater vest. She com-
posed herself in front of a mirror, tried to make sense of her unruly
blond mop. She dabbed on powder and lipstick, scowling at even
more lines marking a face she hardly recognized. Banks took a
deep breath and returned to the Bridges living room and the
campaign team, now embroiled in a heated exchange about a
public strategy to force Holland's concession.

"Senator," she said to the man hunched over a briefing book,
"can I speak to you in your study?" The president-elect looked
around the table, and narrowed his gaze.

"Of course," he said, excusing himself to lead Banks into the
nearby room lined with dark walnut shelves holding hundreds of
books on politics, history, and the law—the standard assortment
belonging to public figures. "So what's this about?"

Banks looked at Bridges, folded her arms behind her head,
and stretched to relieve a lingering headache. She paused, then
leaned directly into Bridges' impatient gaze. "Senator, they're
going after our electors."

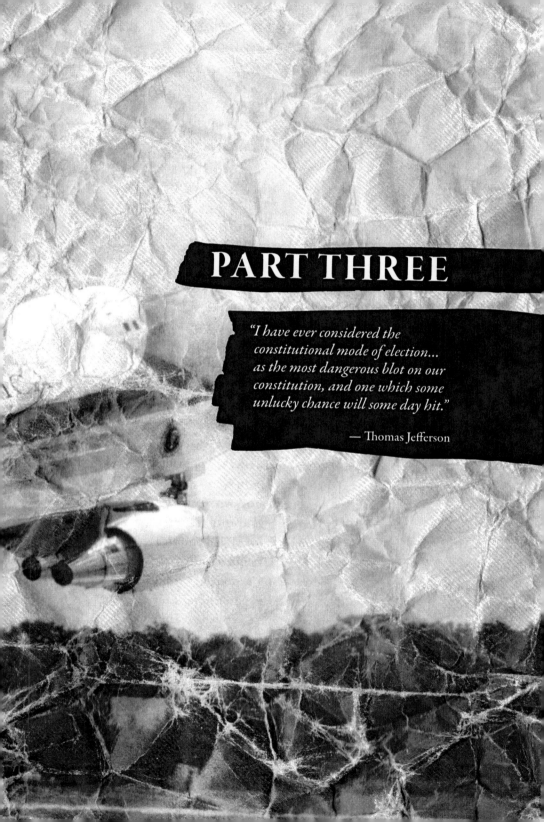

PART THREE

"I have ever considered the constitutional mode of election... as the most dangerous blot on our constitution, and one which some unlucky chance will some day hit."

— Thomas Jefferson

CHAPTER 28

"This is beginning to look a lot like Christmas," beamed Carlton Espy as he and Mann reviewed the state of their targeted converts. "Vaughn and Hartsell all solid, Granberry almost there and Moulton seems to have come around. And Stanning has turned up some new stuff on a guy in upstate New York and one in Illinois."

"We dropped Cusimano, right?" Mann wanted to be sure the New Orleans supervisor-turned-gangster would be off-limits. So far the only laws broken by his team were illegal surveillance, a forged NSA memo, and a couple pilfered emails from the Bridges campaign staff. Bad enough, but he could handle those problems. "Tell me about the two new targets."

Espy launched into the backgrounds of John Geer, a political science professor at U-Illinois in Bloomington, and Freeman Davis, a retired Marine from upstate New York. Geer had been denied tenure and was angry with everyone. Davis had been telling his pals at the local coffee shop he thought the President was showing real leadership by going after the Islamic radicals.

"Bridges has no *cojones*!" complained the Marine to his pals over donuts and bagels. "You lead from strength, not cooperation."

"All right, let's see if they bite," said Mann. "But we've only got six days to wrap them up. And we've got to stay on top of the other four. Frankly, the colonel looks like a better bet, but I'll leave it to you and your folks to find out."

Mann returned to the White House with mixed emotions about the state of the project. He was encouraged by the result of the outreach and Espy's assurances that four Democratic electors appeared ready to jump ship, and that two more were on the line. He needed only three, but as he reviewed the plan, Mann was reminded of its sheer audaciousness. No elector had ever changed his vote when it mattered. The rare close elections when a few electoral votes would have made a difference—Gore and Bush most recently—ended without incident, as the loser's concession effectively shut down any rebellion.

Behind his desk in the roomy West Wing office space fifteen steps from the Oval Office, Mann ran through every possibility that could derail his plan— Last minute cold feet among his converts (most likely). Switches by Republican electors (highly unlikely). Legal challenges by Calvin Bridges and the Democratic Party (all but certain). Legislative maneuvering by Bridges' advocates in Congress, federal court actions (definitely).

The list gave Mann a splitting headache.

This is insane. There's no way we can pull it off, he thought. *Too much can go wrong. And if it blows up, I may just go straight to jail. No stopping at Go to collect $200. No get out of jail cards in this deck.*

Yet, he acknowledged, they had skillfully managed every step of the project so far, including the carefully orchestrated, limited television appearances by the President to keep the battle against terrorism front and center in the American psyche. *And Jesus, the bombing? How good was that?* he smiled.

While politicians and the media continued to blast Holland for failing to concede the election, public support for his military actions in the Mideast was sky high. The Vice President was out of sight, holed up in his Wisconsin home and under the watchful eye of the Secret Service and a nearby Mann staffer.

Critical to their plan, there was no law forcing the President to concede. Espy had a first-class team handling the targeted electors. If they could maintain their current gains, it just might be successful. No one would ever know of Mann's extraordinary achievement, possibly the most remarkable in American political history, but that didn't matter. He would head to a cushy ambassadorial post or lucrative corporate consulting and enjoy the next few years away from the madness of D.C.. He rubbed his temples and downed two more Exedrines as he thumbed through the growing stack of phone calls that wouldn't be returned, briefing memos that would have to wait.

Adding to Mann's growing stress was the President's increasingly restlessness, under virtual house arrest in Orlando. "I'm going crazy down here," he barked to Mann on their latest call. "I know it's part of the plan, but the country needs to see me doing something, anything, other than sitting on my ass here in Florida watching the fucking oranges grow."

Mann agreed to fly down that afternoon with the President's political team to chart a safe strategy for the frustrated Commander in Chief. In the comfortable leather seats of a Gulfstream he had borrowed from Air Force inventory, Mann began to plot a game plan to navigate the legal and congressional challenges that would unfold after the Electoral College vote in a few days.

"Eldon, I need to know all this is legal," said the President. "I wanna win this goddamn election, but I don't wanna be chased by some fucking prosecutor for the rest of my life."

"Absolutely," said Mann, wondering if their conversation was being recorded. He made a mental note to find out if Holland had installed any hidden recording devices in his Orlando office. "All we've done is convince a few principled Democrats that the U.S. will be better off if you continue in office."

"Let's talk about your schedule for next week," said Mann. He wanted to move on, to avoid delving into any detail that would make the President uncomfortable and risk a setback. "We have you leaving here early Monday morning for a three-day fly-around, to show the country you're hard at work and in control after the bombing. Here's the block schedule and the topics of your speeches at each appearance."

Mann constructed the schedule to not only dramatize the President's leadership but to send discreet, compelling messages to the defecting electors. In Lexington, Kentucky, in the wake of an attack coming from an unstable Mideast, he would reaffirm the Administration's commitment to a comprehensive energy policy to exploit every resource possible to guarantee the nation's energy independence—all written to bolster Winston Granberry's contempt for Senator Bridges' zero-carbon policies that had destroyed his father.

Deplaning in Phoenix from Air Force One, the ultimate political backdrop, Holland would stress the value of loyalty in a world torn apart by terrorism. It was a message that would resonate with Wayne Hartsell, who would still be seething at the loss of a coveted ambassadorship.

Touring a Catholic orphanage in Pittsburg with a group of nuns in tow, the President would laud the courage and sacrifice of women who had delivered their babies while pressured to seek an abortion. Holland would handle the issue deftly, the speech draft reading "I will not criticize those who choose otherwise. The Bible warns us to not stand in judgment. But these babies are a testimony to our need to preserve life at all cost." Those words could clinch the deal for Richard Moulton.

Continuing to Albany and on to Hudson, Holland would identify with the leadership of FDR as he nudged the nation into war. "No president seeks war," the speech would read. "But a nation unwilling to unmask and defeat its mortal enemies will be a nation of fear. And I will not stand by as our enemies plan yet another devastating attack on American soil." The speech was orchestrated to inflame elector Freeman Davis's pro-military doubts about Calvin Bridges. There was no compelling reason to reveal to his boss the real reason behind the upcoming trip.

CHAPTER 29

The traveling manifest for the President's national swing included the usual contingent of staff, military aides, Secret Service agents, the President's personal physician, and a gaggle of VIPs placed in the wide seats behind the spacious conference room aboard Air Force One. An invitation to join the President on an AF1 flight was near the top of the wish list of any ambitious politician, donor, or cabinet member. On this flight, a dozen members of Congress, all staunch Holland loyalists, had traveled to Orlando to join the AF1 manifest. At Mann's direction, a deputy ushered one or two at a time into the office suite in the nose of the Boeing 747 behemoth for their moment with the President.

Holland shed his suit coat for the navy bomber jacket worn only for these flights. He thanked each of his guests for their support during the current crisis as he offered coffee and chocolate chip cookies from the steward. "Here, Dick, take the cup with you. I'll get you a box of 'em for your kids!" The President loved these opportunities, holding forth as Commander in Chief, with supplicant passengers craving every moment aboard his aircraft. He knew how to stroke and cajole and reward, and Air Force One was the best possible venue for that exercise.

Each of the VIP guests would receive souvenir glasses, blankets, pens, and a certificate noting they had flown on AF1. Most would make a phone call from the air to family or girlfriends to boast about the flight while surreptitiously stuffing more embossed "chum" into their bags.

Mann's approved manifest included Congressman Lismore and, reluctantly, allowed him to bring the lobbyist Tommy Thompson along as a guest. The White House needed Lismore to help put down a growing insurrection among Republican lawmakers uneasy about the election stalemate, so Thompson was added to the list at Lismore's request before takeoff in Orlando. He could have his moment in the sky, but Mann would make sure the lobbyist would not appear in any photo opportunity with the President.

"Jesus, Eldon, can you believe that idiot? Move the Capitol to Kansas! What a crazy ass idea." Holland vented to his Chief of Staff, who reminded him that Lismore could be critical to the President in the coming weeks if the elector project succeeded. "I had to sign their stupid relocation study bill, but just keep me out of it. And how the fuck did that clown Thompson get on the plane?"

Mann deftly eased him out of his tirade and back to routine business; he pushed the President to sharpen his speech before the first stop in Lexington. The speechwriters were ushered into the office as Mann excused himself and moved a few steps down the aircraft bulkhead to the compartment reserved for the Chief of Staff. The space was compact and efficient, with a large swivel chair that would recline into a bed, and two smaller chairs for visitors. Three large monitors allowed Mann to pull up any telecast or internet feed, or conduct a videoconference with as many as thirty participants. He had personally ordered the hardware and technical capabilities to be installed in the space after he arrived at the White House four years earlier.

Air Force One was the ultimate flying office, every feature replicated in a second 747 that served as a backup plane for the

President and a cattle car for the dozens of media that regularly accompanied any movement by POTUS. It was generally believed by the media that the second plane was used as a decoy to confuse terrorists attempting to down AF1. "Not a bad strategy to improve press coverage," laughed a Holland aide to an unamused reporter.

Every president had been savaged by the political opposition for using Air Force One for trips that were only marginally official, with fundraising events after a public appearances intended for the evening news. The operating cost for the plane was more than $200,000 per hour, not counting the cost of moving, housing, and feeding the hundreds of staff and security personnel who were required in advance of such trips. But the sheer political power of the image of Air Force One as a backdrop for the president could not be overstated, so the budget impact and political criticism were generally ignored.

From his private space, Mann reached Carlton Espy on a secure line. The more success Espy and Stanning achieved in intercepting electronic communications to and from their targets, the more paranoid Mann became about his own calls and texts.

"Any news?" he queried Espy.

"Good feedback from New York. The Illinois contact may not pan out. We'll know more tonight. Call me around midnight my time." Mann signed off, cranked his seat back to nearly flat, and closed his eyes for twenty minutes before the plane would land in Kentucky.

CHAPTER 30

December 10

Pima Grantham sat on a cushioned bench in the small room of the Phillips Collection that housed her favorite painting, Renoir's "Luncheon of the Boating Party". Since her days as an undergraduate intern at the *Post*, she came here often to take in Renoir's large masterpiece. Her art history degree may not have landed her a job, but it continued to give Grantham a near spiritual connection to great art and architecture. Melody Banks was a half hour late for their rendezvous, but she made the wait pleasant by gazing at the painting's subjects having a fine summer outing along a river south of Paris. As she was about to go into a hypnotic state, the tall blonde entered the gallery and took a space next to Grantham.

"It's beautiful, isn't it?" said Grantham, staring at the painting.

"Stunning," replied Banks, dressed in tall boots, black tights, and an olive oilskin coat from Orvis. Washington had been hit with an early ice storm and freezing temperatures. The Phillips was nearly empty as the two women sat side by side and began a guarded conversation. A nearby docent was too close for Bank's comfort.

"Want to get lunch?" asked Melody, who was famished and not particularly interested in art at this point. The two left the gallery and walked three blocks to P Street and Pizza Paradiso, where they found a rear table near the fireplace.

"I liked the old restaurant better," said Banks, shedding the heavy coat and rubbing her cold hands to jumpstart circulation. She was convinced that her lack of serious exercise these past few weeks had left her body vulnerable to all kinds of health issues. "But the pizzas are the best in town." They ordered—a Napolitano for Banks and a Margherita for Grantham, arugula salad to share —with a half carafe of the house red.

"So," began the reporter, "how's it going? When we last talked Senator Bridges was going down the tubes and you were planning your post-campaign vacation. You've had some excitement since then, I guess."

"Pima, how do we do this? Can we make this conversation deep background for now?" Ground rules established, Banks recounted the events of the past month, withholding the ultra-sensitive information about Jackson Cripple's intelligence gathering. Closing with her suspicion that the President's people were trying to convert Bridges' electors, Banks realized that her pizza had become cold. "So what do you think?" She nearly swallowed a slice whole as Grantham took in the story and launched into her own.

"Melody, we've spent nearly a month trying to figure out Holland's strategy. We've done countless interviews with every election expert, every state party chair from every state that matters. We brought in facilitators to help us game this all out, looking for clues we might have missed, anything to get a handle on the President's thinking."

"At first, like everyone else, we figured it was the bombing at the Capitol, Holland trying to look presidential, go out with his reputation as a leader elevated somehow. The drone raids all over the Mideast seemed to confirm that theory, and we shifted to covering the analysts and critics of these attacks. We even found a couple jihadists in Pakistan who claimed credit for the bombing. We put together a week-long feature on the new war on terrorism."

"But," Grantham said, "we've gotten nowhere on the election issue. If anyone knows what Holland is doing, they aren't talking, even on background. And you can always get someone to talk to you, whether they want to grind an ax or trash a colleague, or if they just like seeing their unattributed quotes in print, so to speak. It's beyond weird."

"We did a spread on how the electoral vote shakes out," she continued. "But we never, ever considered that Holland would be out there trying to get electors to switch their votes. How could they pull it off?"

Banks received her own briefing on the Electoral College a day earlier from Todd Campbell, the campaign's in-house expert on election law, with the conclusion similar to Lyndon Polk's presentation to the President. "Pima, not only is it possible, I'm convinced that it's happening as we speak. I can't prove it yet, and I don't even know where to go with it from here, but there's got to be a way to blow this up."

"Have you talked to the *Times*, or the *Post* or anyone else?" Grantham asked.

"Not yet. I need something more to give them. But I thought you might work this a bit, maybe send people to talk to a few electors, see if they've been contacted by anyone to switch."

"But there are hundreds of them, right? Where could we start?" Grantham warmed to the chase but quickly saw the logistical issues confronting *Politico* and the short fuse involved.

"I've got some names that might be productive. We have information that these two electors may have been contacted by a Republican operative since the election." Banks was careful to limit this information, especially protective of her source. She gave the reporter a three by five card with the names and cell numbers of Winston Granberry and Wayne Hartsell. "But you have to move quickly. This is over in five days."

"Let me see what I can do," said Grantham, pocketing the card in her backpack and retrieving her buzzing phone, summoning

her back to the office. "But there's one thing, Melody. We can't
be in the business of doing work for the Bridges campaign. If we
find out Holland is actively trying to steal the election, we're all
over it, and after we report it, so will every outlet in the country.
But there are limits, you've got to know."

"Sure," replied Banks. "If they're doing what I think they're
doing, the country needs to know about it, and damn soon."

Grantham paid the check and left the restaurant with Banks,
who was shivering uncontrollably. "You OK, Melody? You don't
look well." Grantham rubbed Melody's arms and looked up at
a woman who clearly needed a hot bath and a massage, not to
mention an end to the nightmarish political events that had enveloped both of them.

Grantham stopped at Dupont Circle and confronted Banks.
""Oh, one more thing. What happened to Vice President West?
Since that bizarre appearance on CNN he's disappeared. Do you
think he could have anything to do with the elector issue?"

"Anything is possible, but I sort of doubt it," said Banks, who
now just wanted to get out of the cold and back to Annapolis.
"He's not the type to play fast and loose with the old school rules.
But it's worth checking in with him to see if he knows anything. If
nothing else he can give you a read on POTUS and Eldon Mann."

Grantham made a mental note to track down the Vice President, ideally for another face-to-face interview. It would make
good copy while *Politico* was trying to get the big story. On the
subway ride back to Rosslyn she constructed a checklist for the
afternoon work:

1. Meet with the election team.
2. Divide up the list of Democratic electors for contacts.
3. Organize questions to ask each elector.
4. Contact Wayne Hartsell and Winston Granberry.
5. Find the Vice President

CHAPTER 31

The President's fly-around had gone smoothly, with dozens of meet-and-greets with local officials and strategically-placed "real people" in tarmac crowds, carefully screened by the advance teams, who cheered wildly as Holland and his wife descended the stairs from Air Force One and worked the rope lines to their limousine. Local and regional press coverage was generally positive, the national media overwhelmingly negative, laced with harsh criticism of the soft events designed to bolster Holland's standing while the country was in a political and national security upheaval. Holland's refusal to discuss the disputed election result was excoriated by the traveling press. Internal polling showed virtually no movement in the President's popularity and, worse, a trend downward among Republican rank and file voters.

Eldon Mann was neither surprised nor concerned about the public impression of the trip. He had accomplished two goals: getting Holland out of his Florida funk and onto Air Force One, the President's favorite perk, and delivering messages that would hopefully fortify his defecting Democratic electors. Back in Florida, safely ensconced in his Orlando compound, Grady Holland could do little harm.

Meeting at Carlton Espy's club a mile north of the DC line, Mann reluctantly changed into golf attire and joined Espy near the first tee. The weather had warmed considerably since a recent cold snap and Espy was dying to get out on the course. Eldon Mann hated everything about golf. It takes too long to play. Expensive, lousy exercise, and worse, impossibly difficult. Why anyone would take up the game was beyond his comprehension. Yet he wanted a good block of time with Espy to discuss recent developments as they headed into the final weekend before the electors would meet. After closing the Leesburg office they needed privacy and this very private golf course offered that advantage.

"Just don't make me swing a golf club," Mann groused as the two revved the golf cart down the first fairway, a short but treacherous par four with water lining the fairway. "I mean, really. Why do you waste your time with this ridiculous game?"

"Hah!" laughed Espy, who lifted a seven iron to within three feet of the pin. "You should get into this, Eldon. It would relieve all that stress. You might even enjoy it." After watching Espy finish the hole and return to the cart, Mann launched into his laundry list of last minute concerns. *Who is hand holding these people? Can we get into the room when they cast their votes? What's the plan for getting them out of there when all hell breaks loose? Are the lawyers ready?*

"Everything is in place," said Espy, who nearly drove his ball onto the fifth green, a short par four that rewarded a risky tee shot. "Look at that, Eldon. This is fun!"

Mann, unamused, was about to tell Espy to call it quits and return to the clubhouse for lunch when Espy's secure cellphone blasted an emergency signal.

"Yes?" he answered. "When did this happen?" After a minute of concentrated conversation, Espy ordered, "All right. Set up a call for me with Lydia Elving and Brad Cantwell in ten minutes."

His golf swagger now evaporated, Espy turned to Mann. "They're on to us. A reporter got to Granberry and Hartsell. We're checking now to find out if Vaughn and Moulton or any others have been contacted."

From the beginning of the project, Mann feared some reporter, informed by political analysts or Democratic operatives, would raise the specter of an Electoral College strategy. "Let's get out of here. Is there a private room in the clubhouse we can use?"

During brief conversations with Elving and Cantwell, each denied any knowledge of a breach in discretion. Both were instructed to immediately check in with their targets. An hour later they reported their findings to Espy, now holed up in the card room of the stately old clubhouse. A nearby tray of club sandwiches lay untouched. Espy had not revealed to the two attorneys that Mann was in the room, or for that matter even involved in the project. Both determined that the fewer who knew the President's Chief of Staff was in charge, the better.

"Hartsell and Vaughn are still on board. But I'm worried about Granberry and Moulton. Lydia will stay on top of Granberry by phone but it's not safe to send her back to Kentucky at this point," Espy said, reviewing his notes from the briefing calls. "And we found out that every Democratic elector is being contacted by *Politico*. Sooner or later they'll talk to Moulton and I don't know how stable he'll be if he's cornered. The *Politico* story will run overnight and the Post and the Times and everyone else'll pick it up. The White House will get hammered with questions from the press. You'll have to push back, it may get out of control."

"How the hell did that reporter find out about Elving's visit with Granberry and Hartsell?" asked Mann. Espy had learned on the emergency call that Pima Grantham had confronted both targeted electors with the question Mann most feared would come. "Has anyone from the Holland campaign or any Republican organization urged you to switch your vote from Senator Bridges to the President?"

Wayne Hartsell, the supremely cocky Scottsdale developer, told Grantham to go fuck herself, and that he wouldn't talk to her. But Granberry, the aging Kentucky gentleman, balked at the question and nervously told the journalist he would have to get back to her. Those reactions gave Grantham all she needed to take her investigation to the next level.

"So that leaves us with two likely votes and two now questionable." Mann said. "And we need three. Any progress with that professor or the Marine?"

"John Geer won't fly. Seems he's left town, to Puerto Rico. Told his state chair that he won't go to the vote on Monday, so they're using an alternate." Espy had withheld this bad news from Mann, believing Geer would not be needed. "Freeman Davis is still a possibility. Brad Cantwell is with him today in New York. We should know more tonight."

"Well, if we don't get one of them, we're dead. If we deadlock at 269 there's no way the Congress will take it away from Bridges. We need the majority by the end of the day on Monday or it's over." Mann turned away from the table and walked to a window. Looking out over the sylvan golf course he pushed away a dark vision of the consequences of failure and began to consider options for turning around their precarious situation. Espy was on the phone with Cantwell in New York as Mann returned to the card room.

"The Marine is a no go," said a dejected Espy. "Bridges just put out a statement that he will ask the President's national defense team to stay on in his administration, and that he—and I'm quoting here—'will aggressively pursue the terrorists responsible for the Capitol bombing, and all those who would threaten our nation's security.' Obviously that means nothing, but it was enough for our guy to back off. Cantwell says it's no use to keep pursuing him. And there's no one else in the pipeline."

Mann drew a deep breath, exhaled and drummed his pen on the table for what seemed to Espy an interminable silence. "There may be a way to get the Congress to go our way if there is a deadlock in the College. It would be hard to pull off, and I don't know if Holland will go for it, but we've got to consider every option now. We've gone too far to throw in the towel. Can we get Stanning's team up and running again?"

"Probably," said Espy. "But there's no way we can produce anything helpful in the next seventy-two hours."

"I'm not talking about the electors," said Mann. "I want to find out as much as possible about certain members of the House and Senate."

"Jesus, Eldon, we're playing with some serious fire here. Look, I'm confident we can avoid any blowback from what we've done with the electors. Stanning is solid, and his people have no incentive to talk." Espy was shaken by Mann's instructions. "But members of Congress? We'd be crucified if it got out. In fact, we'd be prosecuted."

"I understand all that," said Mann. "But if we're smart we can do this, and we can cover our tracks. And beside, if I'm right, the people I want to target would never go public. Let me know tonight if Stanning can do it. We'll start tomorrow."

Figuring Washington was now off-limits for a reorganized Stanning team of cyber sleuths, Espy found an empty suite of offices in Dallas belonging to a discreet friend of his law partner. Stanning rounded up five of his best hackers with their special equipment in tow, for the newest round of data mining. By evening they were ready for instructions from Espy. Eldon Mann raised the necessary millions within thirty minutes. There seemed to be a bottomless reservoir of very rich men intent on keeping Calvin Bridges and his liberal agenda out of the White House.

Twenty names were on the list Mann forwarded within hours of their aborted golf outing. "Here's what we're looking for," instructed Mann. "Republicans who could lead the pro-Holland debate if the Electoral College was thrown into the Congress. Democrats who might for some secret reason support the President. Or, most important, Republican fence dwellers who might need a shove."

"If we can find soft spots in the private affairs of any of these congressmen or Senators we might have a wedge to turn the count to Holland at the last minute."

But first he needed no worse than a tie vote in the Electoral College, and that was by no means assured. While Stanning's team worked nonstop through the weekend, Mann drove to his now empty home, downed an Ambien and slept soundly for six hours before waking to more bad news.

"We've got some data on ten of the names you gave me," reported Espy. "Something that could help with the Speaker. But most of it is pretty mild stuff, except for the affairs you probably already know about and a few prostitutes, and a couple of questionable real estate deals. You may be able to work with some of it."

"But we've got another problem," Espy added. "I've had the team monitoring our targets, and it looks like we've lost Moulton and Granberry. When *Politico* got around to talking to Moulton, he told her that he'd been contacted, but that he had no intention of switching his vote. We listened to the call, had our guy get to him immediately and he confirmed that he wouldn't do it."

"And Granberry?" Mann said, his voice now weary. "What happened to him?"

"Lydia Elving talked to him and he assured her he was ok. But an hour later he called her back and said he'd changed his mind. We picked up a text he had sent his wife: *I can't do it, dear. I'm sick and tired of our party, but I just can't do it.* Seems he had been agonizing over this with his wife, who pushed back. Elving says she can be in Hazard in two hours, but she thinks his decision is likely final."

"We've still got Moulton's secret abortion issue, the shooting of the doctor," said Mann after a long moment. "But that would involve blackmailing him. I'll give it some thought, but I'm not inclined to go there. Send me what the team dug up and I'll get back to you later this morning."

"Eldon, there's one more thing," said Espy. "Congressman Lismore's son had a drug arrest and a sex offender charge as a minor. Both were later expunged but there's evidence that there was a payoff of some kind to the mother of the young man he apparently seduced in a St. Louis bar. We're trying to track it down."

"OK, let me know what you find," Mann desperately wanted to return to bed and the sleep he wouldn't get for the next seventy-two hours. Instead he plugged in the coffee pot and prepared for a call to the President he had dreaded since learning of their predicament.

"Well, Eldon, I can't say I'm surprised. It never seemed like a realistic plan, but I can't fault you for trying," President Holland was in an uncharacteristically light mood, which was more annoying to Mann than an irate boss. He knew how to handle the latter. "So you need to tie up any loose ends and come on down here. I'll need to go ahead and call Bridges and make a concession speech before the Electoral College meets on Tuesday. I guess that's the right thing to do. When can you get here?"

Mann withheld that he was pursuing other avenues to turn around their recent reversals, but he knew he had to prevent Holland from making the concession if Mann was to launch a new strategy. "Mr. President, I can be there tonight, but I want you to consider holding off on calling Senator Bridges or making any concession. At least until we talk."

"That makes no fuckin' sense, Eldon," Holland sounded like he was laughing and making an aside to someone nearby.

"Mr. President, are you alone? We need to be discreet."

"Yeah, that was just Tony Kornheiser on Sports Center. Crazy bastard is picking Alabama to win the SEC. It's gonna be the goddamn Gators! I may even place a bet in Vegas after this game is over. Holy shit! Touchdown! Hooha!" Mann suspected the President was into his third rum and tonic, not a good frame of mind for serious discussion.

CHAPTER 32

Carefully negotiating the icy sidewalk between her small Portsmouth row house on the edge of downtown and the pharmacist, Virginia Sullivan walked with labored breath to retrieve a new batch of medications before the major storm predicted for the evening. As a younger, fitter woman she had managed the New England winters with relative ease, but at sixty-nine and carrying more than three hundred pounds, it was all she could do to get through each day without a calamity. Widowed for a decade, with few close friends, Sullivan had no fear of death but she was petrified by the prospect of a disabling fall and a slow decline in some godawful nursing home.

Since her husband Errol's death, Virginia had two remaining loves: edgy television dramas and politics. When she wasn't organizing online voter registration for the state party, she was glued to her high definition flat screen and episodes *of Highcliff Murders* or the ninth season of *House of Cards* or a fifth viewing of her collector's edition of *Breaking Bad*, Virginia's all-time favorite. For her sixtieth birthday the California state party chairman had arranged a call from Bryan Cranston to Sullivan. Ending his call, Cranston lowered his voice and closed with "Happy birthday,

Virginia, and always remember, *You* are the danger!" Cranston's iconic line from *Breaking Bad* thrilled her. Virginia wore a tattered *Better Call Saul* apron to prepare every dinner.

For most of her adult life, Sullivan had passionately promoted Democrats running for office at every level of government. Until recently her energy and focus had been exceeded only by her remarkable political instincts. Anyone who wanted to get elected in New Hampshire went through Sullivan for advice and organizing help. Her success record was spectacular, her candidates having lost only twice in decades of elections.

When presidential aspirants made the trek to New Hampshire every four years, a visit with Virginia was mandatory. Signed photos with Obama, Bill and Hillary Clinton, Gore, Biden, and Kennedy filled her walls with grateful notations. Obama even offered her a federal appointment to a sought-after commission in 2009, but she turned it down, immobilized by the idea of traveling to Washington for meetings. Calvin Bridges had not visited, though his campaign team regularly asked her help in organizing the state.

Her life of politics and television kept her busy enough, but she was seriously depressed, morbidly obese, and broke. An intensely private woman, she had shielded her financial situation from her few friends and sank into denial about her mounting debt. The mortgage company was threatening to foreclose on her home. Her credit cards had been canceled and collectors were calling incessantly on her cellphone, which was about to be shut off. An aging Toyota sat idle in her driveway with a busted transmission. Medicare was threatening to cancel her Part B and prescription coverage unless back payments were made immediately.

Virginia's reclusiveness shielded her from the cruel jokes that moved around the Portsmouth political community, but one not intended for her ears had deeply wounded her. A local party chair had circulated a bad joke by email referring to Sullivan as a "walking mountain of fat, a heart attack on two elephant legs." When a colleague piled on with a follow-up response he inadvertently including Virginia on the string. She said nothing to the two men but privately stewed for weeks. Her selection as a New Hampshire Democratic elector had done little to soothe her resentment.

Virginia drastically curtailed her activity during the recent campaign cycle, begging off most requests for her help or advice or contacts, citing health issues. In reality, she was tired of the constant demands and disillusioned with the cynical manner in which candidates pursued their superficial relationship with her and others like her, who gave their time and money to get the politicians elected.

Sullivan trudged back to her house with a large bag of pills to bring down an alarming blood pressure level, statins to stabilize artery-clogging cholesterol, insulin for her recently diagnosed diabetes, and a substantially increased dose of antidepressants. Virginia was by any measure a physical and mental basket case. Complicating her emotional state was the revelation that the child she had given up for adoption at sixteen had recently surfaced and sought to reconnect with her mother.

Ignoring several contacts, Virginia finally agreed to a meeting in nearby York, Maine, where the woman now lived. If the reunion had not been stressful enough, the news that her daughter had been diagnosed with a potentially fatal cancer drove Virginia into a deep funk. A single mother also living on the edge of financial ruin, Virginia's daughter had been prodded to find the mother who had abandoned her a half century earlier.

Her phone buzzed as she unpacked the bag of meds. Virginia considered ignoring the call, assuming the worst from bill collectors, but she was waiting on a message from an acquaintance in Manchester who might take her in. The number on the screen was unfamiliar, but she answered. "Virginia, is that you?" a loud male voice came over the line.

"Who is this?" she responded.

"It's Wayne Hartsell, from Scottsdale. You remember we met at the convention. You weren't having much of a time, but we had a drink in the DNC suite the night before Bridges' speech."

Sullivan sat down on a rickety kitchen chair and cradled the phone as she opened medications. "What can I do for you, Mr. Hartsell? I was just getting ready to go out," she lied.

"I'm going to be in Portsmouth tomorrow and just wanted to drop by and say hi, and get your advice about a project I'm working on." Hartsell's voice was cheerful, but Sullivan was in no mood for a political contact that had to be a request for a favor.

"Well, I'm kind of busy, and I've got a couple doctor appointments tomorrow. And I'm really not doing much politically these days, if that's what it's about." She reached for a small pile of mail on the table and began sorting through bills and solicitations.

"Reschedule them, Virginia. I really want to see you. I promise you won't regret it."

"Oh, all right. What time will you be here?" She noted Hartsell's tone had turned more insistent than pleasant.

They made plans for coffee at Seems Beans at ten am and rang off. Sullivan dismissed Hartsell's call as another political plan she wanted no part of at this grim point in her life. She sorted the pills into the plastic boxes marked with days of the week, sighed, and painfully lowered herself into a large pillowed chair. Downloading season five of *Breaking Bad*, she settled into Jesse Pinkman's drama as a tortured drug dealer. *I'm so tired of all these assholes,* she muttered to herself.

▲ ▲ ▲

"Eldon, I really think this will work," said Carlton Espy as he led Mann up another hill in Rock Creek Park. "Elving is convinced that Hartsell can be trusted. He's certainly motivated."

Mann reviewed Espy's notes over coffee before he drove the short distance from his Chevy Chase home to the park trail head.

The project team had uncovered a potentially promising set of data on a New Hampshire elector and Espy was anxious to brief Mann that morning, now less than four days before the Electoral College outcome would be decided.

"She's desperate, and she's not well. She's got a huge financial problem, and, best of all, she's angry about the cards she's been dealt." Espy reiterated what he had forwarded to Mann overnight. "Hartsell is meeting her in Portsmouth early tomorrow morning. He's been told that we won't authorize or encourage any payment to Sullivan, but he thinks he can talk her into changing her vote." Espy knew Hartsell was prepared to relieve the woman of all debt and pay all costs for her daughter's medical treatments, but he kept this information from Mann.

"Make damn sure there's a paper trail between Elving and Hartsell that clearly states we will not sanction any financial considerations, that we are solely interested in making the case for the President on policy grounds. You'll do this, right?" Mann was certain that Espy was not entirely forthcoming about the intentions of the Arizona developer, but he decided that it was now all or nothing. "I'm headed back now. Call me as soon as you get some feedback about the meeting. And Carlton, next time we'll meet at a bar somewhere. I never want to see this fucking park again."

Mann lumbered down the hill to his car and sat motionless for minutes, taking in Espy's proposition and the odds of its success. *A lifelong Democrat with little more than her political activity to keep her going, willing to betray her party and a candidate on the verge of a historic victory? Highly unlikely. But people can be unpredictable when they're sick and under stress. Let's just hope she doesn't implode and take us all with her.* Mann made a mental note to start his Plan B checklist. Item one: a new passport.

CHAPTER 33

Secret Service agents trailed Melody Banks and the President-elect as the two walked to Bridges' dock at the end of the Senator's expansive lawn. Their hiking boots left a trail of footprints in an overnight dusting of snow. Bridges pulled a cigar from his jacket and smiled. "You know, Melody, I helped Obama end the sanctions against Cuba. Some of my best work in the Senate. And what did it get me? Everlasting hatred from the anti-Castro nutters, and a box of Cuba's best cigars. Not a bad trade-off, eh?"

Banks tried to think of some response that would give Bridges confidence in his team's preparations. For the past thirty-six hours more than a dozen top political and legal minds had camped out in the Bridges' Maryland home to prepare for the anticipated corruption of the Electoral College process and the legal and legislative moves to follow. The campaign counsel had organized teams in every state won by Bridges to monitor each vote. Mort Abramowitz, the renowned Constitutional lawyer, was preparing arguments to halt the process should the President's scheme prevail. State party officials were in hourly contact with each elector to detect any defections.

"We've done all we can do," said Bridges, exhaling a cloud of smoke. The Senator seemed to Melody strangely at peace with the prospect of unprecedented chaos two days away. "Our problem is those states where we'll get no help from the governors and state legislatures controlled by Republicans. We saw it in 2000 in Florida and we may see it again next Tuesday." Bridges sighed and paused, savoring the fine cigar as if it were his last.

Banks ended the conversation with pleasantries about the view from the dock and left Bridges to reflect on the coming battle. She returned to the house and to the bedroom now set up as a make-shift office. She considered a brief nap, but instead called Jackson Cripple for an update, any news which might be used to avert what was shaping up as a Constitutional crisis.

"Nothing from Vaughn or Hartsell, though our Scottsdale hot-shot has booked his plane for a trip tomorrow to Boston," said Cripple. Like Banks, he had been battling sleepless nights as well. "We haven't picked up anything that gives us a hint why Boston, but we're still digging. Vaughn has gone totally quiet. He's at his lake house north of Bismarck, though for God's sake I can't imagine why. It's ten below there today. He's not used his cellphone or been online for two days."

"OK, stay in touch," responded a weary Banks. She rang off and lay on the bed, rubbed her eyes and tried to focus. She now had a fully engaged team of lawyers and consultants hard at work and was finally feeling that she needn't carry the burden of this effort alone. *There's got to be something we've missed. There must be...* Nodding off, she fell into a deep sleep that would be interrupted by a call an hour later.

"Melody, it's Pima. I just got back from Wisconsin," said a breath-less Grantham. "I spent three hours with the Vice President and got an earful. It has nothing to do with your situation with the electors, but he did say one thing you might want to look into immediately."

Banks was still groggy from sleep and asked the *Politico* reporter to repeat herself. Grantham recounted her success in reaching West, who overruled White House staff objecting to an interview in Madison.

"I've never seen anything like it," said Grantham. "There were four staffers and a bunch of Secret Service guys there in his house— ostensibly protecting the Vice President. West is convinced they're monitoring every call or email he sends or receives. They won't let him go anywhere they can't control. I get there and they interrogate me about my interview and insist they sit in while I talk to West. They say that given what they called the Vice President's recent mental breakdown, there are national security issues they worry he'll talk about."

"It's all bullshit, of course, but the Vice President has no choice but to take their orders. We sit in his study with two White House guys and two Secret Service agents and a doc-tor—a fucking doctor, Melody! And I do my interview. Every time I get to the Electoral College question they interrupt and I change the subject. I'm getting really pissed, but I decide that I'll go along and try to figure out a way to get back to the reason I went there."

"But West is way ahead of me. As I'm wrapping up the mun-dane stuff—his legacy and so on—he slips me a note out of sight of the staff. "Meet me in two hours at Taliesin East, in the women's restroom at the visitor center". Either the Vice President has something serious to tell me, or he's one fucked up guy. Could be both, I thought."

Banks still couldn't connect Grantham's story to her own pressing challenge, but she encouraged the reporter to continue.

"So I get back in my car and head out of Madison to Spring Green, about an hour west of town. You know the place, right? Frank Lloyd Wright's home, his masterpiece. I studied it at Yale and did research there my senior year. It's amazing. I'm think-ing, why Taliesin? And I remember that West is a history buff and he actually hosted an event there for the Arts Endowment a few years ago."

Banks was vaguely familiar with the historic site, and feigned recognition, but was agitated and wanted Grantham to get to the point.

"I was driving about a hundred miles an hour and got there a bit early and hung around the bookstore until the time we were supposed to meet. Pretty soon I see two black Suburbans and the Vice President's limo pull into the parking area next to the visitor center. Ordinary folks can't get that close to the house but that's obviously not a problem for West."

OK, wrap it up, Pima, thought Banks. *I'm bone tired and I've got work to do.*

"So I slip into the women's restroom and wait. I see why West has picked this particular spot—it's through a door and immediately next to the men's room. If he gets through there without his guards he can find me. And sure enough, in a minute I'm standing in the women's room with the Vice President of the United States. He locks the door behind him and launches into this amazing story."

"West is talking fast now, nothing like the guy I was interviewing earlier in Washington. He tells me about a call he had received the day before from a major campaign donor. Turns out this guy recently forwarded a very large pot of money to some enterprise run by Eldon Mann. He's apparently looking for an ambassadorship in the next administration and was sealing the deal with Mann and the money."

"Might be just a last minute bundling for the campaign legal fund or the Inauguration," said Banks, suppressing a heavy yawn. "We've done the same thing. It's pretty much legal."

"Yeah, but that's not what's happening here," said Grantham. "This guy had a few too many margaritas out on his boat off Santa Barbara and his wife started pounding on him, demanding that the posting in Argentina be guaranteed somehow. He's cornered and the only way he can get her off his back is to call someone in the White House to assure her that the deal is solid."

"How does the Vice President come into this?" asked Banks, now fully alert.

"It was the Vice President who had offered the appointment to the guy weeks ago, at the insistence of Eldon Mann,' she continued. "And since he couldn't get to the President or Mann, it was the Vice President this guy called to sweet talk his wife."

Banks thought the story was convoluted, but she trusted Grantham's sense of urgency in passing it along. "OK, Pima, go on."

"So here's the bottom line. The guy gets through to West at his home up here and tells the Vice President that he wants a guarantee that she'll get the ambassadorship. West pushes back and tells him there are no guarantees and that, as a matter of fact, West won't be in a second Holland administration, so he should take this up with the Chief of Staff."

"The guy then loses it. He starts yelling at West and tells him that by God he's paid for the damn thing and he'd sure better get it or – and this is where I have the Vice President's exact words—*he'll take the whole fucking place down*. West then presses him and the guy says he's given Eldon Mann ten million dollars to run some kind of operation that will take back the election from Bridges."

"At this point West's getting nervous and he knows he doesn't have much time to talk. He closes it off, and he says—and I made a note of this—"Eldon Mann is a criminal. He's destroying the President. You have to expose him"."

"About that time the Secret Service agent starts banging on the restroom door, calling for him. He's obviously planned for this, so he waves me into a stall and opens the door and acts confused, says he thought he was in the men's room. They look around the space and haul him out and I wait a bit and get out of there and drive back to Madison. I'm pretty sure they never saw me."

"Jesus, Pima," Banks tried to merge Grantham's report with Jackson Cripple's intelligence, but it wasn't processing. "Who is this guy in California? Have you talked to him?"

"No, he sobered up and won't talk to me. He sounded shocked when I told him I 'd spoken to the Vice President," said Grantham. "I'm flying out to Santa Barbara in the morning to track him down."

"We're trying to get Mann to respond, but we're getting nowhere. I can't write it until I get something more, and the Vice President refuses to go on the record or even background with this. He assumes that my story will simply be a recap of his career and his departure as Vice President. But for some reason he wanted to tell me all this other stuff."

"So that's it. But protect me on this. If you have to tell Senator Bridges or anyone else any what I've told you, say I was following up on a lead I'd gotten, which is sort of true."

"And Melody," closed Grantham, "good luck next Tuesday. I hear your folks have hundreds of people on the ground all over the country for the vote. We're writing about that tomorrow."

Banks hung up and called Jackson Cripple. "I need you to get me all you can on William Branson, a rich guy in Santa Barbara. It's urgent. Really urgent." She returned to the meeting where the team was poring over a large political map covering one wall of the room. Each state was color coded—blue for safe elector states won by Bridges, those with no likely defectors and Democratic governors and legislatures—only four of those. Purple for a dozen states won by Bridges but in control of Republicans. Red for twenty-one states won by Holland. And white for Bridges, thirteen states where trouble was possible. New Hampshire had not raised any red flags for the team.

CHAPTER 34

Hartsell arrived at the Portsmouth coffee shop a half hour early and settled into a booth with the best cappuccino he'd had in months. *Can't get this in Arizona,* he thought. *Maybe I'll buy a coffee shop in Scottsdale and hire the guy that runs this one. Beats real estate any day.* He reread the notes from his conversation with Lydia Elving and rehearsed his pitch as instructed by the Nashville lawyer. She had cautioned him to avoid making any promises to Sullivan, financial or otherwise, and to put nothing on paper or in an email or text. Hartsell had a different strategy. If Sullivan was desperate for money, that's where he would head. It always worked for him. And Elving didn't need to know. The outcome was what mattered.

"Hello again, Mr. Hartsell." Virginia managed a thin smile and squeezed into the booth across from the Arizona developer. "Can you get me a decaf latte, no sugar? Thanks."

Returning with the coffee, Hartsell made small talk until the group behind their booth had left. The shop was now almost empty so their conversation would not likely be overheard.

"Virginia, I hear that you've had some real setbacks recently. Real tough stuff, financially and health-wise. I want to help."

"Don't know where you heard that," she said, "but it's none of your business. I've got things under control."

"I'm sure you do," he said. "You're a remarkable woman who's been a rock for so many people, a real rock. But I don't think people have been as good to you as you have to them. I mean, look how many politicians have climbed on your back to win campaigns here in New Hampshire."

Sullivan took in a deep breath and rose to leave. "Mr. Hartsell, my affairs are my own and I'd appreciate you staying out of them. Now I have to go. I'm late for a meeting and I don't have anything more to say to you. Thanks for the coffee."

"Virginia, please wait," he pleaded. "I want you to hear something."

Hartsell dialed a number on his smartphone and when the party answered he switched to Facetime to bring a video image onto the screen. He turned the image toward Sullivan.

"Mother! I can't believe this! What you've done is....you've saved my life!" Virginia's long lost daughter Constance was crying as she tried to gain her composure. "I'm seeing a doctor in Boston tomorrow morning. He came here for a consultation just now and he's confident the cancer can be controlled. Here, say hi to Janine!" Virginia's granddaughter came into the picture and hugged her mother. "Thank you, Grandma. Thank you!"

Sullivan was dumbstruck and unable to speak until nudged by Hartsell. "Well, Constance, that's great. But, you know, I...I...I hope it goes well. I'd love to see you again soon. But I have to go now." The York couple waved goodbye and Hartsell signed off.

"What have you done?" she angrily demanded, now standing beside Hartsell, steadying herself against a wall. She felt her heart racing and feared a serious attack.

"Just sit back down, Virginia. Let's talk."

For nearly an hour Hartsell gently laid out his maneuvering to obtain first-rate medical help for Virginia's daughter and his quiet payment of her debts. A new car was being delivered to her house as they spoke. His lawyer had prepared a consulting agreement and arranged an advance on a book Sullivan would write, or not. Her financial windfall would be entirely legal, accounted for, and taxes paid. If she liked, Hartsell would relocate her to any place in the country, in the world for that matter. He recommended a spa he owned in the Arizona desert, a wonderful place to regroup, get healthy, and consider her next phase. She deserved a new life.

Hartsell shared his own story of likely rejection by Senator Bridges' transition team, and his permanent estrangement from the political process in general and the Democratic Party in particular. Then he dropped the bomb on her.

"Virginia, I'm switching my vote to Holland when the electors meet next week. I want to encourage you to do the same."

"You can't do that," she exclaimed. "You can't just change your vote! Bridges won this state." Hartsell then explained the "faithless elector" principle and the ramification of a switched vote. "I know it would be hard for you, a lifelong Democrat. It will for me, too. But you can handle it. We've got to send a message. And beside, Holland's doing a damn good job with this terrorist thing and the economy and so on. He'll be good for the country. I can't say that about Calvin Bridges, can you?"

"So if I don't do this my daughter won't get the treatment and all that money will disappear, right?" Sullivan was incredulous at Hartsell's proposal and figured it was all some kind of scam. "That's what this is, right? Some kind of weird bait and switch."

"No, Virginia. It's all yours and your daughter's, whatever you decide to do. I can leave Portsmouth today and you'll never hear from me again other than to discuss the book deal if you're interested. You've got a hell of a story. And by the way, it will be even more of a story if you vote as I will next Tuesday." Hartsell knew this was a gamble, but he couldn't renege at this point. All the chips were on the table.

"This is insane," she said, nodding back and forth, head down and obviously in pain as she rose to leave the coffee shop. "And I still don't believe you can do it."

"Please, take this number and call me in a few hours. I'll stay around town for the rest of the day in case you want to get back together."

He held her arm and helped her out of the shop. Rebuffing his offer to walk her home, Virginia slowly returned to her house. Turning the corner onto her street she saw a shiny new Prius sitting where her ancient, dead Camry had rested earlier that morning. "Oh, Jesus. Oh, Jesus," she muttered, pausing to run her hand over the roof of the automobile and shaking her head.

Wayne Hartsell occupied himself with an afternoon of football games at a nearby sports bar, with a pitcher of Smuttynose and a plate of chicken wings. He resisted the urge to call his new best friend Lydia Elving, to recount the conversation with Virginia. He wanted to report total success. He had begun to think of a different kind of relationship with the slender brunette man-killer lawyer from Nashville.

His Arizona State Sun Devils were up by three touchdowns when his phone buzzed. "Hello, Virginia. I was hoping you'd call. Of course, I'll come now. No, I know the address. See you soon." Hartsell downed the last half glass of beer and dropped a fifty on the bar to cover his tab. No credit card charges, warned Elving. Use only the secure phone. Leave your own phone in the plane. *Check, check, check.* Hartsell smiled as he left the bar and gave his driver Virginia Brown's address.

Without fanfare, every state election official certified the popular vote count from election night and reported the numbers to Washington. The media announced the news on websites– "It's Official—Bridges Wins Election" *(New York Times),* "Bridges Election Certified" *(Washington Post)* – with stories about the coming Electoral College vote and the President's ongoing refusal to concede to Bridges. The Wall Street Journal was the only major outlet to get it right—"Not So Fast: Bridges Has One More Hurdle". CNN scrolled the result below news of another Kardashian meltdown.

CHAPTER 35

Billy Branson's sleek 170 foot Baglietto sat moored at the end of a wide dock separated from the lesser craft tied up at the Santa Barbara Yacht Club. Delivered from the famous Italian marine builder a year earlier, the yacht was exceptional even in the rarefied waters off this glamorous California village. At 700 tons, with twelve staterooms, a Hermes-designed dining room, a movie theater, and a speed of twenty knots, *Tanya's Dreamcloud* cost Branson a cool thirty million, plus a million a year in crew and maintenance. It was the wedding present his new wife had chosen while the two were cruising the Mediterranean and shopping for baubles.

"Totally sick!" exclaimed Tanya, who squealed with delight when he showed her the photos on their wedding night. The paunchy, balding hedge fund wiz had learned that the lingo of a twenty five year old was not what he'd remembered as a kid. But her many obvious charms more than made up for any misgivings about their age difference.

The December sun was fading as he finished a second cocktail and about to call the steward for another when a voice beckoned from the dock. "Mr. Branson, it's Pima Grantham. From *Politico*. We spoke yesterday. Can I come on board?"

Fuck. Fuck! Branson thought he had successfully blown off the reporter over the phone. "No! How'd you get on this dock? It's private. I'm going to call security if you don't leave now."

"No! Please! I need to talk to you," Grantham shielded her eyes from the blinding sunset and waved a sheaf of papers to try to grab his attention. "You'll want to hear me out, I promise."

Branson made a show of speaking into his phone to a marina guard to have her removed. "You've got about thirty seconds to get off this dock or you'll be arrested for trespassing." He turned to enter the ship but was stopped short when she yelled.

"I know about the Deepwater negotiations, Mr. Branson. I have the documents here," said Grantham, brandishing the papers again. "If you won't talk with me, I'm writing about it tonight."

Branson looked back at her, head cocked, not believing what the young reporter was saying. *No one knows about Deepwater. No one except me and the lawyers and the Saudis. No one. She's bluffing. Trying to get my goat to talk about Holland and that stupid call I made to West.* He stared at her for what felt like minutes to Grantham before finally responding.

"Come on board. We'll talk but you're not going to get anything you can use," he tried to sound defiant and intimidating but suspected it came across more as defeated as Pima Grantham smiled sweetly and pulled herself onto the deck of *Tanya's Dreamcloud.* Armed with deeply sensitive information provided by Melody Banks, Grantham had readied a line of questioning that would put Branson back on his heels and soften him for some answers about his deal with Eldon Mann. The secret business file was none of her concern, just bait for the bear.

"Beautiful boat!" she exclaimed. "I used to sail with my boyfriend when I was in school in New Haven, but wow, nothing remotely like this!"

"What do you want from me? It's Paula, right?"

"It's Pima, Mr. Branson. Pima Grantham. As I said on the phone last night, I'm a reporter from *Politico* and I'm looking into several things. First, let me put you at ease. I don't care about the Deepwater business deal. I know everything about it, and I can give it to the *Post* or the *Times* or the *Journal*. But not if you can tell me about your arrangement with Eldon Mann, the White House Chief of Staff."

Branson stiffened, remembering her call the night before, mentioning a conversation with the Vice President. *West must have talked to her. Sonofabitch. I should have waited to talk to Mann.* "I haven't got any arrangement, as you put it. Of course I know Eldon Mann. I'm a big supporter of the President. You obviously know that. I'm pissed that he's lost this goddamn election. The country will regret it."

"Well," said Grantham, "he may not lose it yet. There seems to be a plan underway to get some of the Democratic electors to bail on Senator Bridges when the electoral votes are counted next week. And there is reason to believe that you may have helped make this happen. What can you tell me about that?"

"Look, Miss Grantham. I give a lot of money to political campaigns." Branson was trying hard to not get angry or defensive, but the nerve of this woman coming on to his boat and questioning him was hard to take. "I'm a conservative, okay? I believe in what they're trying to do. It's all legal. You can check it out."

"Mr. Branson, did you recently give the White House Chief of Staff ten million dollars for a special operation?" Grantham knew she had precious little time to extract anything helpful from Branson before he threw her off his yacht.

As Branson stood up his pullover rode high above his large, deeply tanned stomach. He made a clumsy effort to pull it down while juggling a cigar and martini glass. Exasperated and desperate to end the conversation, he stared down at Grantham and lowered his voice. "As I said, I give a lot of money to campaigns. Since the election I've given the Holland campaign some money for its legal fund and for its transition planning. Something to deal with the election stalemate. I don't know anything about electoral votes. Whatever, it's all kosher." Branson was now pacing the deck, waving the empty cocktail glass. "Now that's all I've got to say. So if you'll excuse me, my wife and I are late for dinner."

"Oh, Mrs. Branson!," said Grantham as the billionaire's trophy wife came into view from the bow of *Tanya's Dreamcloud*, clad in the skimpiest bikini Grantham had seen, a wispy thong below and a thin band of ribbon covering substantially enhanced breasts.

"Hi there!" greeted Tanya Branson. "If I'd known we had comp'ny I'd of come down earlier. Didn't mean to be rude! I've had way too much sun today! Sweetheart, are you gonna offer this gal a drink?" She retrieved a cutoff *Go, Dawgs!* t-shirt and pulled it over her glorious, long blonde curls.

"Did you go to the University of Georgia?" asked Grantham, hoping to extend the visit as long as possible.

"Nah, just visited there a couple times. Had a boyfriend who played ball for them, but..." she lowered her voice for her agitated husband's benefit, "we don't mention him around here. Right, honey?"

"Whatever," interjected Branson. "Miss Grantham was just leaving, weren't you?" A deck hand appeared from above and motioned for Grantham to follow him. The gesture was not meant to be friendly.

"Bye there!" waved Tanya as the two disappeared into the bowels of the yacht. *This woman will be an interesting ambassador, for sure*, thought the reporter as she rose to leave the ship. *I'm definitely covering her confirmation hearing.*

While Branson had revealed nothing about the electoral conspiracy, he had confirmed the payment to Eldon Mann. And he was on the record, whether he knew it or not. *That's the closest thing I have to a smoking gun. I hope the boss will go with it.*

Since her red-eye from LAX wasn't departing until nearly midnight, Grantham headed to Trattoria Mollie, a favorite of celebrities and local rich folk in nearby Montecito. She had read that it was Oprah's hangout and *Bon Appetit* reported the abalone gnocchi and roasted artichokes were to die for. It would blow her expense account budget for dinner alone but she figured the last few days had earned her a great meal. She left the harbor and hailed a taxi, with tomorrow's *Politico* story beginning to take form. And she would forward the secret file on Branson's Deepwater scheme to a friendly *Post* reporter.

CHAPTER 36

"Okay, here's where we are." Carlton Espy pushed a file folder across the table in Mann's dining room. The late evening session would run through a checklist of preparations for the next day's gathering of electors throughout the country. "We've shut down all the recount operations in Virginia, New Mexico, and Ohio. They got us the attention we wanted."

"They know we're trying to move votes away from Bridges, and that we may have succeeded with Hartsell and Vaughn. So it's like a high-stakes chess match."

"Last week we put a bunch of people in Pennsylvania and Missouri and made no secret of it, figuring the Bridges lawyers would bite and focus on those states. Seems to be working. They've figured out what we're doing in Arizona and North Dakota, so we've moved all the recount lawyers to Phoenix and Bismarck to handle the blowback there on Monday. When Vaughn and Hartsell vote we want to be ready with guns blazing to keep the Democrats from stopping the process. If Hartsell succeeds with Sullivan in Portsmouth we've got a team ready to go there tonight."

"The state officials in Arizona, North Dakota, and New Hampshire are all our people and they'll immediately gather the ballots for us. We figure in all the confusion we can make that happen. We've got three charters stationed nearby to fly the documents to Washington. It's a complicated process but we've got every step covered."

"We've not spent much time thinking about our own 267 electors. It's not impossible that one or more of them could switch to Bridges if they believe the system was corrupted. But we're certain that no one on Bridges' side has made any effort to contact them. Our state chairmen have made repeated calls to their electors and we haven't picked up any remote evidence that we have a problem there. And anyway, our people won't even show up to vote since they believe it's over."

"And one final precaution. Each of these three delegations will vote shortly after noon, by written ballot. We're making sure that our targets vote last." Mann nodded, pleased with Espy's thoroughness and sheer cool as the critical test neared. *Nothing rattles this guy,* he thought.

He and Espy had planned well. Arizona and North Dakota, though narrowly won by Bridges, were in the political control of Holland's party. Republican governors and legislative leaders from both states had been briefed earlier that morning and were on board with the plan. Their legal and political talking points provided arguable cover for certifying extraordinary outcomes. The Constitution protected "faithless electors" and, after all, the Constitution was sacred.

If Hartsell and Vaughn held, the Electoral College vote would be tied: Holland 269, Bridges 269. Whatever happened with Hartsell's overture to Virginia Sullivan in New Hampshire, the election would either belong to the President or be thrown into the Republican Congress. And there they had a better than even chance to prevail.

"I just got a text from Lydia," said Espy, looking down at his phone. "Hartsell's with Sullivan now. Says he'll call and report tonight. We just have to wait and see."

"Okay. Let's get back to the plan for tomorrow." Mann marveled at Espy's calm, as Mann was churning inside. But Mann knew that it would be he, not Espy, who would meet the executioner's blade if the project backfired. Espy would soon be on a plane to Cabo for a delayed, extended vacation. Earlier in the day Mann had idly Googled "countries with no extradition treaties with the U.S."

As the two were reviewing the assignment of Constitutional lawyers prepared to meet the press after the storm subsided, Espy's phone vibrated loudly, sending the device buzzing across the table. "It's Lydia," he noted to Mann.

"Unbelievable," he spoke into the phone, showing no facial reaction to whatever news Elving was reporting. "Incredible. And he toed the line on not offering anything to her? This is amazing, Lydia. Make sure Hartsell checks in with her early tomorrow morning, and call me as soon as you hear from him, okay? Yeah, Pine Valley. We'll make that happen whenever you want to go."

Espy took a deep breath and smiled. "See, Eldon, I told you that golf is a great sport. We got our gal. Sullivan is on board."

The President turned down the volume on the Cowboys-Redskins game to take the call from his Chief of Staff. Holland publicly backed the Florida NFL teams from Miami, Tampa, and Jacksonville, but privately he was a die-hard Dallas fan and even had his personal aide place more than a few bets on America's Team. He hated the Redskins, hated having to sit in the pompous owner's suite during a couple games each season. His autographed photos of Roger Staubach and Tony Romo hung in his Orlando study alongside a formal photo of himself and Ronald Reagan while Holland was a White House intern in the eighties.

"So what're we lookin' at tomorrow, Eldon?" The President had long since reconciled himself to a losing outcome, despite Mann's assurances that the audacious scheme might succeed. He had spent part of his Sunday going over a draft statement that would finally concede the election to Senator Bridges.

"Mr. President, I'm confident that tomorrow the Electoral College vote will reverse the outcome of the election and you'll be serving a second term," Mann decided to be direct and brief, suspecting that Holland was in no shape to discuss detailed strategy. He waited a moment to let his words sink in. "Three Democratic electors will switch from Senator Bridges to you, giving you the necessary 270 votes to be declared the winner."

"Eldon, I don't know how you did this. I don't wanna know. And I still can't believe it can happen." Holland's skepticism was apparent in his voice. "And there'll be hell to pay in Congress if it does go that way. I hope you've thought of that. And what do I say?"

"I'm forwarding a document that will outline the procedure tomorrow and what we expect to happen." Mann needed to have Holland clear headed and prepared for the events that would unfold. "You'll recall our briefing with the Electoral College scholar last month—the Constitutional foundation for this action is solid. There are a number of court cases that..."

"Never mind, we'll leave it that way for tonight. Call me if you have anything more," interrupted the President. Mann heard the football game audio return as the President ended the call.

We may have stolen this election for you, you ungrateful bastard. And we may go to prison for it. And all you can say is never mind? You've got to get back to that goddamn game? Mann, exhausted and stressed to the max, fought back the urge to tell the President of the United States to go fuck himself.

CHAPTER 37

Melody Banks and the Bridges team worked deep into the night to check their own preparations for the Electoral College vote, now only hours away. Senator Bridges entered the room frequently between calls to DNC officials and fellow office holders, pacing like a caged animal awaiting a fight. "Melody, do we have anything more on those two electors?"

"The guy from North Dakota can't be found," Banks said, barely looking up from her laptop. "We believe our friend in Arizona is holed up somewhere near Tucson, won't take calls from the state chairman or anyone else. We even put in a call to him from you, but his line goes to voicemail. I think we can assume he's going to bolt."

"So if nothing changes that leaves us tied," said Bridges, arms crossed and swaying back and forth, a tic he exhibited when frustrated. "I know our lawyers are out there, but do we have any confidence that we can reverse any outcome when they vote? I reread the case law on past court challenges and it's not promising."

Todd Campbell entered the room talking on one cellphone and holding another call on a second phone. "Let me get back to you. I know, you need an answer, but I have to meet with Senator Bridges. Just stay there."

"Any more news on replacing Hartsell and Vaughn?" Despite Bridges' ability to forgive and forget when staff let him down, he had exploded the previous week when he was told the campaign lawyers had missed the opportunity to have North Dakota and Arizona replace the two suspicious electors. The law was clear that any changes in elector selection must be completed not less than six days before the Electoral College met to vote, and the Bridges team had missed the deadline by eight hours. A sheepish Campbell took the blame, and hadn't fully recovered his composure over the coming days, knowing that this one mistake might have lost the presidency for Calvin Bridges.

"No, Senator. The states rejected our last ditch appeal last night. I meant to tell you first thing this morning." Campbell would never live down the failings of his legal team.

"But we have new filings ready to go if it blows up tomorrow," he said to the room. "We've got a good shot in the two lower courts, but if we win there there'll be an urgent appeal to the Supreme Court by Holland's lawyers to allow the electoral votes to move forward. Abramowitz is eager to make the case when it gets to the Court, but we all know how this court is likely to go, especially if they take a strictly constructionist view of the Constitutional issues. There's one wrinkle that could help us. If neither of these two electors show up today the state party can run in substitutes that will vote as pledged."

"And if it's a tie?" asked Bridges, who knew the answer but once more wanted to review all possibilities. Every legal and political scenario had been discussed *ad nauseam* by Bridges and his advisors since Banks had revealed her intelligence about the likely direction of the President's strategy, but the Senator wanted another update. Campbell patiently ran through his checklist once again, noting the historical precedents for actions by faithless electors, the current vote count, state and federal laws governing the process, and the implication for each possible scenario. After nearly an hour of conversation both men took calls deemed urgent and the team went back to work, looking for a magic bullet to prevent what all feared would be a catastrophic day.

Even armed with Jackson Cripple's explosive information about Eldon Mann's operations, Banks had lost an internal debate with the campaign legal team days earlier. Bridges' advisors had been convinced that state by state recounts were the basis of Holland's refusal to concede, and discounted Bank's speculations. Campbell had directed most of their legal resources into those states where Bridges had won by the smallest margins. The presence of scores of Republican election lawyers swarming the courthouses in Virginia and Missouri and elsewhere seemed to confirm that strategy until petitions for recount were withdrawn and the Holland lawyers pulled out of those states. Left with no good answer for their boss, the Bridges team went back to the drawing board, drafting legal challenges and staffing for a court battle to counter the likely actions of their turncoat electors.

Chairman Lismore awoke to honking geese outside the window of his Kansas ranch. The Congressman had been up late pouring over a revised legislative package flown out by Tommy Thompson, who was asleep in the guesthouse nearby. Thompson had also brought a case of rare Highcliff whiskey the lobbyist had procured on his most recent golf outing to Scotland with two of Lismore's colleagues.

The Rake had long ago figured out how to get around the House ethics rules that torpedoed members of Congress who in years past had lusted for gifts and junkets. Thompson's largess perched barely on the edge of legal. He became everyone's best friend by loading on the perks, yet keeping them out of the investigators' lenses.

Thompson and Lismore had polished off a bottle of the scotch while adding new elements to their plan. Two senior Lismore staffers took notes and plotted details on easels of newsprint stationed around the room. There would be three junkets—"official fact finding missions" — to Canberra, Brasilia, and Berlin, departing the following week with members of Congress sympathetic to their efforts. The stated objective would be detailed discussions with government officials about those countries' success with relocating national governments to new capitals.

The Canberra trip, with spouses and staff aboard a comfortable Air Force jet, would stop for several days each in Hawaii and New Zealand to rest for the arduous meetings ahead. The Brasilia congressional delegation, or "CODEL", would return through Puerto Rico and the Virgin Islands, and the Berlin group scheduled for foreign policy briefings in Paris and London when their fact finding was complete. Shopping and sightseeing outings would be managed by U. S. embassy staffs and made comfortable in government limos. No detail had been ignored.

The Security Relocation Congressional Caucus, now numbering more than a hundred members, would begin its informal hearings shortly before Christmas. Lismore's own Committee would be called into session in early January for a field hearing in Topeka, when industry and state officials would testify about the exceptional welcome the newly sited federal government would receive in that area.

The Congressional Budget Office, ostensibly nonpartisan, was overseen by a close colleague of Lismore's and would issue a finding that would show the relocation program to be not only revenue neutral, but a net fiscal gain for the taxpayers.

Lismore's local supporters organized a Congressional field trip to the country's geographical center, about two miles from downtown Lebanon, Kansas. A huge banner welcomed the delegation—"America's New Federal Home" – with a gigantic

Stars and Stripes covering a field with a plaque noting the precise center of the United States. Over ribs and corn pudding and apple pies in a heated tent, members of Congress were treated to a multimedia show touting the region's natural and cultural offerings. Each participant came away with a hospitality bag full of local treats and a very valuable gold coin set minted for the event, a special gift pre-cleared by Lismore's friends on the House Ethics Committee.

To fund the off-budget expenses for the Caucus and the massive lobbying campaign they envisioned, Thompson created the New Freedom Fund, an "educational" nonprofit that could receive unlimited, thinly reported money from virtually any source.

Lismore placed two of his trusted political associates in charge of the operation and within two weeks raised fifteen million dollars toward a goal of fifty. The myriad of industry groups that would profit from such a massive endeavor lined up to write checks. Thompson's lobbying firm was retained at fifty thousand dollars a month to launch a vigorous legislative campaign for the National Security Relocation Act.

The national media, of course, was skeptical in the extreme. Even the perennial Washington bashers at Fox railed at the plan. The city's leading think tanks, liberal and conservative, placed the cost of such a relocation between two and three trillion dollars, enough, stated the *Post*, to fund three Iraq wars.

Neither Lismore nor The Rake were concerned about the criticism. Lismore was one of the most politically secure members of Congress, and The Rake knew that any press, as long as it didn't involve an indictment, was good for his business.

"Damn! The Electoral College votes today. I nearly forgot," exclaimed Lismore, handing Thompson a cup of coffee as the two reassembled next to a roaring fireplace. "Did you see that *Politico* story? Looks like Holland's trying to pull a goddamn rabbit out of a hat."

"I haven't seen any overnight news," responded Thompson, still drugged from the liquor and huge steaks and more liquor. "What's he doing? Stalling the vote until the recounts are done?"

"No, dammit! They're saying that two or more Democratic electors may switch to Holland. Seems crazy, but what the hell, more power to 'em!" Lismore hoisted his cup and took a deep gulp. "Damn that's good coffee! Cuba! That's about the only good thing Calvin Bridges ever did, so I'll give him that. Otherwise he's a self-righteous, smug, pseudo-aristocratic sonofabitch and I hope Holland screws him good. Now let's get back to work."

Virginia Sullivan pulled herself slowly from the creaking bed, sitting for a spell before rising with the help of a cane. Shuffling to the kitchen for coffee, she opened the box of pastries left earlier by Wayne Hartsell and chose a chocolate covered, cream-filled doughnut, always her favorite, though prohibited by her doctors.

She slowly walked to a smaller second bedroom and sat in a sturdy rocker facing a sealed fireplace. Virginia kept this room away from the few guests she entertained, certain they would find it creepy. She gazed along four walls of faded paint, covered with momentos of her dead husband's hobbies. Errol had rarely held a job for more than a year and even those were minimum wage with no benefits. But he was devoted to Virginia, and his passion for his unusual collections was boundless.

Half of one wall was a display of towels from various motels, arrayed in a giant fan announcing Holiday Inns or Howard Johnsons in Bangor, Manchester, Boston, and other New England cities. Each towel was festooned with a room key pinned next to the name of the establishment. Below this were a hundred hotel and bar ashtrays mounted with super glue. The largest wall was reserved for Errol's bowling trophies and the team shirts he wore for those victories. Each trophy rested on its own small shelf with the date and score labeled below.

Above the fireplace hung his most prized possession—six shelves of model trains, all lead by an historic steam locomotive pulling a full consist of passenger or freight cars. Alongside each train was a speaker that would play on command the actual sound of those locomotives in action. The room's full effect was breathtaking.

Every square inch of the fourth wall was covered with front pages of newspapers around the country, each trumpeting a major news event. The project had begun when Errol came across a copy of the *Dallas Morning Herald* the day after Kennedy's assassination. Mounting that, he proceeded to add dozens more: Robert Kennedy's murder in Los Angeles, Nixon's impeachment and later his resignation, the Jonestown mass suicides, Carter, Reagan, and Clinton's elections, explosion of the Challenger space shuttle, and various international events that struck Errol Sullivan as dramatic and memorable. Each of these pages he affixed to the wall with paste that rendered them permanent. The collection ended after the final open space was filled with the *New York Times* special edition after the 9/11 attacks.

The value of this oddball assortment of memorabilia and toys was meaningless to Sullivan, but during the years since his death, she could summon up his ghost when she visited the room. He was a gentle, good-hearted man who made her laugh, her only real friend and confidant, and that was more than enough for Virginia. She missed him mightily.

Virginia often retired to Errol's room to reflect on a problem or challenge. She had successfully concocted more than one campaign plan in that rocking chair. But lately, with failing health and a growing disillusionment with politics and life itself, she no longer felt Errol in the room—she no longer felt energy or hope.

I'm not sure I can do this. It will be so hard, she thought. *Seems like my whole life has been wrapped up in these people and their*

*politics. I used to think it was appreciated. But not now. And I'm
dying, and my daughter is dying, and I've missed a lifetime with
her and a granddaughter I didn't know. What's it been worth?*

Her coffee grew cold while she rocked, trying to make sense
of the opportunity presented by this ridiculous man from Arizona. Opening her laptop, Virginia downloaded a template for
do-it-yourself wills and completed the form. It was a simple
process, as she had little money and few possessions, if you didn't
count Wayne Hartsell's car and the book advance. Everything
would go to her daughter and granddaughter. She printed two
copies of the document, signed both and placed one in an envelope to leave in a desk drawer in the space off her kitchen that
she used for paperwork. The other she addressed to her friend
Andy Vorkink, a law professor at UNH who had befriended her
during his research on unique Portsmouth architecture.

*"Andy, I've enclosed a copy of my will, completed today. I've been
meaning to do this for years. I haven't asked, but I hope you'll be
willing to serve as executor.*

*The will is pretty clear cut, so it shouldn't be too difficult. I've
noted the contact information for my daughter below (yes, I have a
daughter, and a granddaughter. Just recently reunited with them.)
She needs a lot of help, but others have arranged to do that."*

*"You'll find the papers to a new car in the desk drawer, along
with another copy of this will. There's only a little money in my
checking account, and there may be more coming from a new project
I may work on soon.*

*Everything should go to my daughter and granddaughter. You
can take my cat Errol to the shelter but I hope you can find a home
for him. He's a good cat and someone might like him."*

*"Thank you for doing this. I really don't have anyone else to ask.
If we need to discuss this further, I'll be with the Electoral College
group today and tomorrow. I don't know where I'll be after that
but we'll be in touch. And you have my cell number and can reach
me that way. Sincerely, Virginia."*

Sullivan affixed a stamp on the letter and placed it in the mailbox to be picked up later in the day. She showered, dressed in a dark suit saved for special events, and waited for her ride to Concord, where her colleagues would soon cast New Hampshire's four electoral votes for the next President of the United States.

PART FOUR

"Democracy is the art and science of running the circus from the monkey cage."

— H.L. Mencken

CHAPTER 38

North Dakota's three Democratic electors could have met in a downtown tavern, but the occasion demanded a more regal setting. The state's governor, a rough hewn former cattle rancher who had made his fortune during the great oil and gas boom of the early 21ˢᵗ century, opened the ceremonies in the state House chamber with a prayer and Pledge of Allegiance. He then called upon the Lieutenant Governor to chair the proceedings. The Democrats designated one of their own to call the roll as dictated by precedent for the winning party.

After counting the votes, three certificates would be signed and forwarded to the appropriate officials in Washington. Congress would receive the vote count early in January and formally certify the President and Vice President, who would be sworn in on the 20ᵗʰ as required by the Constitution. It was a complicated process that amounted to no more than a rubber-stamping of the outcome on election day in early November. But this day would be different.

The rules were read for casting ballots, which would be written on a three by five card and handed to the Chair. As each name was called the elector acknowledged his or her vote. The room grew tense, since rumors about a possible controversy had arisen days before and now the gallery was packed with media and followers of the two candidates. Two of the electors had adamantly denied any intention of changing their vote. The state Democratic chair, worried about Stanley Vaughn's complete absence from Bismarck over the past two weeks, designated an alternate to take his place should Vaughn not show. He never accepted the speculation that Vaughn would betray the party ticket.

After Stanley's two colleagues acknowledged their vote for the Democratic ticket, the chair asked, "Mr. Vaughn, your ballot indicates that you have voted for President Holland and Vice President West." The room exploded, with shouts of "Fraud! Turncoat!" and various profanities from Bridges' backers. The Lt. Governor was barely heard to shout to Vaughn, "Do you acknowledge this vote?"

The other two Democratic electors rushed to confront Vaughn. The state party chair, a small beefy woman who had been publicly crowing about a new dawn for Democrats in a state long controlled by the opposition, screamed to the Lt. Governor, "You must stop the vote count. You can't continue. This is illegal!" As she approached the riser she stumbled and fell face down on the red carpet laid for the event. Bloodied, she rose and continued her challenge. The scene deteriorated as partisans in the spectator's gallery were coming to blows. The Governor's security team was unable to restore order until state troopers arrived to empty the chamber and cordon off the building. Guards ushered the electors into an anteroom, with the exception of Stanley Vaughn, who disappeared on the arm of a dark suited young attorney from Galveston.

Brad Cantwell directed Stanley into a Town Car parked in the Governor's private space in the garage under the State Capitol. He instructed Vaughn to sign the five certificates required for each elector to verify their vote, gave the certificates to an aide to be returned to the Lt. Governor, and tapped the driver, "Go. Now!" Their departure route had been carefully plotted to avoid the crowd gathered in a courtyard facing the stately federalist building. Despite temperatures nearing zero with strong winds howling down from Canada, several hundred angry Democrats gathered on the pavement, with no leader to focus their protest, no ready target available for their fury. Inside, Republican officials disingenuously sought to assure the two stunned Democrats that they had no idea Vaughn would switch.

"You expect us to believe that, you goddamn asshole!" shouted a burly Fargo labor organizer who had waited a lifetime to see North Dakota elect a Democratic president. He had his eyes on a plum job in the Bridges administration and was beyond furious at the day's outcome. "You people'll do anything to win an election, won't you? You did it in 2000, in 2004, and now this. What'd you pay Stanley to switch? And where the fuck is he, huh?" A colleague tried to restrain the organizer, who was now openly threatening the Lt. Governor, who was trying to find a safe exit. The injured state party chairwoman sat bleeding in a nearby chair, sobbing uncontrollably.

"It's over," said Brad Cantwell, offering the Bismarck car dealer a tumbler of good bourbon from the limo's bar. "You did well."

"Now what?" said Vaughn, who stared ahead, motionless as the car sped through downtown Bismarck to the private air terminal. "I really can't go home again, can I?"

"Of course you will," said Cantwell, patting Vaughn's forearm. "It'll settle down quicker than you think. Remember, this is still really a conservative Republican state. You won't be welcome in liberal circles—but then how many of those are there around here? And you're a hero with everyone else—how good is that!" He roared an unconvincing laugh that did nothing to raise Stanley's spirits.

Cantwell tried another direction. "Of course, you've got your cabin on the lake. And that beautiful young friend to keep you company. You'll be fine." Cantwell thought he spotted a slight smile from Vaughn.

"And don't forget, we'll be there for you for anything you need. But for now, let's get you somewhere warm and fun where no one will know you and you can relax. We've taken care of everything."

The car pulled alongside a new Cessna Citation X+ with engines warmed for the six-hour flight to the eastern Caribbean island of St. Kitts and a small resort owned by Bloch Systems, an Oklahoma energy conglomerate and a client of Carlton Espy's. Stanley brightened immediately upon seeing Eva lounging mid-cabin. "Sweetie! I got a pina colada for you! Isn't this so cool?"

After a short briefing about their travel plans, Brad retired to the rear of the plane to allow the two lovebirds to reconnect after Vaughn's harrowing experience in the Capitol an hour earlier. He called Carlton Espy to report their movements and a fuller version of the vote counting events. Espy had been given a min-ute-by-minute account by Cantwell's associate on site, but was unsure how Vaughn was managing the blowback.

"Oh, I think he'll be fine, Carlton. Just fine. A month from now, I don't know. But for now, Stanley Vaughn is like a pig in mud." Cantwell glanced at the couple snuggling on the spacious chaise and pulled on eyeshades for the flight south. He would drop off his passengers, who would be met by staff to take care of the couple for the next three weeks, and Cantwell would take the plane back to Dallas. Though the team was confident no one could know Vaughn's whereabouts, one of Espy's younger charges would be nearby to monitor any disruption. *Maybe twenty-four hours on the island would be ok,* thought Cantwell as he cranked up George Strait and hummed along.

"*All my ex's live in Texas and Texas is the place I'd dearly love to be, but all my ex's live in Texas and therefore I reside in Tennessee.*

Some folks think I'm hidin'. It's been rumored that I died. But I'm alive and well in Tennessee…"

An early winter storm whipped through New England, bringing a foot of unexpected snow and ice to lower New Hampshire. By mid morning roads became treacherous, slowing travel in and out of the state's capitol. When only three of the four electors found their way to the governor's office for the vote, the chief executive instructed the chair of the session to postpone the vote until all participants were present.

Virginia Sullivan arrived on time, chauffeured in a Wayne Hartsell-hired all-terrain SUV, and was shown to a comfortable waiting room near the governor's office. She made small talk with her colleagues and tried to quell a growing anxiety. *This will be over soon. I have to be steady.*

An aide entered the room and announced that the final late elector, driving from upstate Berlin, would not likely make Concord until four pm. A luncheon with the governor had been prepared for the group, but Virginia begged off, too nervous to eat. At two pm, a nearby television screen flashed a bulletin from North Dakota. A Democratic elector had changed his vote to President Holland, sending political reporters into frenzy. On CNN Wolf Blitzer and John King were attempting analysis with little information. The luncheon group returned to the waiting room to take in the commentary as the electors sat stunned and disbelieving. Sullivan watched the programming for a few minutes, then excused herself to a nearby ladies room, short of breath and sweating profusely.

Wayne Hartsell drove the 120 miles from his Tucson hideaway to the State Capitol on West Washington Street in downtown Phoenix, at a leisurely pace. He wanted to arrive no earlier than 11:45 am. The other ten Democratic electors were already seated in the grand legislative chamber in the classical revival building, but Hartsell and Lydia Elving were determined to avoid the gaggle of press gathered at the building's entrance. Hartsell managed to stay out of sight for the past three weeks. He made his stealth trip to Boston and Portsmouth without detection, but today he would have to face not only the press but also ten fellow Democrats who would soon want his scalp.

As their car entered Phoenix, Elving took a call from Carlton Espy with the news from Bismarck, and reporting a large crowd convened at the Arizona Capitol. A rear underground entrance was secured for Hartsell's arrival, and the governor's staff was ready to escort him to the room to join the official delegation. Hartsell had been thoroughly briefed on his instructions and introduced by phone to the team that would make certain he signed all required documents and exited the building quickly.

To put state party officials off the scent as much as possible, at Elving's direction Hartsell had made several calls to Democratic colleagues and responded to carefully selected press queries to stifle rumors that he was wavering on his vote. The Bridges campaign and the DNC had urged that Hartsell be replaced, but local organizers balked, citing Hartsell's longtime financial support and assurances that he would stick with the party when the voting began. The overwhelmingly Republican state legislature refused to get involved in an effort to enforce loyalty by electors, so Hartsell's position in Arizona's Electoral College process was protected.

Standing out of sight in a passageway next to the chamber, Elving marveled at her convert's steely resolve as he entered and took a seat with his partisan delegation. Several rose to greet Hartsell, the state chairman sternly gripping his hand for more than a welcome handshake. Elving thought she saw him mouthing the words *Wayne, you're okay, right?* Hartsell belted out a loud laugh and slapped his questioner on the back. "Let's get started with this party!" said the smiling land developer, enjoying the drama of it all. *Incredible,* thought Elving. *Who is this guy?*

Following the ritual that had been observed in eastern states and the District of Columbia hours earlier – New Hampshire delayed by weather—the Arizona Electoral College was formally convened by a state official and introductory comments were made. The process was explained for onlookers, and electors designated one of their own, who then asked each to cast their vote. One by one, each marked their ballot for Calvin Bridges and voiced their preference to the chairman. "I only have ten ballots here. Who's missing?" asked the chairman, who paused, realizing that Hartsell was the only holdout. "Wayne?"

"Mr. Chairman, I proudly cast my vote for President Grady Holland!" said Hartsell, loud enough to be heard clearly throughout the chamber. Pandemonium ensued, cameras moving from Hartsell's pronouncement to the audience section, where shouting and shoving brought a phalanx of the governor's guards. Elving's aide moved onto the chamber floor and grabbed Hartsell's arm to exit the area, but the physically imposing man stood looking around the room at the mayhem he had caused. "We have to go, Mr. Hartsell! Now!" Elving met him in the hallway out of sight of reporters and cameras and managed to move her charge into an anteroom and down steps to the VIP parking lot and their car.

"My God, that was unbelievable!" he said as they pulled away from the Capitol grounds, now teeming with television reporters feeding the news to viewers across Phoenix and the country. "It was like some out of body experience! I can't tell you how amazing it was. And you know what? I looked at those assholes on both sides and I just thought *Fuck you.* I didn't give a damn what they thought of me." He pushed a button and the seat in the sleek Lexus sedan reclined to a flat position, an expensive feature Hartsell ordered for his latest auto.

Elving placed a call to Carlton Espy, who was awaiting details with Eldon Mann in Washington. Her report was succinct. She knew the news would set off a hurricane in national political circles but her job was done. She followed Hartsell's lead, lowered her seat and instructed the driver to head south back to Tucson, where he would board his plane to Mexico and she to a waiting jet that would return her to life as a overworked Nashville attorney. *This has been exciting,* she thought, *but I have to make a living. At least there's golf to look forward to in the spring, maybe meet Jordan Speith. I'm not too old for him...*

CHAPTER 39

"Well, that's that," Calvin Bridges shrugged as the news came in from Phoenix. "Looks like we're going to Congress for a showdown. What's the plan, gang?" The Senator was drained from watching the day's events unfold. Todd Campbell's lawyers checked in with whatever scraps of information they could glean from North Dakota and Arizona officials but offered little in the way of encouraging news. Both state party chairs were inconsolable, and Bridges and his team were in no mood to comfort them.

"We let them control the process. We fucked up." Campbell blurted. "We'll go to court first thing in the morning. There were obviously lots of irregularities with both those votes and we'll be all over that."

"We still have to hear from the remaining five western states where we won," continued Campbell. "But all of them have ironclad laws that would prevent a switched vote. Oh, and New Hampshire is still waiting for an elector to arrive in the snowstorm up there, but we don't expect any problem. That'll leave us tied, 269 each. Senator, we're going to win this. Trust me."

Campbell shook his head, looking into the distance, then excused himself to take a call, grateful for a reason to leave the meeting. Defeat is one thing. Being responsible for that defeat is an unpardonable sin in the high stakes game of presidential politics. Campbell left the house to brief the campaign staff two miles away.

While television and online journals blasted the drama out of Bismarck and Phoenix, the conversation at the campaign headquarters had turned to critical gaffs by the Bridges team. One staffer recalled the five-week recount in 2000. The lore had it that Senator Joe Lieberman, without authorization, announced that the Gore team would not challenge late absentee ballots from military personnel overseas. The decision proved crucial as hundreds of potentially invalid Bush votes were allowed in Florida, more than enough to overcome Bush's slim margin during the recount. A few days later Gore conceded the election.

"You think James Baker would have done that?" said one political consultant exasperated with the Bridges legal team. "He was one mean sonofabitch, but he was really, really good. He would have gotten every damn one of those ballots thrown out, even if they'd come from wounded paraplegic Medal of Honor winners. We needed a Jim Baker." Campbell caught the tail end of the conversation as he arrived, and the sting was severe.

"Listen up, everyone. We lost two electoral votes today, possibly sending the election to Congress to settle," he began. "We'll be in court tomorrow morning with a challenge to the process in those states and we've got a good case. Meanwhile we need to get ready for the fight in Congress. I don't have to tell you how brutal this is going to be. The situation is completely unprecedented. It's been nearly two hundred years since a presidential election was thrown into the House. No one really knows how it'll work, but the Constitution is pretty clear. There will be challenges to the electoral votes, but if those fail, the House will then elect the president. Each state gets one vote, so we have to win twenty-six states."

The room filled with cries of "holy shit!" and "what the fuck?" as the campaign aides absorbed Campbell's update. "I know, it sounds crazy—Wyoming gets the same vote as California. But that's the way it is. We'll be working through the night to figure this out, and we'll meet again tomorrow after we've talked to the Democratic leadership in both houses. Melody will be here shortly with more information." Campbell left the room and returned to the Bridges home, feeling unwelcome in either location.

Melody Banks stood on a side porch, fighting off the anger and recriminations, trying to make sense of the day's events. The scant December daylight was quickly fading as storm clouds blanketed the quiet Chesapeake countryside. She had been grateful for the campaign's decision to locate here, miles from Washington's political fishbowl and all its distractions. But this evening she longed for her favorite watering holes and restaurants and friends with whom she could commiserate. She longed to be a "civilian" as the election drama grew more bizarrely grim. Her contemplation was interrupted by a shout from the room where the group had gathered around a large television.

"Melody! Get in here!" came one of the voices glued to a TV monitor. "It's New Hampshire. Something's going on there."

At half past four the final Democratic elector trudged through a snow bank to enter the North Main Street steps of the Greek revival State House, the nation's oldest. Greeted by a state trooper and escorted up a grand staircase to the legislative chamber, Walter Carney joined his three colleagues outside the governor's office.

"That's really some storm," said the upstate retired civil servant, as he removed a heavy coat and slipped off his shoe rubbers. "Sorry I'm late. Are we ready to go?"

"Have you been following what happened in North Dakota and Arizona?" asked the state Democratic chair. "We lost two votes out there. Makes us the tie votes. Crazy way to make history." Carney, who had not been following the news on the ride from Berlin, was confused, but he followed the group into the

legislative chamber to get on with their business. The weather
was turning worse and everyone wanted to get home or into a
local hotel as soon as possible.

Vera Sample, the New Hampshire Secretary of State, a protégé
of the governor and an up and coming Republican star, had been
pulled aside by a lawyer from Carlton Espy's team and briefed
that one of the electors might change her vote. Stunned, she
nevertheless took in her instructions and made final notes to
properly orchestrate the process.

"We were going to have the ceremonial vote here in the anteroom and let you folks go, but there are some press and a few
observers in the chamber, so we'll move in there." The official
wanted to get through the proceedings as soon as possible to
avoid the furor she witnessed a few minutes earlier on CNN.
"Everyone ready?"

"Wait, I think Virginia's in the ladies room," said the state party
chair. As she moved toward the restroom, Sullivan emerged. "I'm
here", she said softly, dabbing the perspiration from her forehead.
"Let's go."

Dispensing with any speeches, pledges, or prayers, the official quickly moved to the formal vote, reminding the electors
of the rules and ordering the distribution of ballots to the four.
Carney was selected to formally record the votes. Sullivan's
three colleagues marked their ballots and returned them to the
Carney, who read their markings. Each verified their vote for
Senator Bridges.

"Virginia, can I have your ballot?" The Secretary of State, who
now understood where the voting was headed, repeated, "Virginia? Are you all right?"

Sullivan sat slumped in her chair, breathing heavily, eyes open
but unresponsive. The group came close to the large woman they
had known for decades as a pillar in state Democratic circles.
Someone cried and another called out for a doctor. Standing
helplessly in a circle around the still body, no one knew what

more to do for her but wait for medical assistance. "Should we lay her down and try CPR?" asked one.

The audience rose from their gallery seats to get a better view of the confusion on the chamber floor, while the handful of press grabbed phones to call editors. Television cameras zoomed in on the chaos unfolding around Sullivan.

An emergency medical team arrived shortly and checked Virginia's vital signs. Finding a rapidly fading pulse, they lowered her heavy body onto a gurney and started to move her to a waiting ambulance.

"She's slipping away," whispered one EMT nurse to another. A doctor appeared from the hallway and moved the group aside to attend to Sullivan. After a minute of examination, he shook his head and stood. "Let's get her to the ambulance. Call St. Mary's to be ready for us."

The Secretary of State noticed Virginia's ballot as it fell from the woman's swollen, pale fingers. She reached down to retrieve it but thought better of the move. "Walter, I know this is indelicate, but we have a Constitutional process to resolve and we have to do it soon, given all that's happened today. Can you pick up her ballot and report her vote?"

"Well, I don't know, Vera. Is that allowed? Tammy, what do you think?" Carney asked of his party chairwoman. "I guess so," she said. "At least that way we could get this over and get to the hospital and check on Virginia." Carney retrieved the ballot from the floor and read her scribbled words.

"No, this can't be right!" he said. "She wrote Holland! She was obviously confused!"

The Secretary of State took the ballot from a stunned Carney and placed it with the other ballots. "The voting is adjourned. Let's pray for Virginia."

"No! You can't do this! There's no way she would have voted for Holland! You can't count her ballot!" Carney was apoplectic but unsure where to take his tirade. "This is outrageous!"

"Walter, she wrote down Holland and she signed the other documents. We'll just have to let the lawyers work it out." With that final declaration Sample left the Statehouse Chamber and returned to her office, where two election lawyers assigned by the governor attested the validity of the elector's ballots and certificates of attainment, made the requisite number of copies and sealed the envelopes in a pouch for transfer to Washington to join electors' documents from the other states voting on that day to elect the next President of the United States.

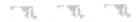

The Bridges team, reeling from the day's earlier events, stood gaping at the newscast coming from Concord. "Get somebody there now!" yelled Todd Campbell to a deputy, who was on the phone to the state chairwoman.

Two lawyers from the state party were en route to the State House. Senator Bridges ordered a call to the Democratic senator from New Hampshire, hoping to make some sense of the mess unfolding in the last state to cast its electoral votes.

Melody Banks slipped into her bedroom office and closed the door. She dialed a number that she had hoped she could lose but was now frantic to call. "Jackson, it's Melody. Have you been watching? Yeah, it's a nightmare. But it all makes sense now. That's what all this was about. Eldon Mann somehow converted three of our votes. At least we think it's three. The third was in the hand of a woman who may have died just as she was voting. That'll be fun for the lawyers."

"I don't know where all this is heading, but can you run one more check on Hartsell and Vaughn and now this woman Sullivan? I'll get you some data on her. If the lawyers can't overturn these votes right away, we're going to need something to go on if we're going to get anywhere with the Congress next month."

Obtaining a reluctant agreement from Cripple to jumpstart his now unfunded operation, Banks returned to the room, now crawling with advisors with no idea of what to do next. Of all the strange aftermaths of presidential elections, this took the cake. The day began with anxiety and now turned into outright madness.

Otherwise measured lawyers were screaming into cell phones, several juggling two devices. The senator who started the day as the President-elect gestured wildly at his top legal aide, who was also yelling at someone on the other end of his cellphone. Melody Banks sat in the nearest chair, dropped her head between her knees, closed her eyes, and covered her ears. *This simply can't be happening. And there is absolutely nothing I can do to stop it.*

"Senator, I need to speak to you," she placed her hand on Bridges' back and steered him into the nearby kitchen.

"Can't this wait, Melody? I got this call with Senator Towns."

"It'll only take a minute, I promise." Banks was trembling. "I think I know what happened today and how it was done. I need to get away for a couple days and figure it out and come up with a plan. And beside, this mess is in the lawyers' hands. I don't have much to add at this point."

"Well, if you think you find something that can turn this around, fine. But stay in regular touch with me. I can't have you off some-place where I can't find you quickly." He took a cellphone from his personal body man and spoke into the receiver. "Norm, thanks for taking the call. Yes, we've been watching. Unbelievable. What can you tell me about this woman Sullivan? And what can we do about it?"

As Bridges listened to the New Hampshire senator, Banks moved from the kitchen through the chaotic living room scene, stopping briefly to interrupt Campbell, letting him know she would be out for a while, but that she could be reached on her cell. She packed the few clothes she had brought to the Bridges home weeks earlier, stuffed her backpack with her laptop and various charging cords and papers, and slipped quietly out a side door to her car.

She drove slowly across the Severn River into the historic town that had briefly served as the infant nation's capitol. She turned onto Main Street and slowed at the large plaque marking Mann's Tavern, site of the 1786 Annapolis Convention, which created the Constitutional Convention. The latter event crafted the document that created the Electoral College. *They sure fucked that up*, she thought, forcing a smile as she realized the irony of the connection.

CHAPTER 40

The Bridges campaign filed a dozen legal briefs in Arizona and North Dakota, each citing numerous irregularities in the states' electoral voting. Todd Campbell's team camped out in Federal district court in Boston to challenge the New Hampshire vote count, claiming that Virginia Sullivan, now on life support in a Concord hospital, was incapacitated during the proceedings. Moreover, that the handling of the ballots was tainted by the Republican Secretary of State.

"Of course, even if we win the argument on Sullivan, we still have a big problem," noted the lead attorney in Boston during a call to Campbell and Senator Bridges in Annapolis. "If we kick out her vote our people can't re-vote with a friendly elector. You can't go back and have a do-over. The law is pretty clear about that. Her vote would simply go away and we'd only get three out of New Hampshire, leaving us under 270. Same thing's the case in Arizona and North Dakota."

"So what's our strategy here?" asked Bridges, groggy after a full night of calls and meetings. "If the court agrees with your assessment, where are we? Do we just go out and concede the election? I'm just not understanding this."

"Senator, we have a lot of options left before we even remotely consider a concession. In fact, I think we could win a stay on the counting of the electoral votes, which would freeze the process. And who knows how the Supreme Court will rule." Todd Campbell had rebounded from his guilt-ridden angst of the previous day and was in fighting litigation mode. "And we'll have overwhelming public opinion on our side. That's significant, especially if this is thrown into the Congress. Those guys won't want to go against the outrage at what Holland has done."

"I'm not so sure about that," replied Bridges. "These people running the Congress are tough bastards. They're immune to reason and seem to care less what critics say. I'd give us no more than a forty percent chance of prevailing in Congress. There's not a Republican down there who will bolt from the leadership and see me elected. We have to win this in the courts. And we need to find a smoking gun that would somehow link these three people to the Holland campaign."

"Does anyone know where Melody is?" he shouted to the group.

Melody Banks and Pima Grantham hovered over bowls of pho at Grantham's favorite Vietnamese restaurant a few blocks from the *Politico* offices. Finishing the dish of broth and noodles with a loud slurp, Grantham downed her tea and continued to update Banks, who had eaten in silence since their order arrived.

"The DNC and the congressional leadership are bouncing off the walls," she said. "Every one of those guys is absolutely confident that the switched votes won't hold and that the courts will reverse. But I'm not so sure. I spent last night talking with Stan Brand, you know, used to be senior counsel for the Speaker."

"He's a rock solid Democrat," she continued, "but he told me your folks are in trouble, that whatever the state and lower courts do, the Supreme Court is likely to leave those votes in place. The only possible challenge is whether or not the Sullivan woman actually marked her ballot and signed the certifications herself."

"But even then," interrupted Banks, "they can't order a re-vote, so if those one or two or three votes are thrown out we don't have a majority and it goes to the House, where we are really screwed."

"Unless...unless," said Grantham, who had already gamed out the scenario. "You can somehow prove that these votes were bought—promise of an appointment, money, or anything of value. You get that and bam! Bob's your uncle." The quaint phrase inherited from her grandmother had always pleased Grantham, though most who heard it were left puzzled.

"The Vice President told you that Eldon Mann had to be stopped, that he was a criminal," said Banks. "What do you think he meant?"

"Hard to say. He clearly believes Mann is unethical, that he wasn't serving the President's best interests. But we were cut off when the Secret Service started pounding on the restroom door. I've tried to get back in touch with him but no luck."

"It's got to be him," replied Banks. "No one else could have pulled this off. And we know he set up that operation in Leesburg. But he's smart enough to cover his tracks. He'd have put some distance between himself and whoever got to these people. There's only one person we know who spoke to Hartsell and another elector—a Nashville lawyer named Lydia Elving. She's wired into serious Republican circles. Our lawyers are serving her to be deposed as soon as possible. Can you look into her?"

"Sure, I'll call her myself." Grantham made a brief note on her phone, paid the bill and left Banks to place a new call to Jackson Cripple.

"Why don't you come out here so we can talk without distractions?" asked Cripple. "I need to go over what we pulled up on Virginia Sullivan. I don't want to do this on the phone, secure or not, probably not."

Banks didn't want to make the ninety-minute drive to Cripple's country house near Sperryville, where she would likely drink too

much wine and crash in yet another strange bed. She was still sleep
deprived and needed to get healthy quickly. That meant no late
nights and no alcohol. Cripple was a very bad influence. Yet she
knew his work was crucial to any success the Bridges team might
have in the coming weeks. She set out along I-66 and missed the
proper exit. Backtracking from Front Royal, she arrived at the
dirt road leading to Cripple's house as the winter sun disappeared
behind threatening clouds.

"Melody!" shouted her ace investigator as she trudged up the
hill to his porch. Several cats scrambled as she climbed the steps to
the large antebellum home Cripple had owned since abandoning
Washington a decade earlier. "D'you have any problem finding it?
It's been awhile. I should have sent a car for you." If he hoped his
high spirits would lift Banks from her funk, he was disappointed.

"No, no problem," she said. "Pretty far out of the way, though.
Don't you get bored out here?"

"I don't know that word," he laughed. "Come on in. I've got
a fire going and a really magnificent Chateauneuf de Pape I've
opened just for you."

"OK, Jackson, but just one glass. We've got work to do.
Where's Bonnie?" she asked after Cripple's longtime girlfriend
and collaborator.

"She's coming from town. Wanted to pick up some good bread
and cheese," he said. "We're gonna eat well tonight. And you're
going to be here awhile. You won't be going to sleep anytime soon.
The guest room is all yours."

Banks sighed and gave in to his control of the evening's affairs.
And anyway, she needed a break, someone else to take charge. He
steered her into a large foyer fronting a massive spiral staircase
leading to the two upper floors. They entered an inviting study
with deep upholstered loveseats facing each other, a crackling
fireplace along a nearby wall. The room was lined with walnut
paneling and photos of Cripple's dogs. No political memorabilia
or ego photos with politicians. A large original Ansel Adams print

of Yosemite's Half Dome hung over the fireplace mantel, a bauble Cripple gave himself after a particularly lucrative project. A thick file rested on the table between them, next to two glasses and the bottle of the stunning Rhone wine. *This is going to be ok,* thought Banks. *I'm just going to enjoy myself.* For the first time in months she let her phone die and didn't look for a charger.

Over a dinner of Bonnie's lamb chops, roasted root veggies and wine, they traded news and gossip about mutual friends and old boyfriends and girlfriends, consciously avoiding work. Cripple decided they would need clear heads and sharp judgment the next morning, and steered the conversation away from his most recent discoveries.

After downing large bowls of salted caramel gelato, they moved back to the fireplace for more wine and no talk of campaigns, electors, or the legal and Constitutional issues dominating the national news at that moment. At ten, Melody collapsed under a down comforter and slept soundly for twelve hours.

CHAPTER 41

After checking the online summaries, The Rake skimmed newspapers neatly arranged on his huge oriental redwood desk, looking for articles about the National Security Relocation Act. Columnists from every ideological corner blasted the idea since Chairman Lismore had gone public with the legislation. The coverage was scathing, and in different hands, that would have been enough to torpedo the plan. However, Lismore was a stubborn, tireless promoter of his pet interests and he had a hold on enough House colleagues to give the Act some semblance of credibility.

Thompson was invisible in the press accounts, and that suited him just fine. His payoff would not be in publicity but in the financial windfall that would accompany the legislation's progress. Lismore would maneuver potential clients to The Rake's firm, and each would pay upwards of forty thousand a month for the privilege of being represented by one of Washington's most influential lobbyists.

A special trade group of these companies would be established by Thompson, given a patriotic sounding name – "Building a More Secure Future" – and staffed with Thompson loyalists and handpicked Capitol Hill veterans. If they could keep the

Act alive for a year or more, Thompson would reap millions in retainers. After strategic contributions to Lismore's cosponsors' upcoming campaigns, he figured he could net twenty, even thirty million dollars.

A Thompson staffer entered the office, near breathless after digesting the endless press commentary about the Electoral College meltdown. "Tommy, this is crazy! What's going to happen next?"

"I don't care," he said. "In fact, you shouldn't care. Aren't you supposed to get me the data on those companies that would benefit most from the Lismore bill? I need to get that to Lismore today, dammit. And the CEO contact info on each one of them. Got it? Now go!"

Thompson had learned to shut out all information that wasn't relevant to the project at hand, and a Constitutional crisis was not only irrelevant, it was a bothersome distraction. On the other hand, the electoral mess would give cover to his "pigeons" – as The Rake referred to his covey of friendly Congressmen – as they embarked on their important fact finding missions to Australia, Brazil, and Berlin. He reviewed his checklist of to-dos, assigning key staffers to coddle and indulge spouses and staff traveling with the CODELs. *We want the pigeons to come home to roost in our pen,* he thought.

"Jimmy!" he yelled into the speakerphone to Congressman Lismore. "You ready for Sydney? I've got some great stuff for you to do there. My good friend Don Henry has arranged an amazing tour of the Hunter Valley vineyards. Sending it along now. Check your email. And Jimmy, that list you asked for, it'll be in your inbox by the end of the day. If you could make a few of those calls before you leave tomorrow it would be great. I'm gearing up here and throwing every resource I've got at the bill."

Receiving assurances, Thompson wrapped up the call with chitchat about the election nightmare – "Yeah, it's unbelievable. I've been reading everything and I can't make heads or tails of it.

But it looks like the President might actually pull this out. That's damn good for the country."

Like a buzzard on a telephone line, The Rake surveyed the political landscape, and only saw endless roadkill.

CHAPTER 42

Banks had worked nonstop since rising two days earlier to review Cripple's new data. After a long sleep and a vigorous run, she was refreshed. She set about the task of briefing Senator Bridges and Todd Campbell's legal team by phone. She decided to stay on Cripple's farm until she had all the pieces in place. Cripple was wired with every imaginable communication and research tool, and she was now grateful for the distance between her and the Washington-Annapolis axis that had been her life for six weeks since election day.

"Jackson," she said, "you've got to help me frame all this information to make the country angry. That's the only way we'll convince Congress to do the right thing."

"And we have to lay the whole damn illegal conspiracy at Eldon Mann's feet. That's the only way we'll get to the President."

Pima Grantham had been calling Banks daily to exchange updates and Banks agreed, with the team's approval, to a background *Politico* interview on the Bridges strategy. "It's time to toss a grenade into Holland's rats nest," she explained to the Senator's advisors still sequestered in Annapolis.

The President's speech to the nation after the Electoral College fiasco had been a *tour de force*, or at least he thought so.

"My fellow Americans, the events of this week surrounding the Electoral College vote have been remarkable, to say the least. I have reached out to Senator Bridges to offer any assistance needed to help make sense of the voting and bring an end to the long confusion we have endured to elect our next president. My campaign and White House staff will do everything we can to settle this election once and for all. Supporters of both campaigns deserve that. The American people deserve it."

"In the meantime, I will continue to serve our nation as your President and Commander in Chief during this difficult time. As you know, last week we struck another resounding blow to terrorist factions determined to harm this country and its citizens. Last night I ordered air strikes against Islamic radicals in Yemen and along the Syrian border."

"I am pleased to report that our heroic military units in the field have overwhelmed terrorist strongholds in western Pakistan and near the Afghanistan border with Tajikistan. Our commanders there report three dozen senior Islamic State leaders have been captured or killed. We are determined in our resolve: we will not rest until every jihadist responsible for the heinous October attack has been caught or killed. "

"As we near the sacred holiday season I want to assure each of you that our top priority is to make our nation secure. As Americans we cherish our freedom, and it is my responsibility to protect that freedom at all cost. Thank you for having me in your home tonight. God bless your family and God bless America."

Holland failed to tell the nation that a near-unanimous sentiment among his intelligence advisors was a totally different assessment of the Capitol bombing. Earlier that morning Holland reviewed the CIA's latest report.

TOP SECRET MEMORANDUM

December 18, 0700

To: The President

Via: The Chief of Staff

From: Director of Intelligence Services, Central Intelligence Agency Director, Federal Bureau of Investigations Director of Weapons Programs, Department of Energy

We have concluded our analysis of the Capitol bomb fragments, and obtained verifiable intelligence that establishes the source of the device and the possible suspects involved in its transport and detonation.

In early October an individual of eastern European origin managed to enter the U. S. on the Mexican border, with a shipment of small medical devices. His import papers were in order and he was allowed entry. There are no radiation detectors at this location. Sometime earlier the suspect acquired a quantity of explosive material from former Soviet bloc scientists and assembled the device that was detonated at the Capitol.

We have initiated an international search for the individual who brought the device into the U.S., and for suspects involved in its transport to Washington and detonation. As noted earlier, we are also investigating the malfunction of radiation detectors deployed around the city.

While we continue to find no connection to any terrorist cells in the Mideast, we will continue to pursue that possibility.

"Well, that's interesting," said the President to Alistair Muse, as the CIA briefers left the room. "But until we're certain we're gonna keep up the pressure on these people. They took credit for the attack, and beside, even if they didn't set it off they'd have done it if they could've. And they're sure as hell out to kill Americans wherever they can."

"Now if you'll excuse me I have to get to Gainesville. I've got a football game to attend." The President dismissed his staff with a wave.

Mann had tried to discourage the President's travel for recreation that weekend, especially with the election legal battle beginning. But Holland was growing increasingly restless, holed up in the Orlando White House. A steady stream of visits from old Florida pals and endless ESPN programming had grown thin. Each morning photos of Holland meeting with advisors and consulting foreign leaders were orchestrated to present a Commander in Chief on top of the crisis.

During the drive to the Air Force base and Marine One, Holland took a call from Eldon Mann. "Mr. President, it's a dangerous moment in this election process and we can't expose you to problems out there. Soon enough it'll lighten up, but until then we've got to be extra careful."

"Eldon, you can handle all these details, but I've got to get out of here more, see some real people. Watch a goddamn football game. How dangerous can that be? Not counting the nut cases out there who wanna shoot me."

Mann doubled the security detail and other traveling staff to make sure the President was surrounded by a protective bubble. Each moment was now managed to keep the President from disrupting the maneuvering Mann had put in place to reverse the election.

"I want to put some pressure on him!" yelled Calvin Bridges to his advisors, as Holland finished his televised address. "And this offer of cooperation? What the hell is that? Has his office reached out to us in any way?"

"He had his deputy call me," said Bridges' counsel. "Said they were contacting Justice to help if they do start an investigation. Totally useless."

"So is that it, Todd? That's all he had to say?" groused a frustrated advisor. "Maybe we should ask the President to *order* a goddamn investigation. "Or maybe appoint a special prosecutor," said another. "Why don't you just call him back and tell him thanks a lot, but he can kiss your ass."

"All right, guys, let's calm down," said Bridges. "What'd we expect the President to say? He's conceding and calling on Congress to reverse the electors' votes? They're gonna play this out till the bitter end, one way or the other. Todd, let's go through the court cases."

Campbell walked the team through their appeals in the three state courts that had jurisdiction over how electors were appointed. "Unfortunately, we haven't settled on a compelling argument that the electors were selected in some unlawful manner, and, barring some clear evidence of coercion or bribery, that's likely what the cases will hinge on in the states. The Constitution simply says that the states will decide how electors are chosen. These three electors were chosen by the book."

"OK, so what can we expect in the federal courts?" asked Bridges. "We better do better there or we may not even get all the Democratic votes in the House next month."

"As you know, Melody's intelligence has opened up some new areas for us, and we're devoting all we've got to create a case for prosecutorial involvement," Campbell said. "But that's a tightrope walk, since we can't expect Justice Department intervention unless there's a credible smoking gun."

"We may be able to find a sympathetic judge...sort of what John Sirica did for the Watergate investigations, by kicking ass and holding the burglars by the throat until they squealed on John Mitchell." Watergate was a goldmine of analogies.

"We believe there was coercion of these electors by the President's team and even bribery and obstruction of justice. If we can prove that over the next few weeks we've got a good shot. A lot of the President's people had a hand in this. And if we can get some of them hauled before a judge, if nothing else we'll grab the high ground if the election is thrown into the House." He was unconvincing in his speculation that such a judge could be found.

Campbell's confidence had soared when Melody Banks gave him a preliminary briefing in advance of her call with the team. She had shielded Cripple's operation from the campaign's top lawyer, knowing that information could corrupt the legal strategy and even subject her – and certainly Jackson Cripple – to their own brutal examination.

"Todd, all this makes sense," said Bridges. "You and Melody have done an amazing job pulling all this together and getting us back on track. But it's still pretty thin stuff. We'll need a lot more before we can prove election tampering, much less criminal behavior by the President or his Chief of Staff."

"We'll get back together tomorrow to regroup. Now I need fresh air and some exercise." Senator Bridges pulled on a windbreaker and left the house with his Secret Service detail for a cigar and an evening jog around the property with his two golden Labs.

CHAPTER 43

The Democratic National Committee was in full message attack mode. Top party officials, members of Congress, and partisan talking heads shuttled from MSNBC to CNN to the network shows. All were still trying to absorb the Electoral College explosion five days earlier.

"This is a travesty against not only American democracy but against the American people!" shouted one liberal, a former Gore campaign manager who recalled the 2000 nightmare in draconian terms. Her counterpart, an aging Reagan aide, invoked a constructionist interpretation of the laws governing the Electoral College.

"Donna, it was certainly unexpected, but not unprecedented. Moreover, read what the Founding Fathers said. What these principled electors did was conscience driven and entirely legal. They simply believed that President Holland was better for our country than Senator Bridges. Just get over it."

Liberal groups funded by Silicon Valley and Wall Street billionaires were buying every minute of television advertising time available, pushing their spots into every living room, messages designed to cast the President and his allies as immoral political thieves, hell bent on destroying the one man – one vote principle of American democracy.

Conservative groups pushed back with their own campaigns, screaming, "Don't let left wing liberals undermine the Constitution". Social media sites were swamped with $100 million in messages in one week alone. Search engine optimization companies made record profits pitting one side against the other. By weeks end the country was saturated with a national debate that was more confusing than ever.

Analysts charting media coverage determined that editorials were running 70–30% condemning the electoral betrayers. "It is a dark day in our country when three individuals can reverse the will of sixty-six million," read one column. "A day that will live in infamy." lead a scathing column in the *Times*. Others trashed the Electoral College itself, repeating a refrain heard after every close presidential election. The President's approval rating dropped to below twenty percent, lowest since Nixon during Watergate.

Eldon Mann was concerned with the public outcry only insofar as it might affect a later vote in Congress. So he accepted an invitation to meet with the Republican leadership of both houses of Congress to address their confusion about the coming battle. Gathering in Nashville at the home of the Senate Majority Leader, Mann faced his party's dozen top elected officials and as many senior staff.

"Eldon," opened Senator Crump of Tennessee, "what's happened here is certainly extraordinary. Yes, it could benefit our party and keep our President in office for another four years. That would be a welcome outcome. But it's putting us in a difficult position. We're getting a lot of heat from our constituents."

"Let me add to that," drawled the House Majority Leader, a Deep South political warhorse, and the most conservative member of the lower body. "I don't want Calvin Bridges in the White House. I don't think he's fit to run this country. And he sure won't protect us against our enemies. But Eldon, this is one hell of a mess we're facing in the House next month."

The senior political advisor to the Republican leadership group asked a more direct question of the White House Chief of Staff. "Mr. Mann, can you win these legal challenges in the three states and the federal courts? If not, you're not likely to get a majority of votes in Congress when challenges occur on the floor next month. If the courts determine that your campaign or your electors have acted illegally, you'll lose at least a half dozen Senate Republicans and... "

"Of course, Eldon, you can assure the President that we'll be comforted that nothing untoward was done to influence these electors to switch," interrupted Marshall Chapman, the Speaker of the House, who was no real friend of the President. His own advisors had urged Chapman's caution in managing the political battle, as he was next in line to become president if Holland was forced out of office. The rumors of Vice President West's resignation had been muffled by the electoral drama. *Could be Watergate all over*, his aide advised with a thin, unrestrained smile.

Mann waited until each participant was finished. "Gentlemen, let me assure you that nothing, I repeat, nothing questionable has been done to convince these Democrats to change their votes. And absolutely nothing of material value, or any administration position offered. We are on completely safe ground here."

"Our lawyers are working nonstop on this. We'll comply with any official request for documents or other information. Our hands are clean. But we won't hesitate to defend the process." Mann grew more assertive, not wanting to leave the party leaders believing there were cracks in the President's armor. "The Constitution and election law are clear on this: if neither the President nor Senator Bridges end up with at least 270 electoral votes, the House must act to settle the issue."

"And I don't have to explain to you the consequences of losing the White House to the Democrats," he finished. "Yes, the

President needs your help to see this through. But so does the country. All we're asking you to do is keep your powder dry until the legal cases run their course, probably to the Supreme Court later this month. If it goes to Congress, and we now think it will, we'll put every resource we have behind your work to resolve the election."

Mann rose and made the rounds to shake the hand of each Republican leader, thanking them for their presumed support, and lingering with Marshall Chapman. "Mr. Speaker, I need to come see you sometime next week. There's a matter we need to discuss in private."

"Of course, Eldon, I'll clear my schedule for it," said Chapman. "And be sure to tell the President how much we admire his fortitude and discipline during this difficult time. We've got his back here."

Sonofabitch would slice his mother's throat to get to the White House, thought Mann as he left the antebellum mansion tucked deep into the neighborhood of Belle Meade, the most Republican zip code in America.

After a particularly stressful call with his untethered associates in Florida, Jack Raglan walked a hundred yards to the Jasper, Alberta campground office to again complain about the lack of heat in his cabin, with icicles hanging in the shower. Temperatures had dropped to record lows and had stayed there for weeks.

"We're working on it, Mr. Smith. But we're out of heating oil and the company can't deliver for another two days. I know, I know, the electricity is spotty, too." The front desk clerk tried unsuccessfully to diffuse Raglan's ire, offering a space heater that Raglan knew wouldn't dent the bitter cold.

"I don't wanna space heater. I want heat," he said, trying hard not to frighten the clerk into making a call to his manager. "If I can't get heat today I'm outta here."

Raglan trudged alongside a snow bank, hating the endless cold and even more, hating JoJo and Delores for complicating his disappearance. The two had been at each other's throats for nearly a week, and JoJo had lost any control he had over his unbalanced wife. *Fucking idiots*, thought Raglan, entering the cabin. *Fucking Canada. Fucking goddamn winter.* Early the following morning, his bedroom more suited for freezing beef carcasses, Jack packed his bags and set out for Florida.

There was the matter of the second bomb hidden in the back of his SUV. Raglan considered dumping the device in the frozen Athabasca River, but decided that it might be useful at a later date. On the drive to Calgary he pulled into a state park and buried the lethal duffel bag near a campsite. As he neared the city he pulled into a used car lot in Bearspaw and negotiated four hundred dollars for the tired Jeep, and a ride to the airport, carrying only a dirty wad of clothing and several hundred thousand dollars in cash.

From the Jacksonville airport he took a taxi to a seedy strip mall along US-17 and a shop he had researched online, told the driver to wait, made his purchase and returned to the airport to await his ride. He did not want JoJo involved in this shopping outing.

"Goddammit JoJo, I've been waiting a half hour for you to get here. How fucking hard is it to find the goddamn airport?" Raglan was tired and cranky after a delayed flight to Chicago and on to Florida. Stuck between two large teenagers headed to Disney World, Raglan had been unable to sleep.

"Fuck it, let's stop at Waffle House," he ordered JoJo, who was vigorously fingering a bloody ear, a tic that sent Raglan up the wall. "Dammit JoJo, stop that! You're gonna infect that thing!" After downing a late breakfast of eggs, sausage, waffles, and three cups of bad coffee, Jack confronted JoJo. "So tell me what the hell is going on with you two? Start at the beginning."

"Well, Jack, it's complicated. Really complicated. First of all there was the money problem. Yeah, you helped with that, but

Delores ran through that envelope pretty quick. Then there's the motel room, which frankly I agree with her that it sucks. Smells bad, air conditioning don't work worth a damn. Drunks and hookers coming in all hours of the night. It just ain't workin' for us."

"OK, go on," Raglan held back, wanting to punch the weak, shaky man across the booth from him. "So what else?"

"Well," continued JoJo, who hadn't touched his double patty melt, fries and Coke, "Delores wants to get our boy and head back to Casper. She don't like Florida, don't know anyone here, can't work, you know. There just ain't nothin' good about it for her."

"Fine," said Raglan, pausing to make JoJo even more nervous, lowering his voice and staring into JoJo's eyes. "Go on back. Go today. Here's some more money to get you there. Fuckin' fly if you don't wanna do the drive. I'm tired of your and Delores's bullshit. Just get the fuck out of here and don't ever call me or ask me for anything ever again, you understand, you stupid piece of shit."

"But just remember. You go back and you're gonna be looking over your shoulder every goddamn minute, you understand? If it ain't the cops, it'll be me. And believe me, you don't want me on your ass. It won't be pretty."

"Jack, you know I won't say nothin'. You can count on me. I never let you down. But can you talk to Delores for me?" JoJo had hoped for Raglan's blessing and a little cash to get them on their way. "She won't listen to me."

"All right, let's go talk to Delores." Grim faced and weary, Raglan fell into the passenger seat of the Impala and immediately groaned. "Jesus, JoJo, what the fuck you been doin' in here? It smells like rotten food and dog shit all mixed together!"

"It's been hard, Jack. That's what I been tellin' you. It's been real hard." They pulled into the space in front of the couple's motel room and stood outside while JoJo fumbled for the room key. The sight was as Raglan expected, beer cans and whiskey bottles and fast food wrappers everywhere. He thought he saw a syringe as Delores swept away items from the small coffee table. "Shit, Jack, you coulda knocked. I'm not decent," Delores said, pulling sweatpants up over faded pink underwear and farting loudly.

"Sweetheart, Jack's come to visit. He's gonna help us figure out all this." JoJo didn't know who to fear more, Raglan or his wife.

"JoJo tells me you wanna go back to Casper, that so?"

"Hell yes," she said. "It stinks down here. We're out of money and I'm sick and tired of begging you for nickels and dimes. Don't forget, we know what's happened. You need us to keep quiet. What're you gonna do about that?"

"Delores, you got nothing to worry about. I've got some more money for you. But you can't go back to Wyoming, at least not now. We're not gonna argue about that."

"Fuck you, Jack. Fuck you and the goddamn bomb we delivered to Baltimore. Yeah, we figured that out right away. You fuckin' bombed the Capitol and killed a bunch of people and caused a goddamn war. That's what you did, Jack, and we know it. If you don't give us some money—a lot of money—we're gonna have a nice little talk with the FBI. Right, JoJo?"

"Now Delores, no one said anything about the FBI or talkin' to anyone. Jack, she's acting crazy now." JoJo stood behind Delores, who was high on meth from the pipe Jack spotted on a chair.

"Fuck you, too, JoJo. You're just a pathetic piss ant of a man." Delores was now on a roll and her husband wasn't about to stop her rant. "I mean every word of it, Jack. You take care of us or we're goin' to the Feds. I got the number and the address off the internet and by God I'll go there tomorrow and tell them everything I know. And I know that was Andrea that took the bag from us."

"Delores, I'm real sorry to hear all this," said Raglan. "Real sorry. But you're not gonna do nothin'." With those words Jack withdrew the silencer-fitted pistol he had bought an hour earlier and shot the woman between the eyes.

"Jack, no!" cried JoJo, backing up to the wall and sinking to the floor. Raglan turned to him and shook his head. "JoJo, I didn't want this. Really, I didn't. But you couldn't keep her straight, keep her off the hard stuff, and I couldn't have her go off the rails, especially now. I'm sorry, JoJo." With those parting words he pulled the trigger and killed his longtime cohort with a single bullet to the head.

After searching the drab, filthy room for any evidence of the pair's Wyoming connection, and removing his wallet and her bag, Raglan wiped the gun, removed the silencer and wrapped JoJo's hand around the handle. *Yeah, this looks like a murder-suicide,* he surmised. *Too bad. I really did like JoJo. If it just hadn't been for his crazy woman.* Finding JoJo's car keys, he closed the door and drove to a similarly downtrodden motel fifty miles up I-95.

Raglan slept through the afternoon and rose to find supper at another Waffle House a mile away. He put away a burger, a double order of hash browns and fried onions, and returned to the motel to sleep another ten hours. He awoke somewhat saddened by the deaths of JoJo and Delores and came up with an idea to soften the guilt. Raglan had set aside another five thousand dollars for their upkeep, so he placed this money in an envelope for Delores's aunt in Myrtle Beach. He had found the address on a postcard Delores had addressed to the relative who was keeping her son.

"Dear Mrs. Manson—I am a friend of your niece. I am sad to report that she and JoJo have had a terrible accident and both have died. I know they wanted the little boy to be taken care of, and they asked me to get this money to you to help out. Sincerely, Tom Smith"

Raglan bought stamps at a 7-11 and found a mailbox just off I-95 near Florence and dropped the envelope through the chute. He wanted to avoid post offices, where there might be cameras. Feeling better about the unfortunate events of the past two days, Jack filled up the Impala and headed north. He wanted to make Washington by nightfall.

CHAPTER 44

December 21

Melody Banks returned to the campaign headquarters refreshed from her time in the Virginia countryside. Jackson Cripple had armed her with mounds of evidence to launch a platoon of lawyers to bear down on the Electoral College culprits. Eldon Mann, Lydia Elving, and a half dozen White House and Holland campaign officials were served with papers requiring their appearance for depositions. Republican office holders in North Dakota, Arizona, and New Hampshire were next, though the electors themselves could not yet be reached– Vaughn and Hartsell had disappeared and Virginia Sullivan was still hospitalized in intensive care in Concord.

Todd Campbell and the campaign lawyers held a videoconference briefing for the Democratic Congressional leadership on the legal strategy and Banks organized a coordinated message campaign with their aides. With the holidays around the corner they were limited in their options, as most families were focused on shopping, eating, and sports on television.

The Bridges team and their allies would start with a blizzard of talking points for surrogates and television talkers to pound on members of the House of Representatives to reverse the Electoral

College voting, and to restore Bridges as the President-Elect. With Republicans holding a forty-seat advantage in the House, the task was formidable—twenty-one members of a party passionately opposed to Calvin Bridges had to be convinced to defy their leaders and vote with the Democrats. The Senate margin was just as daunting, but if the House upheld the votes of the faithless electors, the game was all but over.

Banks knew the only way they would prevail in Congress was to produce evidence of illegal behavior by Eldon Mann or his operatives. There wasn't enough time before January 6 to convince prosecutors to aggressively to go after Holland's team, and the chances for unqualified victories in the courts were slim. Banks talked with Jackson Cripple almost hourly, hoping for a break, the smoking gun that would reveal the elector conspiracy she was certain had occurred.

During her days with Cripple in Sperryville, Banks had reviewed the financial transactions Wayne Hartsell had made over the past few weeks. One of his subsidiary companies had purchased a Toyota Prius in Boston while Hartsell was there. A second Hartsell entity, an advertising firm in Chicago, had recently founded a subsidiary publishing house and made its first advance to an author's agent in New York, a one-man operation with a few obscure textbook authors in his inventory. The advance payment of three hundred thousand dollars was more than the revenue for all of the agent's previous clients combined. The money was then transferred to a yet to be identified account in a bank in, of all places, Portsmouth, New Hampshire.

"Sullivan is the key here," said Cripple. "There's a paper trail we will sooner or later be able to document. And if you can get Hartsell on the stand before some tough judge, he'll crack and their little plan will come unraveled. Unfortunately, we haven't found a trace of him or Stanley Vaughn."

"We don't have much time, Jackson. And Sullivan may not be alive to answer questions," said Banks. "Have you found any connection between Vaughn and Hartsell or anyone else we can go after? We've only got sixteen days before Congress votes."

"No, nothing," said Cripple, who had been convinced the Hartsell-Sullivan connection would be sufficient to blow the story wide open. "But surely this Hartsell-Sullivan stuff would light a fire under some prosecutor. We just have to figure out how to do that without tainting the evidence, since it wasn't retrieved in exactly a, uh, traditional manner. Maybe some friendly congressman would run with this. They operate under their own rules, right?"

Since the Capitol bombing, most members of Congress were still away from Washington with no plans to return until the January 6 date for certifying the electoral vote. With the Capitol and nearby offices sealed off for structural and radiation cleanup and repair there was no clear schedule for resuming any routine. Reoccupying the damaged buildings was at least a year away. Alternate space was being prepared to house the thousands of Members and staff necessary to manage the country's business. George Washington University would host the January 6 session and the two weeks of organization meetings Congress would hold to prepare itself for the coming session. Since no permanent legislative location had been found, there was talk of adjourning after the Inauguration until further notice, a proposal few Members of the majority party would argue against.

Other than resolving the Electoral College mess, and swearing in the President on January 20, there was little pressing Congressional business that couldn't wait. For matters that did require immediate attention, committee chairmen would arrange hearings outside Washington. Local officials—and their economies—would welcome the Congressional activity and the attention it would bring during the winter doldrums.

Since all House and Senate committees were controlled by Republicans, the task of provoking a congressional hearing into the electoral fraud allegations was daunting, to say the least. Despite demands from Democratic members, the chairmen of the two Judiciary Committees begged off, noting that the courts must complete their work before the committees would meet. The Republican leaders would shut down any proposal for action in other committees with relevant jurisdiction. There were plenty of excuses.

With two weeks before the showdown in the House, Democratic congressmen and other Bridges allies were forced to hold press conferences and seek appearances on television shows to cry foul. CNN was on the air with four hours of "Government in Crisis!" After interviewing Constitutional scholars describing the legal situation facing both camps, King moved to the flashy set used to project election night results, now covered with national maps indicating congressional districts in red and blue.

"Here is the challenge Senator Bridges faces in the Congress," said King. "Assuming the decision falls to the House next month, the Democrat must win the vote of twenty-six state delegations. Each state has one vote. Alaska, with 500,000 residents, has one. California, with 45 million, has one."

"Now, look at how the states shape up for this vote. Assuming each state House delegation votes along party lines, President Holland gets thirty votes and Senator Bridges gets seventeen. Even if you add the three states with an evenly split delegation, Senator Bridges ends up with only twenty votes. President Holland is re-elected."

"So how does Senator Bridges turn around nine states with a majority of Republican congressmen? That's the question for our panel of experts here today. And we should note that once the president is elected in the House, the Senate would act to elect the vice-president. That's further complicated because the incumbent Vice President may not serve in a second Holland administration. But first, to our panel to try to make sense of this most extraordinary political showdown."

Three liberals and three conservatives then launched into well-rehearsed talking points with little new to explain. After ten minutes of noise King interrupted the group and asked each to make a prediction of the outcome. An outspoken Democratic consultant declared: "I don't know who'll win, but I can damn near guarantee you that people are going to get indicted and go to jail before this is over."

On Christmas Eve the television coverage of the issue diminished to make room for feel-good programming, NFL football, and massive holiday advertising. *The Today Show* expanded its cooking and gift segments, and added an extra segment of carolers to its already shrunken news analysis.

Nightly reports from the Mideast and Gulf region noted thousands killed or injured by U.S. air raids ordered by the President. Retaliation from Islamic extremists produced another thousand casualties. Most had been civilian men, women, and children who had the misfortune of getting between U. S. military actions and terrorist revenge. U.S. forces, with a growing number of troops on the ground, suffered several hundred casualties and the loss of a few helicopters.

At the President's order, four hundred drone attacks were targeted at suspected militants. While the Holland administration reported the capture or death of several hundred radical jihadists, the CIA secretly confirmed only a dozen known terrorists taken out by the U.S. raids.

CHAPTER 45

Holland gave his traditional Christmas Eve televised remarks surrounded by several hundred U. S. Marines and their families. Many had taken part in the recent actions in the Mideast and were celebrating a homecoming with their Commander in Chief.

"My fellow Americans," began Holland. "I'm speaking to you this evening from Fort Bragg, North Carolina, with some real heroes. The men and women of the 33rd Marine Battalion and their families are here in this auditorium celebrating the holiday season, thanking God for a nation that has so many freedoms worth fighting for. We've been sharing egg nog and cookies and stories of Christmases past."

"The past seven weeks have been monumentally challenging. The confusing election results, the terrorist attack on our nation's Capitol, and the conflict in the Mideast have tested American resolve and the very Constitution we treasure. But we are a strong nation and we have come through these challenges intact and with our nation's leadership even stronger around the world."

"As we enjoy the holidays and prepare for the coming year, my family and I want to extend greetings to each and every one of you. I hope you will join me in praying for the safe return of our remaining military men and women in combat and for the lasting peace they are fighting to preserve."

"In closing, let me repeat the parting words of my favorite Christmas character, Tiny Tim, and say to you: "God bless us everyone!""

After the video wrapped, the President growled at his aide. "Dammit, Isidro, I told you to fix the goddamn teleprompter! I said I didn't want that Tiny Tim shit in there. I wrote in the Abraham Lincoln bit, you know, his Christmas message to the troops. What the fuck happened to that? For Christ sake!"

Holland pulled off his mike and stormed away, leaving the shaken young aide fumbling with equipment and once again wondering what other kind of job he might find. As he boarded Air Force One for the flight back to Orlando, he ordered his secretary to find Eldon Mann.

"So now what?" Holland barked into the phone before any pleasantries. "I've got the goddamn Speaker on my ass whining about the problems we're creating with this Electoral College vote and the media going crazy and all you can tell me is to sit tight?"

Mann had his hands full with legal issues emerging from the December 14 vote, and now he had to babysit the President with a positive update every few hours. "Eldon, I want the lawyers down here tomorrow. I want to know everything and I want to know it now."

"Mr. President, tomorrow is Christmas Day. Let's get everyone together in Orlando in two days and get you fully briefed. It's going well, believe me. We've got the law on our side. You should ignore these media polls and the background noise and focus on relaxing and enjoying the holidays with your family. It will get stressful soon enough."

"All right, but I want your team here first thing Sunday—no make that Monday morning. And Eldon, don't bullshit me. I need to be up to speed on this mess."

The President rang off and picked up a folder of urgent national security papers. He waved off an aide's reminder that several telephone calls were scheduled. He ordered a stiff drink and commanded that he not be disturbed. Holland turned on a television monitor to ESPN, where a lively young blond was reviewing the upcoming NFL and college playoffs. *Alistair Muse and the Mideast crisis can wait*, he thought, stretching in his recliner and switching to the NBA, where an aging LeBron James was leading the Cleveland Cavaliers to another win. By halftime he had drifted off, drink in hand.

Melody Banks joined her father for an uncomfortable twenty-four hours of Christmas joy at his retirement village near Philadelphia. Annoyed with her sister's refusal to devote little more than a drop-by with her father, she busied herself with a turkey and stuffing recipe favored by her late mother, stirring the gravy so loved by her father. Melody was determined to make the day as pleasant as possible despite his grumbling and her sister's lame excuses. "Dad, we're ready to sit down at the table."

"Not now, Melody. Can't you see we're watching this game? Your sister and I have a bet." Banks placed three wine glasses on the small table, lit candles, and walked onto the tiny patio facing a courtyard surrounded by dozens of units like her father's. She found the home three years earlier, paid a deposit and waited for her father to consent to move in. Making all arrangements on her own, Banks had juggled work and her father's affairs for nearly a decade, beginning with her mother's slip into dementia.

Barely manageable during normal times, her father's emotional needs had been overwhelming during Bank's 24–7 involvement in the presidential campaign. *And I thought the campaign was exhausting*, she thought. Lighting a rare Marlboro tucked into her purse, she exhaled a long plume of smoke and downed half her glass of pinot grigio. She reminded herself that she must read her sister the riot act as soon as possible if she was to take an extended vacation once the election was settled.

Congressman James Lismore and his CODEL arrived in Australia on Christmas Day with spouses in tow for the fact-finding work down under. The party took three days in Sydney to recover from the grueling first class flight from L.A., followed by a luncheon meeting in Melbourne, where Aussie pros awaited the tennis enthusiasts in the group. Two hours of formal discussions in Canberra, the dull backwater capital, and it would be off to Cairn and the Great Barrier Reef for a day of snorkeling and sun before returning to the States via Hawaii and more R&R after an exhausting Congressional mission. Lismore assured Tommy Thompson that on the return flight he would obtain commitments from the traveling party to help advance the Security Relocation Act, or at least to not trash it in public.

Jack Raglan's week in Washington had been a miserable exercise of hiding and roaming, a disappointing search for the mayhem he hoped to find.

He boarded a Blue Line Metro near his Springfield, Virginia, motel and rode into the District, making his way to Capitol South station, where he exited alongside three massive congressional House office buildings. With the Capitol shrouded in a protective cover, and security fences sealing off the grounds, Raglan could only imagine the damage his bomb had wreaked two months earlier.

He walked slowly around the perimeter of the Capitol grounds, joining a few dozen hardy tourists braving hazardous sidewalks slick with a film of ice. He paused in front of the Supreme Court to get a better view of the building—the white shrink-wrapping nonetheless revealing its caved-in northeast corner. Raglan pinched a batch of snuff from a tin and shoved it under his lip. Spitting a brownish blob on the whitewashed granite steps, he thought *I wish I'd been here to see it.*

As he walked toward Union Station, Raglan began to hatch a new plan of destruction. Deep in the woods of Canada, he had another bomb.

Christmas had never been a favorite time for Eldon Mann. Without his wife to go through the motion of holiday cheer, he made no pretense of celebration. There were no gifts to exchange or friends or relatives to dine with. He packed a small bag and booked an Amtrak train to New York, where he would join a sea of tourists on the busy streets as companion strangers until his return the following morning. Walking through Union Station to catch his train, he nearly collided with an unkempt, wiry figure in a heavy coat gazing at the ceiling.

"Fuck you, asshole!" grumbled the stranger. Apologizing, Mann saw a man he assumed was just another tortured character trying to stay out of the cold on the year's most depressing holiday for those alone. As he walked to the Acela tracks in the rear of the station he looked back at the man with a large spider tattoo covering his neck. Mann frowned and continued to his gate.

Senator Bridges' lawyers were on the courthouse steps in Bismarck, Phoenix, and Concord at nine am Monday, for meetings with state judges. The arguments were simple: the three electors had violated the intent of the state laws governing their selection and actions. The concept of the "faithless elector" was a myth, as every elector was presumed by the Constitution to support the candidate that won his state's popular vote. The three votes must be overturned and applied to Senator Bridges' total in those states.

President Holland's legal teams made an equally simple, but contrary case: the electors were chosen properly under the laws of those states and the Constitution protected their independence. Moreover, those states had taken no steps to bind the electors to any candidate. Both sides would request expedited rulings, as federal appeals were certain.

CHAPTER 46

The President was in a cheerful mood as he offered fresh squeezed orange juice and Danish to Eldon Mann and the legal team that had been waiting for several hours in a nearby holding room while Holland arose, finished his morning swim and a leisurely breakfast by the pool with his grandsons. Just before noon he entered the briefing room in khakis, golf shirt and the ever-present Commander in Chief jacket, ready to learn the state of his political fortunes.

"Any of you watch the Tampa Bay-Dallas game?" he questioned the room. "No? It was brutal. The Bucs get an early field goal, then bam!" he slammed the table with obvious pleasure. "The Cowboys score on eight straight possessions. Damn they're good."

"OK, whatcha got for me this morning? Are we winnin' or losin'?" The President's toddler grandson Henry padded around the room showing off his Christmas present, a talking Elmo doll. "I got Melmo!" he announced with a broad smile. The doll responded "It's Elmo's World!" Mann thought *It sure as hell is.*

"Mr. President, I assume you've read the summaries I sent last night," he began, certain that Holland had not opened the file. "So we'll be brief and bring you up to date and take your questions."

"Sure, makes sense," said Holland. "I've set aside as much time as we need. This is important and I want to be fully up to speed." The President punctuated his greeting with frequent glances at football replays on the monitor along one wall.

Mann and his team of lawyers walked the President through the events of the past two weeks and the legal challenges initiated in the three states. "We expect to get rulings no later than Wednesday. Arizona and North Dakota will likely find for us on the question of the states' role in selecting electors and reject Bridges' demands that the votes be reverted to you. New Hampshire is a question mark, in large part due to the unusual handling of the vote in Concord and the unclear state of the elector in question, Miss Sullivan."

"But however they rule, the cases will be in federal court by the end of the week and the Supreme Court immediately thereafter. Mr. President, I've asked Carson Ravenel to lay out how all this will play out." Mann turned to the esteemed former Solicitor General to continue the briefing.

"Mr. President, the issue before the court will turn on the precise wording in the Constitution that created the Electoral College. Not the *intent*, as Senator Bridges' lawyers will argue, but the actual words. And in this case you're on solid ground. The only legal test over the past two hundred years involved the ability of the states to bind electors. But that's not an issue here, as these three states had no such laws."

"In selecting electors and governing their behavior, the three states acted in strict accordance with the Constitution. The established law reasonably precludes any involvement by the federal courts in the selection of electors by the states. And there is no realistic argument for reversing their votes. Even if there was proven fraud there is no way those votes could revert. Thrown out, possibly. But reverted to Senator Bridges, no." Ravenel concluded, "And given the need to act before the House meets next Wednesday, the Court will likely err on the side of no intervention."

"And this is a friendly court. Seven-two." The President often threw out "seven-two" as shorthand for the judicial backstop for any challenge to the conservative agenda. "I can't imagine this Court acting to give the presidency to Calvin Bridges."

"Of course, we can never predict how the justices will finally rule," continued Ravenel, a distinguished Poppy Bush appointee who occasionally advised conservative causes. "But there is no question that the majority of these justices are originalists who tend to stay close to the literal reading of the Constitution. I can't recall a case during the past four years that they've ruled otherwise."

"So if I'm hearing you guys right, we're likely to win this thing," Holland added another small pour of clear liquid to his orange juice and walked around the perimeter of the conference table, stopping to pat this or that advisor on the shoulder. "I still won't believe it 'til I have my hand on the Bible on January 20, but I gotta say, I'm damn amazed. You've all done one hell of a job. One hell of a job! The country is in your debt."

"Now if you have time, stay for lunch and have a swim. Sure beats Washington right now. Eldon, can I grab you for a moment?" The President motioned for his Chief of Staff to follow him into the adjacent study.

"D'you talk to Marshall Chapman? I thought you said he'd be ok," growled Holland, now pouring another screwdriver into his tumbler. "We're likely gonna have the goddamn House voting on all this next week and the Speaker is telling me he may have to stay neutral. What the fuck's going on?"

"Mr. President," said Mann, holding up a hand to quiet Holland's outburst. "Chapman's a snake, we know that. And we also know he'd like nothing more than to have you go down, with no sitting Vice President, so he can become President. But when the House convenes next week the Speaker will be in the right place and he'll instruct the leadership to be in line."

"How can you be so fuckin' sure? Eldon. Dammit, we can win every fuckin' court case but if the House votes us down it's over.

And it's worst than over, we're totally humiliated and the vultures will set in—hearings, investigations, you name it. These cowards in Congress will jump ship like rats. I wanna know how you're gonna turn around the Speaker. Because if you can't, we should drop the whole goddamn thing right now."

Mann reflected on the nature of cowardice and his boss's willingness to cut and run at every turn. "Mr. President, Speaker Chapman has a personal problem that's about to come to light. If it does it'll cost him his job and destroy him personally. I'm helping make sure that doesn't happen, and he'll soon know it."

"Jesus, Eldon, more shit I don't wanna know. Just stay in close touch with me about this, you understand?" The President retreated into his palatial Florida mansion, leaving Mann to find his team and depart for the airport. There would be no lunch or swim.

CHAPTER 47

"New Hampshire is in," said Todd Campbell, entering Senator Bridges' dining room with one ear glued to his cell. The group looked up from their laptops and the candidate leaned over the table and seemed to pray. "We won on all counts." Repeating what his deputy was reporting from the state courthouse in Concord, he continued. "The Secretary of State has been ordered to inform the Speaker of the U. S. House to withdraw New Hampshire's submission of its four votes for immediate reevaluation for extreme irregularities in the electors' voting process."

Cheers around the table dissipated after Campbell's next report within minutes of the Concord verdict. The North Dakota and Arizona Supreme Courts rejected all arguments of the Bridges team, affirming the counts reported after Vaughn and Hartsell's votes. The discussion turned to the U. S. Supreme Court deliberations that would begin the next day. Campbell made an effort to paint the outcome as not only uncertain but potentially favoring Bridges. "This is completely uncharted territory," he explained. "Yes, I know it's a conservative court, but..."

One advisor after another interrupted to ridicule the notion that the Court might side with the Democratic candidate.

Campbell tried to regain the floor. "All I'm saying is that we have to make the case and wait. What the court states in its opinion could radically affect the deliberations in the House."

The Senator spoke in grim terms. "Todd, I appreciate your optimism, but we've seen this movie before, with Bush v. Gore, and that was with a five-four Court. We're looking at seven-two now. Yeah, the Court could somehow uphold the New Hampshire decision, but even with the restoration of those votes we're left without 270. We have to get ready to win this in Congress, and we have to do it by challenging the sheer immorality of what the President has done."

Melody Banks sat silent through the ninety minute free for all, checking her notes for the trip she would make the next day to Concord, to the hospital room where Virginia Sullivan hung somewhere between life and death.

The Supreme Court set the coming Monday for oral arguments in Bridges v. Holland, less than forty-eight hours before Congress would convene to debate the vote count. Written submissions were already en route to the justices' clerks, who would work furiously to digest the arguments and prepare their judges for the historic proceeding. Legal analysts bombarded the television commentary with predictions of each judge's likely leanings. Yet in such an unprecedented case the analysis usually boiled down to the political. *Seven-two*, repeated one talking head after another.

CHAPTER 48

New Years Day

"Mr. Speaker, thanks so much for seeing me today." Eldon Mann perspired profusely in the gulf coast humidity as he entered Speaker Chapman's antebellum home on the outskirts of Mobile. *Christ, it's January. How do these people live down here?* he thought, as Chapman's butler ushered him into a sitting room filled with antiques and paintings passed down from one Chapman to the next over ten generations of Southern tradition. Portraits of wealthy cotton merchants hung beside three Confederate officers and flattering oils of various Chapman women and children. A large curio cabinet displayed a collection of small pistols and knives sheathed in scabbards of whalebone or silver.

"Johnson, please bring Mr. Mann some of that fresh lemonade, will you?" Chapman motioned Mann to a French Empire loveseat and took the more comfortable, heavy Georgian chair to Mann's right. "All this came over from England and France to New Orleans at the turn of the century—the nineteenth I mean. Old Major Chapman—that's him over the mantle—he fought with Andrew Jackson in the Battle of 1812. Became one of Jackson's biggest supporters when he ran against John Quincy Adams in 1824. When Adams stole that election the Major pretty much carried the South for Jackson four years later. Would have shot Adams if that's what it'd taken. One tough bastard."

"So Eldon, what can I do for you?"

"Mr. Speaker, it's what I can do for you," Mann carefully calibrated his message, fully aware that Chapman's actions over the next week could spell success or doom for the President's reelection. "I was approached a few days ago with this. I can't tell you where it came from. In fact, I don't really know. But I do know that it's from no friend of yours or ours." Mann withdrew a large brown envelope from his bag and placed it on the handsome Hipplewhite coffee table between them. "I'll give you a moment to review this."

Chapman opened the clasp and pulled the first document, an eleven by fourteen black and white photo. The Speaker's face grew slack and ashen. He dropped the material to the table. "Eldon, where did you get this? What is this?"

"As I said, Mr. Speaker, I have no idea who sent it. All I know is that it came to me in the White House last week, no name attached. I asked my assistant to find out who delivered it but they came up dry. I haven't had anyone look at it to try to determine its origin. As you can see, it's best that no one else sees it."

"No message, nothing?" Chapman stuttered. "I mean, this is outrageous!"

"Well, Marshall," said Mann, "there was a message. The next day I got a call telling me that I needed to meet someone to discuss the contents of the envelope. Gave me a time and place and hung up quickly. I met the man in that park off the GW Parkway, you know the one where Vince Foster shot himself."

"So?" Chapman was now shaking. "So what did he want?"

"He wants you to resign. He seems to have had a relationship of some kind with the woman in that photo you just saw. Maybe her father. Says if you don't step down he'll put the full set on the internet. Says he has nothing to lose.."

"Eldon, I don't know what to say. This'll destroy me. It'll destroy my family and all I've built." Chapman turned away from Mann and moved to a large window opening to acres of wildflowers and meticulous landscaping. "I need some time to think about this."

"Mr. Speaker, next Wednesday you'll preside over one of the most historic proceedings the House has ever seen. Your leadership is critical to an outcome that will heal this country and move us ahead. We need you in that chair."

"But...but how can I...with this?" Chapman's shaking hand pointed to the envelope.

"Marshall, I have a plan. I believe we can take care of this guy. You're right—it's outrageous. It's extortion. We cannot let a great public servant be brought down by some grudge holding madman."

"What...what do I do?" the Speaker of the House, always ready for an argument, a debate, was now speechless.

"Do nothing, Marshall. I'll get back to you soon and let you know, but for now don't worry. Burn those photos and all of it. I have no other copies."

Chapman was near tears as he saw Mann to the door and to his waiting car. "Have a safe trip, Eldon. God bless you." As the car turned down the long, magnolia lined pebble driveway, the Chief of Staff turned to see the shaken Speaker in a large window. Mann smiled, recalling the Speaker's discomfort as he viewed photos of the shocking assignation Chapman had with a runaway teenager thirty years earlier.

The Mobile lawyer was serving as her court-appointed guardian while her parents were summoned from Panama. He was married with three children, a solid presence in Alabama legal and political society. In his handsomely appointed office near the federal courthouse, Marshall Chapman brutally beat and sodomized the young girl, who was discouraged from filing a complaint under the threat that she would be immediately deported. What Chapman had not known was that the young girl had a small camera in her bag and photographed the room, Chapman's framed diplomas, and her body, bloodied and bruised, before the attorney returned from his restroom to ease her out of the building.

If that wasn't bad enough, the poor girl got pregnant and had a child. Another photo showed the now forty-eight year old woman and a daughter who appeared to be afflicted with Downs Syndrome. The inscription read: *Maria Chapman, born Nov. 16, 1990. Died December 1, 2020.* A single page included in the material described the results of a DNA test performed on Maria after her death, on the same day the Electoral College had met. A notarized affidavit recounted her encounter with Chapman in the Mobile office, her ensuing pregnancy and childbirth, and her pursuit of justice as the only reason for making her complaint public. She wanted no money and refused to consider a private settlement. She had seen Chapman pontificating on television during the election dispute and was thrown into a deep depression. Her father encouraged her to take action.

Mann, of course, had fabricated the circumstances surrounding his receipt of the incriminating information he had delivered to Chapman. There was no White House delivery. No meeting with a relative of the wronged woman. No threat to the Speaker's political position. The information had been unearthed during one last push by the secret Stanning operation to produce data Mann might use for advantage when the Congress would deliberate the outcome of the election. Jonas Stanning uncovered the Panamanian woman when she called the Speaker's home, asking to meet with him to settle a dispute. Chapman had been one of a dozen Congressional targets submitted by Mann through Carlton Espy. An Espy lieutenant had flown to Panama and retrieved her information, promising to bring Chapman to heel.

The Speaker has a right to be frightened, thought Mann. *And we'll keep him that way for a while.*

278

CHAPTER 49

January 2

Virginia Sullivan was moved from the ICU to a private room in a quiet wing of St. Mary's Hospital in downtown Concord. The constant media scrum that lingered in waiting rooms and on the pavement outside the facility had shrunk to a young television assistant and a local reporter who checked in with the nurses desk every hour or so. The furor that attended Virginia's vote and her collapse three weeks earlier had subsided as the public turned its concern to an early snowstorm that gripped much of New England with winds whipping the region, driving temperatures to record lows. Eighty thousand homes were without power, and local rescue efforts were stymied by blinding whiteouts and ice-covered roads.

Melody Banks had been waylaid in Boston as she made her way toward Concord, hoping to be at Sullivan's side when she emerged from unconsciousness, or at least pick up a shred of information that might lead to something more. It was a long shot for sure, but the only one Banks could conceive as the final political showdown was nearing.

Senator Bridges' team had five days to produce anything that would convince Congress to reverse the electoral fiasco in their favor. There was little confidence in the looming Supreme Court verdict, so Bridges had been calling dozens of colleagues in Congress—Republicans as well as Democrats—to gauge their sense of the coming vote. While each had been cordial and urged him to keep up the fight, he had been given little encouragement that twenty-six House delegations would oppose the President.

Banks was certain Virginia Sullivan was the key to proving the Holland crowd had committed illegal acts in convincing her to switch her vote. There was little in Sullivan's background that would predict such a partisan betrayal, but there was something odd about her behavior hours before the electors met. And there was the matter of Wayne Hartsell and his unusual spending in and around Portsmouth the day before the vote, as discovered by Jackson Cripple's investigations. Pima Grantham had been unable to pry open Sullivan's financial accounts to spot any large deposits, and Hartsell had been unavailable for comment.

Since neither Hartsell nor Stanley Vaughn could be found and served, the Bridges lawyers were left with various state officials to interrogate. Eldon Mann had postponed his own deposition until after the Congressional debate. Sullivan was in no condition to be deposed, though lawyers waited in nearby offices in case she experienced a sudden recovery. The clock was ticking and Bridges' legal options were evaporating.

Finally reaching Concord by hitching a ride with a Boston EMT nurse headed north in an all weather vehicle, Banks arrived at St. Mary's and took a seat in the small waiting space near the nurses' station on Sullivan's floor. A bored uniformed policewoman sat nearby, paging through a stack of gossip magazines. Melody had a brief conversation with the duty nurse and powered her laptop for a conference call with Senator Bridges' team in Annapolis.

Bridges had been none too pleased by Bank's absence as the political team was crashing to develop a strategy for the House vote, but he had come to respect her judgment and gave her room to maneuver. She had been right far more often than wrong, a record he recognized as unique among his team of advisors.

"I'm here in the hospital now," she reported to Annapolis in a hushed voice. "I can't speak up, but there's not much to report anyway. I can tell you that Sullivan is still out of it, there's no chance she'll just pop up and give us what we want, at least not immediately. I'm going to hang around here and talk to some more people. The weather is awful and I don't know how long it'll take me to get back. But I still think Virginia Sullivan is the key and I can't leave until I exhaust every possibility."

"Melody, this is Cal," injected the Senator. "We're bleeding here. No one thinks the Court will help, and I'm not getting anything positive from the Members I've spoken with. You've got to come up with something, and fast. Our friends on the Hill are nervous and no one thinks we can win without a credible smoking gun. Let us know the minute you've found anything. Thanks. And stay warm up there."

After sitting through a half hour of chatter among the legal and political team, Banks signed off and walked the halls, stretching her long, stiff limbs and downing a second bottle of water. She turned toward her chair when she saw a slight female figure emerge from Sullivan's room, accompanied by an middle aged woman and a doctor. The three huddled briefly by the nurses' station and disappeared into a nearby office. Banks hurried to the nurse and asked, "Can you please tell me who those women are who were visiting Miss Sullivan?"

"Not sure, but I think one was her daughter. Had to be relatives since no one else is allowed in her room."

"Thanks," replied Banks. She gathered her laptop and backpack and hurried to the door where the three had entered. Finding it locked, she knocked. There was no response, so she ran to the stairway and down five flights to the lobby, where she hoped to encounter the pair. As she was questioning the desk volunteer, Banks saw Constance Appleby and her daughter exit an elevator.

Breathless, she confronted the couple. "Excuse me, my name is Melody Banks, and I have been here hoping to see Virginia Sullivan when she wakes up. I understand you are her relatives. Can we talk?"

"I don't know," said the older woman, holding tightly onto her daughter's arm. Both seemed unusually fragile, possibly ill. "Are you a reporter?"

"No, I work for Senator Bridges and I'm trying to get some answers about what happened with the Electoral College vote a few weeks ago. It's really important, believe me."

"We don't have much to say about that," replied Constance, shaking her head, looking around the room, seeking a way out of the conversation. "We're just here visiting her. She's in bad shape."

"Can we get a cup of coffee or something to eat? It's too cold to go outside, but there's a cafeteria in the basement." Banks was frantic to question the pair.

"We're trying to get to Portsmouth by dark if we can. They say the interstate is clear now. We need to get to Virginia's house if possible." Appleby shrugged. "If you want to ride with us I guess that would be ok. I've got a big SUV that'll go anywhere. Don't think it'll help you but that's up to you."

Banks closed her eyes and gushed, "Thank you! Thank you so much! I certainly will ride with you!"

⚜   ⚜   ⚜

A soft shower freshened the vast tropical grounds and brushed the bungalow nearest the powdery white beach on an island reserved for the very rich or very famous, or those lesser souls favored by the owners. A little known property of the billionaire Bloch brothers, Sandfly Island had been a private preserve for the past three decades, rarely used but always staffed and stocked with the best wine and food and a resident chef. Rare Australian tree ferns, giant bromeliads, and acres of Birds of Paradise graced the grounds surrounding six luxurious cottages designed by a renowned Japanese architect.

The island complex had been the vision of Robert Bloch's first wife, a Houston debutante who became a passionate Japanophile after a single visit to Japan. She spared no expense in making Sandfly a tropical replica of a treasured Kyoto villa, transporting a teahouse in its entirety from Japan as a welcoming entry. For the past three weeks the only guests were the couple from North Dakota.

Stanley Vaughn rolled off a down comforter and hit the floor with a bang, laughing at his clumsiness. His knee buckled as he rose to greet Eva on their twentieth day in paradise. "Damn, that hurts!" The young woman in his bed yawned and stretched, smiling at Stanley's complaint, patting the space next to her. "Come here, silly. It's too early to get up. I'll call for coffee." With that sweet rebuke, she drew North Dakota's most famous refugee into her arms and kept the news from the north one more day away from his reality.

▨   ▨   ▨

Twenty-five hundred miles west, in Marquelia, Mexico, Wayne Hartsell stuck a tee in the ground and smacked his golf ball toward a green space cut between rocks and the Atlantic Ocean. "Damn! This game is too hard for me," he laughed to his playing partners, a cousin visiting from Albuquerque and a local property developer. After a non-aerobic morning riding in golf carts over the lush course, the trio retired to eggs Benedict and Bloody Marys on the deck of the club Hartsell and his friend had built during the 90's economic boom.

"Wayne, it's a damn good thing you're down here and not in Phoenix," said his cousin, downing the drink made richer with a shot of Don Julio tequila. "This election thing is out of control. They can't serve you here, can they?"

"Nah, I doubt it," replied Hartsell, who had been devouring news coverage of the Electoral College brouhaha and the coming showdown in Congress. "And anyway, what the hell are they gonna do? What I did, I did in public and I stand by it. And by the way, the Constitution protects my right to vote however damn well I please."

"Here's to the Constitution!" shouted the cousin as the three clinked glasses and ordered another round.

CHAPTER 50

During the three-hour slog between Concord and Portsmouth, Banks learned little about Virginia Sullivan but a great deal about her daughter Constance and granddaughter Janine, who slept for most of the journey. Constance recalled her efforts to find her mother, recently successful after years of frustrating third-party contacts. The two had met briefly in York, Maine and promised to spend more time together after the political season ended. Constance had revealed her illness and introduced Virginia's granddaughter. She hoped Janine would develop some kind of relationship with Virginia after Constance's likely death. She wanted nothing from Virginia other than a connection, so when she learned that Sullivan had financed her potentially life-saving treatments, she was both grateful and sheepish that she might have guilt-tripped Virginia into this largess.

"It was just overwhelming," recalled Constance as she opened the door into Sullivan's crumbling Portsmouth house. "It was like God had chosen us that day. God smiled on us, and her face was Virginia's. That's how I felt."

"Make yourself at home," implored Constance as Banks stood shivering in the foyer. The house smelled of mold and rotting cat food after weeks of disuse. "I came down every day or so to feed the cat until the weather got bad, so I took him back to our place in York. The house needs cleaning." She found matches and lit a burner for the kettle. "They turned off her heat but promised me it'd be back on today. I guess they haven't gotten around to it with all this snow and ice. Thank goodness we've still got gas on the stove."

Warming herself with a large mug of black tea and honey, Banks moved through the house, careful to not appear to pry but taking in every inch of the home of one of America's three most notorious presidential electors. She searched for some clue she could take back to Annapolis. As she entered Errol's sanctuary, Constance joined her. "Yeah, it's pretty amazing, isn't it? The guy had some real interesting hobbies, I guess. I love all the newspaper front pages, don't you?"

Banks turned slowly, taking in each wall and cabinet, wondering how Virginia's long dead husband somehow fit into the picture she was creating of the woman. *Trains, history, newspapers—what's all this mean?* thought Melody. *Probably nothing.*

Returning to the kitchen she passed a small desk covered with loose papers, unopened bills, and a photo of Constance and Janine in a plastic frame. As Constance busied herself with a refrigerator full of spoiled milk and limp vegetables, Banks slowly opened the desk drawer and saw the envelope with the writing "Attn: Andrew Vorkink, Atty./Virginia Sullivan Will".

"Constance, do you know an Andrew Vorkink? Is he Virginia's lawyer?" Banks closed the drawer and came close to Appleby, who looked up from the mysterious freezer contents. "No, why?"

"There's an envelope for him in the desk. I'm sorry, I didn't mean to pry," Banks attempted to excuse her violation. "I just thought that perhaps if he's Virginia's attorney he should have this envelope now that she is in such bad shape."

"Where is it?" asked Constance, now annoyed with Banks' snooping. "If it's important, I'll take care of it. What's your plan for getting back to Washington?"

"I'm taking Amtrak tomorrow morning. I'll be at the Marriott tonight," Banks knew she had stepped over a line with Appleby and tried to recover. "Can I take you and Janine to dinner? It's too cold to stay here."

"We'll be fine, thanks. I enjoyed meeting you and our talk. I hope you'll respect Virginia's privacy. She's a good woman and she's had a hard time of it." Constance showed Banks to the door, forcing a smile and a handshake. "Travel safely."

Melody walked the half-mile in bitter cold to the hotel, checking into a blissfully warm room, with a large flat screen television and working wifi. She ordered room service and sat cross-legged on the bed, opened her laptop and called Jackson Cripple. Banks had a lot of work to do and little time to do it.

The Supreme Court heard three hours of oral arguments on Senator Bridges' appeal of the Arizona and North Dakota state verdicts upholding Hartsell's and Vaughn's votes. The Holland team decided not to challenge the New Hampshire ruling, which rejected Virginia Sullivan's vote. The President's lawyers wanted the decision in the lap of the House, where Republicans enjoyed a huge partisan margin. Barring an unexpected decision by the President's "seven-two" court, Bridges v. Holland was little more than a warm-up for the real fight to be waged forty-eight hours later.

"Mr. Chief Justice," began Morton Abramowitz, the fabled liberal attorney for the plaintiff, "the argument in front of this court is not the selection or the process in Arizona and North Dakota that brings us here today. The framers of the Constitution established the Electoral College as a means to level the playing field, ensuring that the smaller, less powerful states would not have their rights trampled as the nation's president was chosen every four years."

"But the rights of all Americans have been trampled by the unprecedented actions of two men determined to reverse the will of the majority of the nation's voters and, indeed, the majority of its electors. To allow this travesty to go forward is to undercut the very foundation of our democracy."

After a vigorous grilling by six of the justices, the court recognized the President's lawyer, who used only five minutes of his allotted time. Quoting the relevant sections of the Constitution, he summarized the core of the President's case.

"You don't have to like the result of the Electoral College vote. You don't have to like the Electoral College. But you do have to acknowledge the words, the words the framers of our Constitution set down as the unequivocal procedure by which we elect the President. And subsequent law has precluded the involvement of the federal courts in resolving what are clearly state electoral matters."

"The two states in question followed every correct procedure. Neither had in place, or attempted to install afterward any procedure to reverse the votes of their electors. These two electors made a conscious decision to reject the winner of the election in their state. A remarkable, even unprecedented decision? Yes. A courageous decision? That depends upon which side of the aisle you sit. But a legal act? Most certainly."

The Court adjourned at noon and retired to chambers to deliberate the outcome of Bridges v. Holland. At six p.m. a spokesman entered the press-room and read the verdict. The Supreme Court found that, despite the dramatic and consequential circumstances, the votes of Hartsell and Vaughn would stand.

The evening television broadcasts were cleared for nonstop commentary by political consultants, legal scholars, members of Congress on both sides, and various campaign officials. Profiles of the three electors were splashed alongside the talking heads every few minutes, and friends and associates were interviewed *ad nauseam*, until there was little more to review.

Several cable shows mimicked CNN's political war room, with wall-to-wall interactive maps outlining the tie vote in the Electoral College, then the potential voting pattern for the upcoming debate in Congress. Online sites lit up the internet with additional coverage, often skewed toward the extreme and inflammatory.

"Okay, here we go," said Eldon Mann to no one in particular. He had joined senior White House staff in the press secretary's office to await the Court verdict and rose to leave as the room erupted in applause. "This was the easy part," he whispered to a nearby aide as he quietly departed, walked down the narrow stairwell leading to the West Wing exit and entered his car waiting on Executive Drive.

CHAPTER 51

"Melody, do you have anything for me?" Pima Grantham called Banks for a story line to distinguish *Politico's* coverage in the hailstorm of media attention the day after the Court's decision. "Is it all over for you guys?"

"No," Banks replied. "There's the Congressional debate tomorrow and who knows where that will go. We're picking up signals that a bunch of Republicans may bolt and support Bridges. But I don't have any proof of that. We're still working the fraud angle. I hope to have something later today."

"May be too late. But good luck." Since the December 14 fiasco, Grantham had filed an impressive array of articles about the potential abuse of the Electoral College and directed a growing team that had interviewed more than a hundred House members to develop a profile of where the issue might head. Unfortunately, she was unable to use any of Bank's most sensitive information, as attribution was impossible and the most important targets—Hartsell and Vaughn—had disappeared, and Virginia Sullivan was still unconscious.

Melody drove the sixty miles to Jackson Cripple's farm and entered the house to find Cripple on two cellphones, directing subordinates while typing on a laptop. The scene was chaotic in his ordinarily sublime place. "Melody, look at this." He handed her the laptop and she read:

Virginia P. Sullivan, First National of Portsmouth. Account entries. Dec. 14 $300,000.00 to checking. Transfer from Chase Manhattan, 42nd St. branch, account of Wilson Parrish & Co., Literary Representatives.

Warner Peebles, M.D., Boston, MA. Statement of patient Constance Appleby, York, ME. $20,000.00 transfer from Saguaro Holdings, Phoenix. Deposit for procedure, date TBD.

"Holy shit. Bastards bought her." Banks had expected some kind of connection between Sullivan and Eldon Mann's operation, and the proof was staring at her on the screen.

"The problem is, Sullivan is no longer the issue, right?" Cripple was now looking over Banks' shoulder. "Unless she's revived overnight and can state that she had no intention of voting for Holland. And even then it wouldn't give you a majority."

"That's correct," said Banks. "But if we can get this out tonight it could affect the debate tomorrow. Even Republicans might not like the idea of their President stealing an election this way." Banks looked at Cripple, seeking a sign of agreement, but both sighed and returned to the computer screen attempting to decipher meaning that would help Senator Bridges' cause. Banks placed a call to Todd Campbell in Annapolis as the lead attorney was briefing the Senator.

"Melody, I need to get back to you. I'm going into this session with Cal."

"No, Todd, it can't wait. Here's the deal—we've uncovered payments made to Virginia Sullivan the day before and after the January 6 vote. Large payments. There's no doubt in my mind they constitute a payoff for her vote."

"Jesus," he said. "Listen, let me do this briefing quickly—there's not a lot of legal stuff to review with them. It's all about the House now. I'll call you back in fifteen minutes."

"Okay, but don't wait." She rang off and returned to Cripple's monitors to scan the crumbs he picked up over the last few days. Other than the Sullivan revelations, there wasn't much to go on. As promised, Campbell called in and resumed their discussion.

"Melody, this is likely the smoking gun we've been looking for, but Congress is going to convene in the morning and I don't see what we can do with it tonight. You say it can't be publicly documented yet. And besides, Sullivan's vote isn't even on the table."

"I'm going to find a way to get it to the media," said Banks. "But don't we have friendly congressmen who can figure out how to put this out on the floor tomorrow without busting my source? Surely it could create some doubt for our side to use?"

"Let me think about it," he said. "I've got to get back to this meeting."

Banks placed a call to Pima Grantham at *Politico*, but she was unavailable. "Pima, please call me as soon as possible. We've found the smoking gun in New Hampshire." She then called through a list of Democratic congressmen who befriended her through the years and got a cordial but skeptical reception from all but one. She forwarded a summary of her findings and asked that it be shared with the Minority Leader, who would manage the Democratic response on the House floor.

Minutes before midnight she took a call from Campbell, who had reviewed the Cripple file with Senator Bridges moments earlier. "Melody, I'm sorry it took so long to get back to you. You can imagine how crazy it is here. Cal has been on the phone all day with Members."

"I understand," she replied. "What do you want to do with the material?"

"We can't use it, Melody. The Senator believes it would be ruled out of order on the floor of either body, much less in a court.

Without Sullivan or Hartsell to corroborate any of this, we have nothing. The Senator is prepared to go with whatever the House and Senate decide tomorrow."

"Then it's over, Todd. We're going to lose all around." Banks slumped into a chair and closed her eyes. *Fuck, fuck, fuck! They're going to get away with it,* she thought. Exhausted, fighting off tears, she placed a call to a friend on the staff of the Democratic Minority Leader. The aide promised to arrange a pull-aside before the vote at GW, if Banks could be available from eight am on. Melody rejoined Cripple in his study for another bottle of red wine, then retreated to her bedroom for a fitful night of troubled sleep.

CHAPTER 52

For two months since the Capitol bombing, preparations had been underway to transform George Washington University into temporary quarters for the upcoming joint session of Congress. Security officials complained that safety precautions would be too porous at the Foggy Bottom location, which was surrounded by hundreds of homes, stores, office buildings, and a Metro stop underneath the University. But GW was the only non-federal institution willing to vacate its entire academic operation for the two months required to support the thousands of members of Congress and staff, as well as media coverage of the historic session and the Presidential Inauguration to follow two weeks later. Students were informed that classes would begin on Feb. 1, and that their presence beforehand would not be required.

The University's gymnasium was outfitted to accommodate separate desks for the 435 House members and one hundred Senators for the joint session. A smaller room nearby was set up as a makeshift Senate chamber.

The gym's press section was turned into a media gallery high above the floor that had been the site of GW basketball games.

The press box was packed two hours before the scheduled opening of the session, as Congressmen began to file onto the floor, disoriented as they sought their assigned desks. Staff milled about, their dark suits and security pins identifying those with floor access. Each carried a large valise with briefing papers, phones, iPads, and laptops, in case their Member had an urgent need for a bit of research or a pithy quote if they were recognized to speak. Most of the Members circulated among their colleagues, sharing their universal incredulity at the proceedings.

In the suite of offices normally housing the University president and his staff, the Speaker of the House gathered his leadership team to review the debate facing the institution. Speaker Chapman welcomed the group and recognized the House chaplain for a prayer. He then turned to the Parliamentarian to explain the day's procedure.

"The debate today is governed by the Electoral Count Act of 1887," began the Parliamentarian. While he ran through the lengthy process Congress would face, the attention of the Republican leaders waned.

"This is crazy! How the hell did Holland pull this off?" said an elderly Member in an aside to a colleague, who was sending a Tweet to his followers.

The Parliamentarian droned on, annoyed with his audience's distraction. "The joint session will formally count the electoral votes forwarded by the states. If there are challenges to any state submission the House and Senate will separate, debate the challenges, and vote,"

"I don't know," said the Tweeter, "but it's pretty damn incredible. How's your mail running?"

"I don't have a clue," laughed the older Member. "I don't see my mail. A computer answers it all."

"The two houses must agree or the state submission will stand," continued the Parliamentarian. *By God they're going to hear all this, whether they like it or not*, he thought.

"Thank you, Joel," Speaker Chapman interrupted. "I think we've got it. You'll be on the dais to keep us honest. Now please excuse us for a few minutes." The Parliamentarian stood and looked over the group before he took his leave. The Speaker thought he detected a slight smirk from the Parliamentarian. "I'll brief the Democratic leadership now with the same information," he said in parting. "I know you all realize what an historic occasion is before you today."

Chapman turned to his colleagues as the Parliamentarian left the room. "All right, the rules aside, the question is simple: are we going to be unified in our support for the President?" The Speaker's intention was firm: he would deliver the vote for Holland—and Eldon Mann—to protect himself from any disclosure of the incriminating material he had viewed three days earlier. But he needed to appear collegial and line up the entire leadership behind the effort.

"As far as I'm concerned it's open and shut," spoke the Majority Leader, who would manage floor debate for the Republicans. "These electors cast their votes and the Constitution backs them up. And if we have to actually vote to end this matter, we have to follow the Constitution."

"But we're gonna catch hell," injected the Majority Whip, the only ideological moderate in the leadership group. "It's gonna be 1824 all over again. There's gonna be a partisan holy war out there, and the press is gonna keep it alive all the way through the next election."

The debate among the five men and one woman careened from raw politics to Constitutional law to the essential matter that bound them all. The Speaker cut the discussion off. "We all know what's at stake here. The power of the Presidency and our access to it. With Grady Holland we have a friend, sort of. We've got the patronage, the perks, the trillions of dollars of federal spending, the military bases, the CODELs, the jobs, all of it. We hand the election to Calvin Bridges and that's gone for four, maybe eight years. Some of us won't even be around when he leaves office."

"Put out the word now. Our people are to vote no on all Democratic motions. If we prevail, and I'm sure we will, we'll recess until tonight to begin voting on Bridges versus Holland. We'll gather the senior Republican in every state to work it beforehand. Everyone clear on this?" Chapman polled each of his team to assure that the party line would hold, then led the group into a large adjacent classroom to meet with their rank and file colleagues, to issue the call for unity.

A chaotic scene unfolded in the Democratic caucus as the members peppered their leaders with questions about strategy after the Parliamentarian had completed his presentation. "Can't we just walk out?" demanded a junior member. "They can't get a quorum without us." The Parliamentarian, who calmly explained the rules governing the proceeding, noted every possible delaying tactic as impractical. The Republican leadership was fully in control of the day's debate.

The Minority Leader, a crafty New York legislator, the woman who served as House Speaker when the Democrats controlled the chamber, cut through the noise to make a simple case. "Every analysis we have indicates that all but a handful of Republicans will vote against all three motions. That leaves us to make the case in our state delegations".

"The Speaker has told me he will set aside six hours for the states to meet and reach a vote. Obviously it doesn't look good. But it's not hopeless. You each have talking points to use in those meetings. Try to keep the debate collegial, appeal to whatever sense of fairness and morality they might bring to this debate." She glanced at a message handed to her by a staffer and deferred colleagues' questions to an aide, leaving the room to meet Melody Banks waiting in the hallway.

"Rosa," began Banks, who was breathless from the run down a long corridor leading to the Democratic caucus space previously housing the university wrestling arena. "Rosa, can you somehow stop the vote? I've got a file that will destroy the President's case on the floor. But it will take some time to explain and brief your team."

The Minority Leader had once mentored the younger political consultant, taking her into her home for several months during Bank's first campaign since graduating from law school. She saw in Banks a version of herself as a passionate community activist in Albany, and made an effort to be available to Banks as her career progressed.

"Melody, I've read the summary you sent to Paul yesterday. The problem is, we simply can't go on the floor to make these accusations against the President. Have you made any progress with the Justice Department?" The Leader knew the answer, but she wanted to give Banks the chance to make her last ditch case.

"No, but I know that if we can have just one week we can break this open." Banks took the older woman's hand in hers and gripped hard. "Just one week. Can you somehow delay..."

"Melody, no one wants Calvin to become President more than I do. You know that." The Congresswoman placed her other hand on Banks' shoulder and shook her head. "In an hour or so we'll start voting and I can't see any way we can raise the charge that the President has committed massive vote fraud in New Hampshire. The Speaker would blow us away. There would be procedural votes to sanction any member who raised these charges. You've just got to understand the situation we're in." She drew Banks to her for an embrace that both understood was a benediction.

Banks walked slowly down the corridor as the voices began to rise from the gymnasium. She waved off an aide who was to escort her to her gallery seat, and left the building to walk eastward down Pennsylvania Avenue. A strong wind buffeted her stride as she crossed over to H Street and into Lafayette Park. Oblivious to the freeze that enveloped her as she sat on a bench facing the White House, Melody punched in the number she had frantically dialed so often over the past weeks. She reached Jackson Cripple as he was watching the House debate begin.

"We've lost, Jackson. They're not going to try to stop the vote. They can't use our stuff. We should have known it from the start." After allowing Cripple a consoling speech, she thanked him for his work and rang off. *What now?* She thought. *I've wanted this over for so long, but now that it's over I don't have a clue what to do next.* Banks took a deep breath and finally felt the bitter cold.

She pulled her coat close and walked briskly into the Hay Adams Hotel, past a friendly car attendant who recognized her and opened the door into the warm lobby that had been visited by so many famous and infamous guests for more than a century. She found "Off the Record", the hotel's legendary bar, and settled into a dark corner. Midway through her double vodka martini Melody made another call, to Paul, her Congressman boyfriend a decade earlier, who was on the floor of the GW gymnasium with his House colleagues.

"Paul, what are you doing after the vote? No, I'm not at GW. I'm at the Hay Adams. Can you come over here? I'm serious. No, not for dinner. Not for a drink. I need you to come be with me. That's right. I need you to come as soon as possible. I'll get a room. Bring some wine. Or something stronger."

She downed her cocktail and approached the front desk, managed to score a room from the manager who had previously turned away two would be guests, and took an elevator to her floor. Filling the spacious tub and adding perfumed bath salts, she stripped and eased her weary body into the steaming bath to await the only man she wanted to see at this moment. She was desperate to feel something other than the extreme disappointment of political failure.

CHAPTER 53

At eleven am the joint House and Senate session was called to order by Vice President West, serving in his role as President of the Senate. Earlier in the week he had been visited by three old friends from Congress. They urged him to delegate his role to the Speaker *pro tem*, the Utah senator who had served in the upper body for fifty years.

"Dan, we're your closest friends, and we only want what's best for you," said one. "We'll cover for you, say to the press that you're still under the weather and have no business getting out in this cold to perform a role that is totally ceremonial to begin with. And in these times no one will challenge that."

"And besides, you're going to be reelected by the Senate," continued another colleague. "Then you can properly resign and get on with your retirement. Hell, I'd love to get out of here!" There were awkward guffaws all around.

The Vice President smiled and thanked his old friends but assured them he would serve as President of the Senate as the Congress met to resolve the election. He wasn't about to miss this event.

After the Chaplain's opening prayer and his own introductory remarks he began the counting of the electoral votes as dictated by law. When the Arizona ballots were read, heated objections arose from Democrats, who called for a vote to reject the state's reported numbers. West then ordered each body to its separate room to debate the question, House members remained on the gymnasium floor for their deliberations.

Once the commotion of Senators vacating the floor had dissipated, the House Speaker gaveled the session open and recognized the Minority Leader for the first motion. The gymnasium's upper deck was packed with spectators who had been forced through hours of security lines and metal screening before entering the facility. Nearly a thousand U. S. and international press credentials had been issued, with seating spilling out of the basketball arena press section into nearby sections. Acoustics were dreadful, and the sound system inadequate for the somber nature of the proceedings.

"Mr. Speaker, today we debate an unprecedented proposition— that is, do we accept a technical reading of the law to reverse the electoral will of nearly sixty million American voters." The Minority Leader summoned all her rhetorical skills in what she knew to be a losing battle. Invoking Thomas Jefferson, Golda Meir, and George Washington, she gave a stirringly emotional speech. But she, like every other member of the House, knew at this point the debate would move few if any from their partisan moorings.

Her Republican counterpart responded with an equally spirited defense of the literal interpretation of the Constitution that gave electors absolute flexibility to vote their conscience. "No one likes the situation we have been placed in here today," he concluded. "We would all preferred to have had this election decided on November third. But it wasn't, and when the Electoral College met the vote left the outcome still undecided. The Constitution speaks to us today, and we must honor its words even if we do not like the outcome."

Each leader recognized colleagues chosen beforehand to give brief speeches, until the time had expired and the vote called on the first motion. With only four Republicans voting with the

Democrats, the motion to reverse the Arizona electoral vote failed. After another hour of debate, the second vote was called on the North Dakota electoral count and the outcome was identical. The vote on the New Hampshire issue was close, with the Republicans prevailing by only two votes.

In the nearby auditorium the Senate conducted a similar debate and vote. On the first two motions the Republicans prevailed, though by a narrower margin. On the question of New Hampshire's elector, the Senate voted to reject Sullivan's vote, a meaningless victory for the Democrats since both Houses had to agree.

Voicing the outrage of every Democratic, the junior Senator from New Jersey led a walkout. "We will no longer take part in this travesty," he shouted. As the forty-one Democrats left the room, their leader announced that they would not attend the later session to elect the Vice President.

Presiding over the Senate debate, Vice President West had little control over the rowdy minority. He still managed to fulfill his role in recognizing speakers and stating rulings from the chair as handed to him by the Senate Parliamentarian.

Prodded to recess the Senate he softly tapped the gavel and spoke just above a whisper. "The Senate will stand in recess until further notice." He stepped down from the platform and steadied himself against a railing. Accepting assistance from a floor staffer, he slowly left the room and summoned an aide to see him to his limo for the short ride to the Naval Observatory. He had enough excitement for one day, and wanted to focus on his plans for the coming weeks without the distraction of a congressional madhouse unfolding in the building.

Speaker Marshall Chapman, in contrast, was firmly in charge of the House action. "Pursuant to the Twelfth Amendment, the House will now move to a vote of the state delegations to elect the President. We will stand in recess until six pm, when debate will begin on the election of the President. Each state will cast one vote. If there is no majority decision within a state delegation, that state's vote will not be counted. Twenty-six votes will be required to conclude the election. Balloting will continue until one candidate receives the necessary majority." He banged the gavel and moved to an adjacent room serving as the Republican cloakroom.

Fifty classrooms were set aside for each state delegation to debate its decision. The shouting could be heard through the walls separating the members. Few touched the luncheon buffet spreads made available for each group as partisan tempers flared. After two hours of rancorous deliberation, Democratic members from twenty states controlled by Republicans abandoned the process and moved to their own cloakroom area to continue fuming. Three states evenly split between the two parties could not reach consensus. The seventeen states with a majority of Democratic House members quickly voted to cast their ballots for Senator Bridges.

In each state caucus, Republicans were warned to avoid argument, to let the process move toward a vote as soon as possible. As Speaker Chapman noted during his party's caucus, the outcome was assured, so keep it civil.

While the state delegations caucused in private, CNN, MSNBC, and Fox cable stations cleared their channels for full coverage of the Congressional deliberations, while the major networks scrolled brief messages about the votes below the daytime shows that were bread and butter revenue sources. At five o'clock ABC, NBC, and CBS finally interrupted regular programming for an hour of reporting from the GWU campus. George Stephanopoulos, the only news anchor with first hand campaign and White House experience, set the tone of the coverage.

"Nearly two hundred years have passed since the United States experienced an election decided not by the American voters, not even by the Electoral College, but by the U. S. House of Representatives. In a few hours 435 members of the House will begin voting to determine the next President. But it is not as simple as that. Here to try to make some sense of this extraordinary political event is perhaps the country's most notable expert on the Electoral College, Professor George Edwards of Texas A&M. Professor Edwards, can you shed some light on what we'll be watching tonight?"

Edwards had been in wide demand for analysis since the dramatic elector votes in Arizona and North Dakota. An ardent critic, he had written compelling arguments for scrapping the Electoral College. As the talking heads droned on about conspiracies and campaign strategies, Edwards summarized the extraordinary situation.

"We have long known that the Electoral College was a ticking time bomb, and it has now exploded. The reversal of the November election and now, a contingent election in the House, have provided ample evidence that our system is completely broken."

"Our democracy is founded on the concept of political equality—that is, no individual vote should count more than another. But the Electoral College turns that principle on its head. As we've seen once again, if you live in Texas or New York, your vote counts less than if you vote in Alaska or North Dakota. And if that's not bad enough, we will now have the House of Representatives taking control of the election, where the state of Wyoming, with barely six hundred thousand citizens, will have the same vote as California, with nearly forty million."

"Imagine a politician proposing that such a disparity be made law today—he would be savaged. But that is what we're now facing."

At the designated hour, the Speaker reconvened the House. Refusing to recognize the Minority Leader or other Democrats seeking to speak, he boomed, "The Clerk will now call the role of the states."

"Alabama," spoke the Clerk in a flat monotone. "Representing the people of the great state of Alabama, its delegation casts its

vote for President Grady Holland," came the response of the
state's senior House member.

The Clerk continued the roll call, the votes flashing on the
massive Jumbotron hanging above the gymnasium floor. Iowa,
Nevada, and New Jersey were placed in a "no decision" column.
Virginia was called as the 45th state to vote, and an eerie hush
descended over the cavernous space.

"Mr. Speaker, recognizing the monumental responsibility facing
this body, and having fully debated the remarkable circumstances
that have brought us here tonight, the Virginia delegation casts
its vote for President Grady Holland."

The gymnasium erupted in protests, drowned out by hundreds
of cheering House Republican staffers given extra tickets for that
purpose. Speaker Chapman banged his gavel repeatedly to call
the proceeding to order. Unsuccessful, he allowed the impromptu
demonstrations to continue for more than five minutes until
bringing down the gavel once more.

"The vote is not finished. The Clerk will continue to call
the roll."

Amid ongoing mayhem, the Clerk completed the voting, with
West Virginia, Wisconsin, and Wyoming delegations adding to
Holland's total and Vermont and Washington to Bridges'. Face
to face confrontations broke out on the floor as Democrats chal-
lenged their colleagues' honesty, patriotism, or manhood, and
Republicans sought retreat from the uncomfortable recriminations.

A young conservative firebrand taunted his Democratic colleagues with a laugh and double thumbs down, provoking an aging
liberal member from California to slam the younger Member to
the floor. Within minutes a dozen fights broke out around the
gymnasium, which looked more like a barroom brawl than the
U. S. House of Representatives.

Chapman was barely audible as he brought down the gavel and
the Jumbotron clock turned to midnight. "The voting concluded,
President Holland has received thirty votes to Senator Bridges'

seventeen. Having won a majority of the state delegations, as required by the Twelfth Amendment, President Holland is hereby declared winner of this Presidential election."

"Hearing no objection, the House is hereby adjourned until January 20 for the Inauguration."

With little fanfare, the Senate met in the adjoining room with no Democrats attending. The fifty-five members of the majority unanimously reelected Vice President Dan West, with the expectation that West would soon resign to allow Holland to select one of their own.

"Damn, that was exciting!" Tommy Thompson entertained his staff in a penthouse atop the posh W Hotel to watch the televised House proceedings with rare tenderloin and a case of prized Italian wine. As the Speaker closed the session, The Rake popped a magnum of Perrier-Jouet champagne and filled glasses as the team yelled their approval at Holland's victory.

"It's all fun tonight," said Thompson. "Tomorrow we get back to work on the Security Relocation Act. It's gonna be a great campaign, and we're gonna make a lot of money with it this year. But tonight, let's have a good time!"

Thompson moved to a quieter corner and dialed Congressman Lismore to congratulate the committee chairman on a great victory and remind Lismore that he would attend the congressman's upcoming fundraising weekend in Palm Springs, and would be bringing a healthy check.

Rebuffing his Democratic colleagues' angry encouragement to continue the fight, Senator Bridges entered the temporary pressroom at GW to make his concession speech.

"First, I want to thank so many wonderful people who took the fight for democracy this far. To my tireless, exhausted staff I want to say there are no more patriotic, dedicated professionals in this city. To my supporters throughout the country, to the millions of Americans who voted for me in November, thank you for your trust and confidence."

"This has been a fight not only for my election but for the democratic principles that make up the foundation of our Constitution. The process is deeply flawed-and I will have more to say about that in the future – but it works every four years, however strangely, to elect a president to lead this country through good times and bad."

"I will continue to speak out on issues critical to my own state of Maryland and to families throughout the country. But for tonight, I want to extend my support to President Holland as he deals with an ongoing national security crisis and the many difficult issues facing this country. Thank you."

Leaving the building with a handful of aides, Bridges encountered dozens of well-wishers. "It's not over, Cal!" "They're gonna regret this day!" He shook hands and forced a smile as the scrum grew around him. As he navigated toward an exit, an aide handed him a cellphone. "Senator, it's the Vice President."

"I'm sorry it had to end this way, Dan," said Bridges, before West could speak. "You deserved better treatment."

"Thanks, Cal," said West. "So did you!" A chuckle emerged from the Vice President. "But you know, politics is sort of like the Lord. It works in strange ways. I suspect we'll be seeing more of each other in the coming years."

Bridges signed off, perplexed by the Vice President's jovial mood, and encountered another large group of friends and colleagues who weren't quite ready to give up the fight.

Holland watched the televised House debate with his family and, in his nearby study, called Eldon Mann. "Unfuckingbelievable," sighed the President. "We actually did it. Damn, Eldon, we actually did it."

"Yes, Mr. President, *we* did it." Mann placed an emphasis on the "we", but the comment was lost on Holland, who was off to receive the concession call from Calvin Bridges and congratulations from scores of sycophants, foreign dignitaries, and a handful of genuine supporters.

CHAPTER 54

The country awoke to headlines screaming *"Constitutional Chaos!"* and *"U.S. Politics Gone Crazy"*. There were not enough election law experts to fill the television commentary seats, so the cable shows resorted to members of Congress and consultants who never refused a spot in front of a camera. The analysis ranged from measured, scholarly legal arguments to partisan screeds thrown at opposing panelists, each armed with the political talking points they relied upon for their TV appearances.

The international press had a field day with the news—*Folie Americain!* read the *Le Monde* headline leading a story eviscerating the U.S. process for electing its president. *Die Zeit's* banner trumpeted *Amerika braucht Aufsicht von Erwachsenen!* USA Today recycled the German headline—*America Needs Adult Supervision!* Russian and Chinese coverage was predictably brutal in ridiculing the American system. One popular Moscow television personality was viewed smirking at a U.S. electoral map and crowing, "And they tell other countries how to manage their affairs? What a joke!"

Mann had arranged for the President's speechwriters to be in Orlando to craft Holland's remarks that were to be delivered early the following morning. At seven am, his staff clearing all networks for the speech, Holland appeared relaxed, American flag pin in place, photos of family in the background.

"My fellow Americans, the long struggle to resolve the Presidential election is over. I want to extend heartfelt thanks to my friend Calvin Bridges, who called me a few hours ago to formally concede the election. I congratulate him on a statesmanlike campaign and his gracious support as we move forward to address the issues facing this great country."

"The road to arrive at last night's decision was difficult, often confusing, and frustrating for all concerned. But the Constitution guided the elected representatives from every corner of the nation. In the end, the words of our founding fathers prevailed, and we can move on."

"Four years ago I took an oath—to faithfully execute the office of President of the United States, and to the best of my ability, preserve, protect and defend the Constitution of the United States. Two weeks from now I will do so again. It is a sacred vow, and I promise to meet the challenges that come with it."

"As we prepare for the next four years, I can assure you that this administration will continue to protect our nation's security, through our fight against terrorism at home and abroad. We will continue to work to create jobs for our families, to grow our economy while protecting our environment."

"Thank you for your support and trust. God bless you, and God bless America."

Eldon Mann watched the speech from behind the press pool camera. Once the President had taken congratulations from family and staff in the adjacent conference room, he joined Mann in his study.

"So what now, Eldon? Have you come up with a plan for the next cabinet? Who stays, who goes?" the President removed his coat, loosened his tie, and poured a spicy tomato juice for both. "Want something in this?"

"No, thank you," replied Mann, who wanted to leave the Orlando White House and return to Washington as soon as possible. "There's a lot to consider. The cabinet overhaul can wait awhile. You need to shake up the White House staff. But first you have to pick a new Vice President. I assume you don't want to encourage West to rescind his resignation."

"Hell no!" growled the President. "West's a goddamn nutcase. For fuck sake he's the reason we got in this situation to begin with. I'm leanin' toward Jim Ramsey. His seat in Oklahoma is safe for Republicans and he'll do the right thing on all the stuff we care about. But you tell me if you have other ideas."

"Ramsey would be a good choice, no problem getting confirmed by the Senate. Liberals will go crazy, especially after all his hearings to debunk global warming. But he'll be fine. As to the White House staff, we have to talk about the Chief of Staff job."

"Later, Eldon. Right now I wanna get some rest and spend some time with my family. Shit, Clarice is gonna leave me if I don't go to my granddaughter's graduation. Can you believe this shit? A graduation ceremony for sixth graders. And when's it gonna be? You got it, same day as the SEC championship game in Atlanta."

Mann expressed his sympathy about the President's scheduling dilemma and excused himself as Holland's wife entered the study. He summoned his car and made the trip to the airport in silence as his driver yammered on about the previous day's drama. *He actually said WE did it. That asshole really believes he had some role in turning around an election the sonofabitch had lost.*

As the Citation lifted from the runway, Mann skimmed the morning papers and news clips delivered to the plane. Coverage was heavy and predictable throughout the world, every headline announcing Holland's victory and virtually every editorial blasting the process that ended in the historic outcome. The House of Representatives came under attack from all but the most conservative editorial writers for its lockstep support for reversal of the November election. Television reporting was generally straightforward until the cable panels weighed in with vitriol from the Left and defensive reliance on the Constitution from the Right. The late evening Senate reelection of Vice President Dan West was almost an afterthought.

Mann took special note of an online feature from Pima Grantham, the *Politico* reporter who had been hounding him since the Electoral College vote. Her story covered the ground other media had plowed, but Grantham's closing paragraphs left Mann with a sudden chill.

"Despite the finality of last night's House action, a number of questions remain about the manner in which President Holland was able to reverse the November 3 national vote. The two faithless Democratic electors who switched their allegiance to the President on December 12 have yet to surface to answer questions that will certainly come. And the third elector in question, Virginia Sullivan, remains in critical condition in New Hampshire, unable to meet with investigators probing the circumstances behind her own vote."

"Over the past few days allegations have surfaced that Sullivan may have been coerced to change her vote, or that financial considerations may have affected her decision. Should that be determined, state and federal prosecutors will certainly make this case a national issue."

Somewhere over South Carolina, Mann resolved to leave Washington as soon as possible. His earlier plan to take an ambassadorial appointment to Australia would be abandoned. Such jobs required Senate confirmation, a process he had no intention of subjecting himself to, after the brutally partisan events of the past two months. He would accept one or two corporate board directorships and quietly consult for the Bloch Brothers empire and the reclusive casino billionaire who had frequently sought Mann's intervention with the administration. Money would not be a problem. Staying under the radar of the post-election investigators and reporters was a different matter.

Mann recalled a Presidential trip to Morocco. After Holland's Inauguration, he could settle into a comfortable house in Rabat or Marrakech, where friends had developed one of the world's most opulent resorts. When the political heat settled he could return to the states; until then he would disappear.

CHAPTER 55

Grady Holland was sworn in on January 20 before the smallest Inauguration crowd in recent history, on the same gymnasium stage where two weeks earlier the Speaker of the House had declared Holland the victor. Several hundred protesters managed to obtain tickets as demand from Holland supporters and congressional offices was slack. The antagonists chanted "POTUS Thief!" until forcibly removed by armed security.

The President's speech, shortened to ten minutes, was neither moving nor memorable. The traditional Inaugural parade, the balls, and attendant parties were canceled. More than two-thirds of the Democratic House and Senate members found excuses to be absent, though Calvin Bridges, the short-lived President-elect, sat quietly in the rear of the section reserved for members of Congress.

Holland expected to use the VIP luncheon to announce his choice to replace Dan West as Vice President during his second term. The word had already gotten out that Senator Ramsey was Holland's choice, and the Oklahoman was receiving boisterous congratulations from his Republican colleagues as the guests sat for their meal.

"Jim," said Holland in his meeting with Ramsey a few days earlier, "you are on the shortest of short lists to be my next Vice President. I need to know you'll be with me, especially in dealing with the mess Dan West created with his goddamn pathetic confession."

"We were doin' fine with the industry guys. Then West has a fucking meltdown and throws the whole country into a fit for what? Did he really think he'd singlehandedly change the way this country does its business? He almost cost us the election! In fact he did cost us the election until we turned a miracle and reversed the fuckin' Electoral College. For the life of me, Jimmy, I have no goddamn idea what he was up to."

"Mr. President," said Senator Ramsey once Holland finished, "I'm with you all the way. We've got some work to do, but there's great opportunity out there. Great opportunity. And not only with our friends in the energy industry, but the telecom companies, the railroads, Wall Street—you name it. We'll make damn sure they know they have friends in the White House."

As the VIP guests settled into their seats for the post-Inauguration gathering, Vice President West rose from his distant table, walked across the room, and placed his hand on Holland's arm. He smiled as he looked down at Holland's cue cards with talking points about Jim Ramsey. "Mr. President, can I have a word with you,"

"Dan, this'll have to wait," replied the greatly annoyed President. "We're getting ready to start the program." Holland looked about the room frantically for Eldon Mann to remove West from the President's table.

"No, Grady, it won't wait. You need to hear this." He gripped Holland more firmly and steered him to a small alcove in the rear of the room. A nearby Secret Service agent joined the two men, but was waved off by West.

"What is this?" Holland looked back and forth across the room, finally saw Mann and motioned to him frantically.

"I'm not resigning," said West.

"What? You can't do that. I have your resignation note! You confirmed it with that goddamn reporter. "

As Eldon Mann joined the two men, West ignored the Chief of Staff and continued. "Two months ago I was on the ballot. And the Senate elected me during that rump session two weeks ago. And if you recall, you never publicly accepted my resignation. That email is meaningless."

Speechless, Holland looked at Eldon Mann for guidance. "Mr. President, we'll get the White House counsel on this. But frankly, the Vice President is probably right." Mann turned away to call a White House lawyer to quickly research the issue, then left the luncheon. He turned to see the President raging at his Vice President. Mann smiled. *Serves you right, asshole.*

Dan West sat in a deep leather chair in his NavObs study in complete silence, refusing all calls from well-wishers, staff, and the media.

Two muted nearby TV monitors resembled wild abstract video art, with a dizzying array of competing images: six screens of political commentators, polling numbers, quotes from various officials, Tweeted comments, and other random excretia from the weeks events.

Weeks earlier, expecting to vacate the residence after the Inauguration, West had supervised the staff packing of his belongings. Hundreds of framed citations and commissions, photos with world leaders, flags, his U. S. Navy officer's uniform, books, and assorted belongings were boxed and labeled and readied for the van that would take away the symbols of his long political career.

Other than his small wardrobe of clothing and a box of gadgets, the rest of the house's contents would remain, to be picked over by his successor's family. They would undoubtedly call for major renovations and upgrades of the furniture, entertainment systems, paintings, and so on, with millions to be raised by the corporate and foreign interests that fronted the costs.

He hoped to have a week after the Inauguration to vacate the property, but not-so-gentle prodding from Eldon Mann's emissaries forced him to accelerate his departure. He had to make way for the Foundation committee that would oversee the upgrades that would welcome the new Vice President. When West asked to move into Blair House in the interim period, Mann waved him off, noting that the German Chancellor would be occupying the grand townhouse on Lafayette Square for the next ten days.

Now West's living arrangements were even more uncertain. The President had no intention of honoring West's change of heart, but the Constitution was unclear about how he could be removed. Their relationship was irreparably damaged, *but what was new about that?* he thought. He had nearly brought down the Holland government with his television appearance and the resignation email, and he would have few supporters within the next Holland administration. In fact, he now had more friends among Democrats in Congress than in his own party.

But he was still the Vice President of the United States. Tomorrow morning, he would ride to the White House, greet the Marine guards at the entrance, gather his staff, and begin his work. It promised to be an interesting year.

The 117th Congress convened in the makeshift GW facility with an agenda of routine business—the budget, Holland's second term cabinet appointments, and the hundreds of committee appointments that leaders would dole out to favored colleagues. But the overwhelming challenge for the 535 House and Senate members was finding adequate work space while Capitol Hill was going through detoxification, a tedious process expected to take at least twelve months.

Special committees were established to oversee the cleanup and temporary housing of both chambers and the members' personal and committee offices. An estimate of several billion dollars soon ballooned to twelve, then twenty billion, touching off a confrontation between budget hawks, construction unions, and the anti-labor politicians who would approve these projects and the accompanying tax and spending measures. The number of Washington lobbyists soared to service the various financial interests in this battle. Fifteen former representatives and senators and hundreds of staffers set up influence shops in nearby Rosslyn, Virginia as they awaited a decision about where the Members would be working.

Much sought after were the special House and Senate Select committees to investigate the potential of a permanent relocation of the U. S. Capitol. Following briefings by Dan Lismore's earlier CODELs, new delegations of members and staff flew off again to Canberra and Brasília to consider the development of an entirely new federal city, built from scratch on a secure site in middle America. These delegations would report to their colleagues that such an undertaking was not only possible, but also advisable given the state of terrorism and the likelihood the recent nuclear attack was only the beginning threat to the nation, especially to its seat of government.

The debate escalated into an all-out battle among advocates for virtually every state except Hawaii and Alaska. The relocation of the entire federal government and the many thousands of highly paid workers was the gold ring for politicians and businesses. Trillions of dollars would flow into local coffers for decades to come.

Wisdom dictated that, in the end, nothing would be decided. The cost would mushroom so high that the public would soundly reject any attempt to move the federal government to Kansas or Iowa or anywhere else for that matter. Homeland Security scientists confirmed that the Capitol would be clean within eighteen months, and reconstruction underway shortly thereafter.

"It'll take that long for this Congress to agree to wipe its ass!" Speaker Chapman roared to a group of friendly lobbyists, over a plate of salmon and rare beef in the private dining room of the Inn at Little Washington, a favorite Chapman hideaway an hour to the west of the Capitol.

As the sun rose on a record cold New Hampshire morning, Virginia Sullivan sat up and began coughing violently. A nurse ran to her bedside and called a nearby doctor to help restrain the woman who had been the Concord hospital's famous patient for more than two months.

"No, please!" she cried as the doctor administered a sedative. "I have to go home! I have to go home! Please let me go!" A powerful sedative sent Sullivan back into a deep sleep while doctors monitored her strengthening vital signs.

The news of Sullivan's sudden awakening traveled fast. Reporters were rebuffed at the nurses' station and soon a barrier was erected to keep unwanted visitors off the floor. Attorneys for the Bridges campaign had long departed Concord since the Senator's concession speech on January 6, but the New Hampshire Democratic Party still wanted a statement from Virginia to determine her actual electoral vote. Her doctor refused their access, but Sullivan overruled him and allowed the state party chair to visit.

"I may have done something terribly wrong," Sullivan declared in a clear, strong voice to her guests. Sitting upright for the first time since her collapse Virginia asked. "Did my vote elect Holland? I remember writing his name but then it all went blank. I had such pain."

"No, Virginia," assured the party chair. "Your vote was thrown out as a result of how that bitch Vera Sample handled the paperwork, pardon my French. The election went to the House and they elected Holland. It was a damn travesty. A real travesty."

"I don't remember much," said Sullivan. "I went to the bathroom. I felt really awful. They tell me I had a pretty bad heart attack."

"So Virginia," asked one of the lawyers. "Why did you write Holland on your ballot?"

"I can't say. I just had a breakdown, I guess." After ten minutes her visitors were shooed out of Virginia's room. She stared at the ceiling for a moment, then asked a nurse if she might have a telephone to make some calls. After a brief emotional conversation with her daughter in Maine, she dialed the number for Andy Vorkink, the friend she asked to handle her affairs.

"Virginia! You look great!" Vorkink arrived with a large bouquet of dried blue hydrangeas he had grown the previous summer. "You sure had us worried. For a while there I thought I'd be executing your will. But look at you!"

"Andy, you're a lawyer. I know, I know—you haven't practiced in a very long time. But still, you're a lawyer." Sullivan had progressed sufficiently to walk to the hospital chapel with her friend, itching to get out of her room, to start the journey back to Portsmouth, and to a new life. "I want you to represent me. Is that possible?"

"Represent you for what?" responded Vorkink, thinking the woman walking with him seemed more energetic than he remembered. For sure she had lost weight, a lot of weight, during her hospitalization. "Why would you need a lawyer?"

"Andy, I've really screwed up. I took some things from a man who convinced me to switch my vote. I shouldn't've done it, but I did. I'm glad my vote didn't matter in the end, but that doesn't change anything."

"Virginia, maybe you shouldn't be telling me this," Vorkink grew uneasy as Sullivan made her revelation.

"But if you're my lawyer it's ok, right?

"Well, yes. But I haven't agreed to be your lawyer." The pair took a pew in the rear of the pretty chapel, a large crucifix staring down at them from behind a simple altar. After a long pause, Vorkink put an arm around Sullivan and smiled. "Oh, what the hell. I'll be your lawyer."

"Good," she said, slapping his thigh, and sighing. "Let's get started tomorrow. You can drive me home and we'll talk on the way."

Unable to mount a protest, Andy Vorkink was drawn deeper into Sullivan's life, which would soon become another national drama.

EPILOGUE

Melody Banks chose Inauguration day as her moment to escape the nightmare of the past three months. She slept for most of the week following the House vote, then began piecing together a new life without politics, far from Washington and the country that seemed prepared to tolerate the most corrupt presidential election in history. Her night with Paul was sweet, and he begged her to stay. But it was time to move on.

Banks notified her landlord she would be giving up the lease on her apartment, which only recently had been declared safe for habitation. She packed up clothes and books for storage and called Goodwill to haul away her pitiful furnishings. She considered trashing her cache of campaign and political memorabilia – pins, posters, signed photos, newspaper clippings and editorial cartoons, stacks of letters, t-shirts, convention hats and flags, the flotsam and jetsam of a life on the run with a candidate. It all represented warm and fuzzy memories for winners, painful reminders of an inglorious defeat for losers. *No. Maybe my grandchildren will be interested in this stuff*, she thought, and sealed the boxes for a later fate.

Joining a few campaign staffers for a joyless dinner in Annapolis the week before, Melody excused herself early, as the group became raucous from alcohol and an incautious joint not yet legal in Maryland. Driving an hour back to DC she took a call from a reporter who had been particularly kind to her in his coverage during and after the election.

"Hey, Melody, how you doin'? Must've been a nightmare." They had shared post-election plans, Melody confiding her intention to disappear to a warm place to get some sun and nurse her wounds.

"Well, I think you should try New Zealand," as a blast of the Rolling Stones nearly washed out his words. "We just met a couple here at our place, they're from an area north of Auckland, the Bay of Islands, and it sounds like heaven. Especially this time of year. It's summer there. Seems just like the place for someone who's been beaten up."

The idea of New Zealand grew on Banks. A million miles away from the hellhole she had sunk into with Calvin Bridges, denied a victory, torched by the machinations of Holland's henchmen. Pulling out her laptop Melody began to eagerly research the country and, in particular, the Bay of Islands. The more she read, the more photos she saw, the more she became convinced this little Commonwealth nation so far away might be just the place for her. It was a culture with a healthy disdain for the self-impressed, crassly ambitious world she desperately sought to leave.

On January 20, as Holland was taking the oath of office, Banks stretched her long limbs in a first class seat on a United flight to Los Angeles—a luxury she indulged herself, with no qualms about the cost. Later that evening in L.A., she would board Air New Zealand flight 101 bound for Auckland.

Her entire luggage consisted of a small carry-on with cosmetics, underwear, three new pairs of shorts, a scant bikini and a more discreet one-piece cobalt blue swimsuit, a couple of tees, new walking shoes, a cute short skirt that couldn't be worn on Washington's K Street, a cashmere scarf which would double as a warm wrap on the plane, her fine Louis Vuitton sunglasses—a gift from the Paris embassy aide a year before—and a new iPad loaded with movies she had missed over the past year, information about her new home, and all the music she could download from her laptop, before selling it on eBay.

Accepting a glass of champagne from a friendly, good looking, fifty-something flight attendant, Banks tried to shove the election fiasco aside and focus on her coming adventure—a year in a lovely flat on the beach near Pahia, three hours north of Auckland. She would drive along the east coast of the North Island, in eighty-degree weather, the sun blazing through puffs of clouds that blew from the Pacific across the island country, west toward the Tasman Sea.

Somewhere over Tennessee a tall, thin man in jeans and turtleneck eased into the empty seat next to Banks. She had closed her eyes and zoned into the Sam Smith ballads on her IPad, not noticing the man beside her until the attendant brought warm nuts and another cocktail.

"Hello, Melody," he said, smiling broadly. Jackson Cripple leaned into Banks, squeezed her arm and smiled. "Jackson! What the hell are you doing here? How did you know I was on this flight?" Banks was shaken but excited and intrigued by the bizarre presence of her seat companion. "Wait, I can imagine how you knew. But why?"

"Well," he said, drawing out the word. "I just thought you needed some interesting reading material on this long, lousy flight." He withdrew a file from his bag and placed it delicately on her tray. "Better take a long draw on that drink before you see this."

Banks downed the cocktail, slowly opened the file, and began reading. Barely into the second page her jaw dropped and she turned and stared at Cripple. "Unbelievable! Stanning was Eldon Mann's guy, right?" Cripple nodded. "You got it."

The first page was a police report, noting the arrest of Jonas Stanning for possession of child pornography, thousands of photographs of very young boys and girls. The second sheet featured a mug shot of the alleged pedophile; a third page noted his arraignment in DC Superior Court two days earlier. An astounding array of sophisticated computer equipment was found in his basement office.

The final document was an email from a federal prosecutor, noting that Stanning wished to speak to someone to discuss a possible deal involving the recent presidential election.

"It's all there," he said, taking a sip of his own strong straight bourbon. "The shit is about to hit the fan."

"So what happens now?" she said, shaken by what she was reading. "Holland was just sworn in a few minutes ago. What can I do with this?"

"That's for you to decide," said Cripple. "This plane lands in L.A. in four hours."

— THE END —

ACKNOWLEDGMENTS

I could not have undertaken this book without the support and encouragement of my wife, Jenny Clad, who provided not only helpful criticism, but also timely nudges.

Each of my children and step-children proved to be insightful readers, providing much-needed feedback. Working with my son Tucker, a talented artist, writer, and professor, as he edited, designed, and illustrated this book, was a particularly inspirational bonding experience.

My longtime pal Steve Wilton became a stalwart editor and cheerleader, helping me avoid many stylistic potholes and preventing the rejection of several favorite characters in this story. Thanks to Phyllis Theroux, whose gracious hospitality and thoughtful suggestions were an inspiration while I was toiling away in her delightful Ashland, Virginia, writer's cottage. I am grateful for advice and encouragement from Sarah Raymont, John Geer, Michael Zibart, Ann Shayne, and others who saw this story as compelling, and frighteningly possible. Pat Anderson, a long time friend and talented writer, provided insightful criticism and extremely helpful support when it really counted.

Linda Lesher's advice and support helped substantially improve the story. *Barn Swallow*, Linda and Grif Lesher's wonderful

Rockport, Maine, bookstore, was a timely sanctuary to bring the book to fruition.

For research I called on many former White House colleagues, journalists, members of Congress and staffers, and other political friends to help me remember details and procedures. While some of the descriptions in this book are fictional, many come straight from experience and observation. The West Wing, Air Force One, and the Vice President's ceremonial office are magnificent settings for any fiction. For the flavor of close-up Presidential interaction with many staffers, friends, and various more-or-less important people, I owe a special thanks to President Bill Clinton, whose intelligence, political skill, and energy bear no resemblance to the President in this story.

Texas A&M professor George Edwards' scholarly text—*Why the Electoral College is Bad for America*—informs much of the political process noted in this story. Dr. Edwards was generous with his time in considering the Constitutional issues front and center in *The Electors*. Stan Brand, the esteemed Washington attorney and lecturer, helped me validate the underlying premise of this story—that is: "faithless electors" can, indeed, legally reverse a presidential election.

I relied on a number of scholarly and popular articles about domestic terrorism, especially Steven Coll's disturbingly informative 2007 *New Yorker* piece, "The Unthinkable". The work of former Senator Sam Nunn's Nuclear Threat Initiative should be required reading for anyone concerned about the potential for a terrorist's domestic nuclear detonation.

While most of the characters in this story are purely fictional, I have taken the liberty to insert many real, living personalities into the plot. Most are men and women I know and admire. I have tried to depict them with respect. For others mentioned in a less flattering way, history may bear me out.

Finally, to Al Gore, my good friend and mentor, thanks for giving me the opportunity to participate in four decades of an extraordinary—and often bizarre—experiment in American democracy. Many men and women set out to save the world. Al Gore may actually have done it.

ABOUT THE
AUTHOR

Roy Neel served as Deputy Chief of Staff to President Bill Clinton and Chief of Staff to Senator, then Vice President Al Gore.
During the 2000 Presidential election cycle he was Gore's Transition Director. During 2004 he briefly managed Howard Dean's
presidential campaign. Neel has been a sportswriter, U. S. Navy
journalist, aerial photographer, and Washington trade association executive. He is an Adjunct Professor of Political Science
at Vanderbilt University and a visiting lecturer at the University
of Melbourne, Australia. He lives in Washington, D.C. with his
wife Jenny Clad.

RECOUNT PRESS

CPSIA information can be obtained at www.ICGtesting.com
Printed in the USA
LVOW07s1148220816

501341LV00004B/292/P